FINDING BRYAN

MATTHEW KESSELMAN

Published in 2021 by Novel Novels, an imprint of Novel Novels LLC

ISBN 9781952974038 (paperback)

ISBN 9781952974052 (hardcover)

ISBN 9781952974045 (ebook)

matthewkesselman.com

novelnovels.com

Dedicated to Kate

CHAPTER 1

I remember after the first honk, I thought to myself: *What in God's name is that elephant-lookin' bitch doin'?*

I seriously thought that. Word for word. Ain't proud of it, but don't take it the wrong way neither—it wasn't no anti-woman thing. No, not at all. My mama woulda thought the same, maybe even said the same if she'd been there with me. A little more polite, though.

You see, we were all locked up in traffic, like deadlocked, like car-movin'-a-foot-every-minute locked. I was bidin' my time, tryin' to stay calm, just tappin' on the wheel, but then, in the middle of the freeze, I spotted this car outta the corner of my right mirror. It was driven by a *beast*—shit, man—her chubby cheeks came dribblin' with chicken-nugget juice and leftover XL Super Gulp Coke, which her quadruple chin gobbled right up.

I thought if she grew any larger, lard chunks would explode outta her ugly ass and cut holes all over her stupid $60K SUV.

After the *second* honk, I fuckin' said it.

"What the fuck is that elephant-lookin' bitch doin'?" I screamed it in my truck so loud my throat started hurtin' and my seat started shakin' and I started sweatin'.

I couldn't hold back. And believe me, I was right. What on God's green earth was she doin'?

Here's what she was doin'—she was ridin' up the road's shoulder, tryin' to merge after skippin' fifty fuckin' people. She was just goin' her merry way, drivin' past everyone, while all the good Samaritans waited like reasonable human beins.

Finally, she realized that the shoulder was gonna end, and she'd needa merge soon. And guess where she was tryin' to merge? Right in fronta me. Right in the three-inch bumper-to-bumper gap between me and my neighbor.

Lord knows, even now, even after all that's happened, my pasty face gets a little red thinkin' bout it. But back then? Back then my brain coulda blown from pure steam. I was bouta have a *conniption*.

So when she finally finished sneakin' in fronta me and honked a *third* time, I couldn't hold back. I did the only thing a reasonable citizen could do at that point. I took my old trusty Ms. Reliable 2006 F-150, put my foot on the pedal, and bumped her. I just rammed right into her car.

Don't worry, it wasn't hard enough to hurt nobody, just enough to send a message. Sometimes you just gotta send a message.

Immediately, she opened her window and *screamed*, "What the *fuck* are you doing?"

I nearly laughed right at her. Her voice was like pure gurglin' piss. Even thirty feet away, I could feel particles of leftover burger oil slap my cheeks.

I opened my window and stared her down, and then it hit me: *Dang, she's even uglier than I thought!* Her fat had rolled over her face, scrunchin' up her nose. You couldn't even see her eyes.

You'd reckon at that point I'd be just gettin' madder, but it was surprisingly the opposite. While we were stopped, a buncha honks ganged up on me, and I started feelin' good. Hell, I was feelin' great. I had a good sweat goin', all peppy and zippy. When I bumped into her, it got my body back into motion and pumped my blood back into all the right places. After seein' her car get crunched, I must be honest, the little guy down low got a little hard. Not proud to admit it, but that's how it happened, and I only tell stories true.

I rolled down the window and said, "Ma'am, what is your name?"

She opened her Big Bird eyes wide, as if I'd just sent Beelzebub after her ass. "It's Macy, you *fuckface!*"

Ah, Macy.

To sum it up: That was how the beginnin' of the end of this past summer started, and I'll never forget it. No, I can't, cause I got all them honks stuck in my head, and cause that was how I was late to my little girl's twelfth birthday party.

But don't worry. I don't cuss around my daughter.

CHAPTER 1 (REDO)

Sorry bout that, y'all. Scratch all that rantin'. I'm restartin'. I already screwed this all up, takin' all my time to talk bout fat Macy and how I smashed her car, while cussin' a whole bunch. That ain't how you tell a story, not how my mama taught me to tell a story.

Here we go with round two:

It was hot as hell this last summer, mid-August. Sun real shiny. My little girl, Casey, had started callin' it "school's eve" cause she'd just learned what "eve" meant, and school was startin' in three weeks, so to her it was the end of summer, beginnin' of school. It was a little cute at first—she's good with words and all—but then it kinda annoyed me. See, there was no eve for me. That entire August, the summer stuck to my face and dripped down my butt. It got damn humid too. Felt like wadin' through a pool all day, every day.

South Virginia can get that way: fun for the kids, stress for Daddy. You get the beach, but you also get the traffic, the work, the occasional weekend work, the long days, the short nights... They all just make a man sweat, especially when he don't really have nobody to talk to.

But let me say this up front—this ain't a story bout me. I see that now. Make sure you understand that loud and clear. That said, I can tell it only how I can tell it: through what I seen, heard, and remember.

So, my words is gonna haveta be enough to show you what I wanna tell you. Or tell you what I wanna show you. I don't fuckin' know. I ain't no word doctor.

No more gettin' sidetracked.

It was school's eve, and I was headin' to my daughter's twelfth birthday, but then I got locked in traffic, and my truck bumped against a woman's SUV, and there was a small tussle, but we resolved it quick enough, after some screamin' and heartburn.

I hit the road again, and around 12:25, my phone went off a second time. Unfortunately, I hadn't noticed the first call, not with the whole Macy business.

Casey's party had started at Saturday noon, and it was kinda a big deal. Last year, we didn't do nothin' special for her eleventh birthday, just cake, cause she told us she didn't want nothin' big, that she "just wanted to hang out with her friends." The problem was that two outta three of her friends no-showed. It was rainin' somethin' fierce.

That got her down for a whole week, got her all kindsa upset. She ain't a screamer, nothin' like that. Honest, sometimes I wish she were. Instead she's an upset-quiet. She'll just go silent, lettin' it boil. We could only tell she was upset cause she'd stare at her food. At least, I could tell. Or she'd go watch some trash on her phone and do nothin' else for an entire day.

I was a little like her that way. When I got upset, I didn't talk much at all, just got angry in my head till I busted. Sandra did most of the day-to-day talkin'.

So for this year, Sandra decided we was gonna go hard and

hire a clown and have him clown outside the house for Casey and her friends. I ain't sure where she got the whole idea from— the girl seemed a little old for clowns—but apparently she vetted it with Casey, who gave the nod, and all of the sudden we had this fool comin' to our house.

I was, am, and likely will remain iffy on clowns. Look at it this way: There's more than enough clownin' goin' on around today to fill everybody's lives. You get it aplenty on the radio, the boob tube, at work, on the phone, and especially at home.

But my opinion on the subject didn't matter none, it seemed. Please understand that I didn't argue with her on the whole value of clowns. No, I had a much better point. My main problem with the whole proposal was that we were broke.

We weren't *broke broke*, like some of my friends, but broke enough to call ourselves broke, if I'mma be honest. A mechanic's salary ain't much to write home bout, and Sandra worked the house, which was fine by me. In fact, I'd asked her to stop workin' after we had Casey, told her the girl would need her mama, but fact of the matter was, we had no money.

So all week, I was thinkin' bout this clown. It was gonna hang around the house for two hours for a hundred bucks, which meant I had to put in an extra weekend shift up at the shop. I wasn't too keen on the idea. My boss, the owner, could be a bit of a dick. He wasn't a big believer in labor laws. His philosophy was: *Stay till the job is done, even if that means a broken back and two lost fingers.*

That said, he also claimed to be a big believer in family, a slightly questionable statement at best, and told me I could leave early to get to Casey's birthday party. He said he'd meet me there later.

So after I left work at 11:20 a.m., I took a small detour, a drive up to the beach. All I wanted was a little me-time before the festivities. I parked, hopped out, pulled off my shoes, and did a mini-sprint to the sand.

It was hot as hell for my feet, but I got over it quick. On the beach, it just works, it always works. I jumped around, feelin' all warm all over my little toes and the sun right on my neck. Then I went up to the edge of the waves. After that, I kinda just zoned out, stared out into the distance. I couldn't even hear the kids screamin' around me or their parents. No, sir, no one was gonna bother me. Not the lovers, not the old folk. It was just me and the waves and their cool little foam tuggin' at my toes.

I lost myself there for a bit. See, I got a good imagination. When I look out, the ocean always looks back at me.

I looked out way far out to the horizon, out where there's nothin' but pure livin'. Fish, sun, water. I'd done it so many times, but still, it came easy. Out there, in the horizon, I imagined someone—an old friend, we'll say—on another distant beach. He was lookin' out too, out onto another sea, onto another horizon. Even so, even bein' so far away, I imagined that maybe one day our eyes would stretch across the water, meet in the middle, and there, there in the water, we'd find each other again. That one day we'd just grab a boat, some beers, and he'd rag on me for all the dumb shit I've done. Just like he did when we were little.

But at some point, a big wave splashed up and got my pants all wet. I stepped back and lost my concentration. It was time to go.

Mind you, I left at a reasonable hour, 11:40, but this is Hampton Roads we're talkin' bout, and these drivers are the worst alive. Back in the day, it wasn't so bad, but over the years, Yankees and goobers have flooded the landscape, come in droves. All the old restaurants changed, all the old faces gone. I can't recognize nothin' at all, and the change is clear as day on the roads.

So what did you think happened? 464 was a disaster.

Someone had probably been textin' while watchin' a movie, while pettin' their dog, while smokin' their cigarette, as they do, and crashed. It was amazin'. Even on Saturday, they found a way to screw up everyone's day.

Through the traffic, I drove and drove, had my joyful time with Macy, which distracted me from the first call, then at 12:25, when I was back to movin', Sandra called again. That time, I didn't pick it up cause I knew what she was gonna say. Instead I put my AC on blast and laser-focused on the car in fronta me. His plate said somethin' dumb like "*PARTE4VR.*" What a piece of work.

By 12:30, I was gettin' closer to the house. It wasn't much of a sight with its chipped paint and the whole termite issue, but it was ours. We scooped it up real cheap too, which helped some.

When my phone went off for a third time, a sudden thought struck me—how Sandra had been askin' me to repaint the house for the last few weeks. Coulda been three, maybe four times. I kept sayin' "I'll do it, I'll do it," and I always wanted to, I really did, but each and every day I planned on takin' care of it, I'd wake up feelin' a little tired, needin' to sleep off the past week. Eventually I'd drift off and fall asleep on the couch watchin' SportsCenter or old Westerns or nothin' at all.

As I reached the house, I realized she'd stopped askin'.

I ROLLED up on the driveway real slow and saw Casey and three of her friends joined around our table on the front lawn, and in fronta them was the clown. And what a clown he was. Man had come prepared.

He had this big red nose, balloons by his belt, and giant striped pants. Not gonna lie, he had some talent, with the way he twisted his balloons with a coupla wrist flicks, and although he was probably sweatin' bullets under all that gear, he seemed happy enough. Within a few seconds, he whipped up this whole balloon dog, which he handed to Casey, and she *grinned*. Her smile stretched across her face wide as a rainbow. I hadn't seen her like that in a minute. Made me all kinda mesmerized.

It also distracted me enough to bump my truck into a tree.

I tried slammin' on the brakes in time, but it wasn't enough. The truck tapped against the oak in fronta our house, pressin' against her bumper. Between Macy and the tree, that sucker was done for. The bumper plopped right off, slid down, crashin' into the dirt and leavin' my baby with two lights exposed and black metal juttin' out her front. My plate stuck out too, like someone stickin' out an aluminum tongue that read *NAYRB-82*.

I backed up, parked, and slowly got out. The kids and the clown were starin' at me, so I just shrugged and waved, and Casey, God bless her, waved back. Then the clown returned to his ballooncraft, and everythin' was fine. Well, everythin' except the giant slab of hot steel sittin' on our front lawn, but there wasn't much I could do bout that.

Unfortunately, the real dilemma wasn't the busted truck at all. No, it was the 300-pound warrior in a 120-pound body standin' in the fronta the house. She had her arms crossed, a frown glued to her face, and her back against the wall.

Sandra.

She gestured at me with two fingers, sayin' *Come here now.* Normally when she got annoyed, she'd become a chatterbox, rattlin' off her major and minor gripes with the world, but when she got mad, truly *mad*, she never needed to say nothin' at all. She knew two mean eyes and two small fingers would do the trick.

I trudged up to her, mainly cause I had nowhere else to go, and she held open the screen door for me. I entered, she glanced at the kids, and then closed it behind her.

Before the torrent was unleashed—I knew it was comin'—I scrambled to the couch so I could at least take the fight sittin' down.

She came over. "What happened to your car? And where on God's green earth have you been?"

"Which one do you want me to answer?"

"Both!"

"I got bumped. I was at work."

"At work?" She looked at me like I'd just told her I'd been on the moon. "All morning? The old man didn't let you off earlier?"

I shook my head. "There was traffic."

"You know your daughter's turning twelve today? You can't even make her birthday?"

Now, some things, most things, I could roll off my shoulders. I'd taken a beatin' of many types—physical, emotional, spiritual, animalistic—but somethin' bout *how* she said it really rubbed me the wrong way.

"Course I know that," I mumbled.

"And yet you're sitting here, thirty minutes late."

"So I am."

I didn't wanna look at her. I'd been facin' down, starin' at my dirty shoes and our creaky floorboards, but at that moment, I knew I needed to talk to her eye to eye.

Sandra was still a looker, even after all these years. It pissed me off, the way she'd stayed so good lookin' with so little work. See, even now, she's the real deal. She's got *sapphires* for eyes, dirty gold hair, and a body that just makes you melt.

So starin' up at her, I couldn't help but think bout all the little things she did that I adored. Those things that make you wanna squeeze a person tight and never let go. Like how when she found an idea she liked, she'd start this funny weird smile outta the corner of her mouth. Or how she laughed like a child, with her whole body. Or how sweet she could be, always takin' care of us.

Sure, over the last decade, she'd picked up a wrinkle or two, but who ain't? I had no grounds to complain. Lyin' under dirty cars didn't do my skin no good, and I can't say I've always kept to my diets.

It was true, even after fourteen years together, even after all our minor and major dramas, even after all the burnt pork chops, she still dazzled me. So as I looked at her pretty little face, a fight broke out in my head, with an angel on one shoulder versus a devil on the other, both tuggin' on me and settin' events into motion I wouldn't understand till weeks later. But my brain thought it knew what it needed to do and managed to beat down my heart. Frustration poured over.

"No," I said.

"No? What do you mean, 'no'?"

"No." I stood up and went to the kitchen for some water. "I ain't gonna sit here and argue with you."

"This isn't an argument, this is a discussion. Don't make this into a fight. You're never around. You weren't even here for the party. That's all I'm saying."

"I'm here right now." I took a sip. "I'll go to the party right now. Is that so bad? Look," I said, pointin' out the window. "Casey's playin' outside while we're in here bickerin' like a broken record, ignorin' our child."

As I walked to the door, she whined behind me. "Now you're trying to make me look like the bad guy."

"No, Sandra." I sighed. "No one's ever the bad guy. It just ain't never that simple."

Then I opened the door and let the summer sun settle on my back.

CHAPTER 2

We met junior year. She was sixteen, I was seventeen. She was hot, I was not, but despite our differences, we found ourselves connected.

After she sat next to me in Ms. Ledawoski's trigonometry class and I caught a whiff of her perfume, with apologies to Mrs. L, I quickly found myself spendin' more time studyin' signs of what Sandra thought bout me than any sine whatnots.

Occasionally, she'd glance my way or ask me what I put on the homework, and I'd act like I didn't care, but each and every time, with every glance, every little thing felt alright, even when I knew nothin' was.

Believe me when I say, in those early days, when we'd play off each other all slyly, I don't know if I've ever been more lifted up in my life.

Well, at least till Casey was born.

See, the year we met was my moody year. The year between the beginnin' and the rest of my life, the year after everythin' went down and changed at home. It got messy for a bit: I smoked, drank, cut class, in general acted like an ass. In my heart, I knew none of it was right. I was always the good son—

Mama and the old man raised me right—but that year Daddy was a little too preoccupied with his own set of regrets and demons to try and strip me of mine.

Lucky for me, Sandra found it endearin', or at least I reckon she did, cause she started lingerin' around me more and more, till we became an item.

Lookin' back, I think she wanted to fix me. She never did realize she couldn't do nothin'. All we can ever do is just become more of ourselves. Still, if you're lucky, if you dig deep enough, you can become all the way yourself, your original self—that all-lovin' and curious child buried inside—the one not yet racked with all the world's bullshit. Trust me, I know. That kid's sittin' there, waitin' for you to find them again.

But ain't nobody gonna dig them out for you.

Soon we were *far* closer than her daddy liked, and some time after that, she was pregnant, and shortly after the end of high school, we were married. Man, what a time. The weddin' was mighty special, featurin' all our friends, family, somewhat friends, neighbors, aunts, uncles, cousins, and cousins' dates. It climbed up to a good hundred fifty people. Yeah, we took on some financial squeeze from that one for a year or two, but her daddy helped us some. We convinced ourselves it was gonna be worth it, and at the time it felt like it was. I remember that day perfectly, starin' into her blue eyes, holdin' her warm body by my side, smellin' her blonde hair and feelin' like everythin' was ours. We were gonna be unstoppable, I whispered in her ear. We could accomplish anything together.

Watchin' Casey tug on that dumb clown's dumb nose, all I could think was how young and stupid we were.

"Casey," I shouted.

I walked over to her and her three pals, Mary Anne, Kat, and Lil Pete. I tagged the boy Lil Pete cause he grew like a beanstalk over the summer, thin and long, and his daddy skipped out a while back, then turned up dead, so in a way I felt obligated to give him a little kindness, even if it came out all garbled up. His mama didn't complain. She was usually three sheets to the wind.

"Yeah?" Casey looked at me with her big, wide eyes. I laughed and tousled her hair. They were all so awkward. Mary Anne and Kat were weirdly shaped white and brown girls respectively, each with gangly arms and clunky feet, and Lil Pete, with his sudden sproutin', was horribly uncoordinated, while Casey's face still had some room to grow to fit her eyes. At twelve, ain't no one properly proportioned for this world. Yet, nowadays, they all got phones that gives them the whole globe, all at once. When I was growin' up, all we had were walkie-talkies, a little imagination, and that was enough.

"Just sayin' hi. Happy birthday, baby girl."

Casey pulled back and ran her hands through her hair. "Did you wash your hands?" All her friends laughed.

"Don't be ugly, Casey."

"I'm sorry." She smiled. "Hi!"

Wasn't a fan of her tone, a little nasty, but I wasn't gonna say nothin' on her birthday.

"Well," I said, "get back to clownin', I guess."

Mr. Clown honked his nose twice and sprayed water on the side of his face. All the kids laughed, and in a strange way, I got jealous. A clown ain't never gotta worry bout a thing.

I walked halfway back to the house but realized I didn't wanna go there. Lookin' back at Mr. Clown and Casey, then at the house again, I decided to walk away from both. I ventured back over to the bumper in our yard and Mr. Oak Tree, and I lay down beside his bark.

On the ground, I studied my hands. Casey wasn't wrong. They were gross, covered with grease, oil, and sweat.

The boss man always said mechanics are holy folk, that

"they're the Big Man's way of givin' automobiles a spiritual cleansin'." He never laughed when he said it neither, so you knew he wasn't jokin'. Once, he said, "Boys, listen up—every time we fix a broken piston ring, we're givin' a baptism."

Bullshit.

"Boys, we're blessin' this here car to ride many miles more. Like the good Lord gave us legs, we give miles."

Bullshit.

The man never knew if he wanted to be a boss, a pastor, or a mechanic.

"Boys... boys... boys..." Bullshit. Bullshit. Bullshit. I hated the way he said "boys." Anytime where that term made any sense had long passed.

Wipin' my hands against the grass, I sighed.

Cars are a strange sorta thing. They unlock the road, let you go anywhere, but their parts don't really matter to ninety-nine percent of folks. They don't know their transmission from their engine, or how to fill their own oil, but honest and strange enough, sometimes I wish I was one of them, blissfully ignorant, and able to just enjoy the freedom with none of the work.

A man can find a profession in many ways: through bravery, through perseverance, through luck, through brains. In my case, I was drafted. I never liked fixin' cars much. I'm passable, maybe even a little bad at it, to be honest. I'd never tell Sandra that, even if she already knew. Don't repeat it, but the issue is I got clumsy hands. They just weren't meant for that kinda work. I didn't inherit the handy gene. I was the unlucky one.

That didn't matter, though. Somebody had to do it. And after the bad year, I was the only candidate left available.

Fuck it, I thought. I stretched out, felt my muscles groan, and slowly closed my eyes.

Then I passed the hell out.

.   .   .

"Wake up, Sleepin' Beauty."

Damnit. I woke facin' up, starin' straight into his crotch.

He nudged me with his heavy black boot, and I rolled over. Always tryin' to look suave and younger than he was. Asshole. He wore these fancy gold aviator glasses and a leather jacket. Then he pulled me up with hands clean as a baby's bottom. Mr. Boss Man was always sharper than me like that, sneakier too. He knew how to throw a dime in the air and have it land as a quarter, while doin' none of the hard liftin'. I ain't here to give advice, but I'll do it this one time: Don't ever trust a mechanic.

I pushed myself up and stood right next to him. He was almost exactly two inches taller than me, and even at seventy-one, he hadn't shrunk a damn millimeter. It drove me crazy—that ain't how nature's supposed to go.

"Forrest," he said.

God knows I hate my name. From '94 on, it just all became *Forrest Gump* jokes. My mama appreciated the connection, absolutely adored the movie—made her feel all Hollywood—but it just ain't a good association. Now, don't get me wrong, I got aplenty of retarded friends, care for them dearly, but no one wants to get called a retard. Not even retards.

"Yessir?" I asked.

"Whatcha doin' layin' out, sleepin' on the grass? And what happened to yer car?"

"I was tired." I nodded. "And a woman bumped into me on the road."

"Ya weren't raised to just fall asleep on the grass. Or get bumped on the road."

I sighed. "Sure, Daddy. Whatever you say."

Yes, Mr. Boss Man was my father. Yes, I'd been workin' for him for the last fourteen years. Yes, I was almost thirty-two, a fuckin' man. And yes, he still treated me like a kid.

I glanced around. No one else was in sight, not Casey, her pals, or Mr. Clown. "Where's Mama?"

My old man shook his head. "She couldn't come. Wasn't feelin' up to it."

For a moment there, he looked old. Real old, like some kinda geezer. It was very tiny, but his voice had wavered, zigged and zagged with his usual cottony gruff tone dragged out, replaced by some weird-soundin' silk string.

"Do you know where the kids went?"

He regained his composure and pointed to the house. "They just went for cake. Let's catch Casey blowin' out the candles, then there's somethin' we needa talk bout."

"What's it?"

He didn't say nothin', just started walkin' to the house. I groaned and followed him in. "I hope they ain't usin' that same Walmart cake from last year. It ain't bad, but I coulda made somethin' much better."

He took off his sunglasses and raised an eyebrow at me. "Ya been bakin' again? Ya made the cake?"

I shook my head. "Naw, but if I had time, I woulda fixed up somethin' much better."

He grunted, either in agreement, disagreement, or to simply grunt. It was always hard to tell with him. He never mixed up his grunts much, and grunts made up a third of his active vocabulary. I assumed agreement, even though I knew it was the least likely of the bunch. I didn't care neither way, though. Really, I didn't. Fact is, I got bakin' baked in my genes, came from my mama.

There's just somethin' bout the smell of cupcakes that gets me goin'. Wakes up the nose. And when I get that whiff of fresh brownies, goodness flows down into my heart. Don't know what it is, but I just like it, and I liked bakin' somethin' fierce with my mama every Sunday growin' up. I like how perfect everythin' comes out, how you got perfect instructions to create a delicious masterpiece. There ain't no surprises, no unwelcome guests. You always know how it's gonna go down. There's somethin' beautiful in that. It's far more satisfyin' than tellin' an angry customer their cruddy rubber timin' belt snapped and now they gotta pay us $2,000, all cause some ass in Detroit was too cheap to pay for real steel.

Followin' my old man into the house, we caught the kids huddled around our tiny kitchen. Sandra loomed over Casey while the burnin' candles lit up the girl's eyes. But the cake looked ugly as a muddy shoe with icin'. Another year, another shitty Walmart cake. As the door behind me swooshed closed, I sighed. I hadn't baked nothin' that whole summer.

They all finished singin' *"Happy Birthday,"* and Sandra asked, "Casey, what are you going to wish for?"

Casey was silent for a moment, then she said, "I decided on something, but if I say it, it won't come true."

My old man said, "Smart girl."

Casey blew out the candles, Kat and Mary Anne clapped, while Lil Pete crossed his arms.

"Daddy, can you cut the cake?"

"Sure, darlin'." I stepped up and made sure to start with a big brick slab that I plopped down on the girl's plate. "There, enough to feed an elephant."

Her granddaddy stepped up and asked her, "Don't I get a hug?"

"Of course you do, Papaw."

He gave her a bear hug that, over my entire lifetime, I never managed to sneak outta him.

She pulled back and asked Sandra, "We want to watch a movie. Is that all right?"

"Yeah, that's fine. Just make sure your friends text their parents when it's finishing up so they can pick everyone up."

You better believe when I was a kid, if I asked Daddy that, he woulda said, "I just gave ya a damn cake. Now ya wanna see a movie?" Mama woulda played it anyways, though, probably.

The kids went to the livin' room, leavin' me, the old man, and Sandra alone. I peeked over at the TV. Looked like an evenin' for *Frozen* for the fourteenth time. Considerin' the current state of my company, I wished I coulda joined them.

"Sandra, how ya doin'?"

My old man and her embraced, and she said, awful cheery, "All is well at home base."

I leaned against the wall. I wanted to get away, go out for a drive, grab a beer. I was tired of the day, tired of listenin' to other people. At the very least, for my sake, the sun coulda gone to sleep already, but those summer days can last an eternity.

"That's good." Then the old man looked at me strange. "Forrest, can we step outside? Discuss that matter?"

"Sure," I said, real slow.

Sandra made a face at me, and I shrugged.

I followed him out, and he waited till the door was closed to speak. "Tomorrow I needya by the house."

"Why?"

"Yer mama wants somethin'."

"What? She ain't feelin' right?"

"She can explain."

I rubbed my forehead with the sweat rollin' down my grimy bangs. "That sounds like some secrecy business. Why can't you just tell me straight? And why didn't you bring this up at work?"

He looked at me, all confused. "It's yer mama's business to tell. And I ain't gonna bring up personal matters at work. That ain't professional, Forrest."

What a ridiculous man. I sighed. "I guess that's true. Well, if you're not gonna tell me, that's just fine and dandy. Can I bring Sandra and Casey?"

"Sure. We'll watch the game. Pre-season's started."

I grunted. An agreement grunt, of course. "That all?"

He nodded, stern, the only way he nods. "Now let's enjoy some cake. Twelve's a big year." He started walkin' toward the house, but then turned back around. "And Forrest—know that ain't none of this was my idea."

He had a single drop of sweat on his crusty old forehead. It got my insides twitchin'.

I almost nearly went up to him, grabbed his shoulders, shook him up, and hollered that he better tell me what this whole business was bout, but then I decided against it.

He was never gonna tell me anyhow.

CHAPTER 3

"Okay. Ready to go sleep now?" I'd been with Casey for a good half an hour. Read her some of a biography of Andrew Jackson, *Andrew Jackson: Young Patriot*. Don't ask me how we landed on Mr. J, but we did.

"I'm not tired."

"Fine." I handed her the book. "You can read more, then go to sleep."

"I don't want to read, not tonight."

Admittedly, with a little heat, I said, "You're gettin' a little old for us to read you stories." Instantly, I knew it'd been the wrong thing to say and felt a little sour bout it, but then I decided I was right. We'd only been readin' to her sporadically over the last few months, and now she was twelve. A whole year older than eleven. She could read herself.

She didn't say nothin'.

I sighed. "Party was fun?"

"Yeah."

"It was good seein' your friends?"

"Yeah."

"Well, then, what's buggin' you, my little jitterbug?"

Casey bit the bottom of her lip. She always does that when she's fixin' to say somethin' she wants. Always tryin' to cute it up. She thinks I can't read it, but course I can. She's smarter at the books than me, but I still have my street wisdom. Don't mean it never works, though.

"Thanks for the pillow, and the phone case, and the water bottle," she started.

Uh-huh.

She continued, "I was thinking of another thing which would make my birthday perfect."

Not again.

"I'd take care of the dog. It'd be my responsibility, one hundred percent mine. I'd walk it, I'd feed it, I'd give it water..."

I shook my head.

"I think you'd really like it too—"

"Casey, we ain't gettin' a dog."

She turned toward her pillow. "Why not?"

"I told you before. Dogs are a bad idea. Too much hassle. No good will come of it, trust me. Yeah, they're cute, but you don't wanna deal with the repercussions."

"Repercussions? What does that even mean? How could a dog have *repercussions*?"

I hopped up and snapped at her. "Jesus, Casey, it means I don't wanna deal with a dog. Whatcha you goin' on bout the way I speak? You my vocab teacher or somethin'? We ain't gettin' a damn dog."

She shut down once more.

After a long quiet, followed by my loud groan, I said, "Listen, I'm sorry, but we can't get a dog. I know you want one, and I know you'd take great care of it, but it ain't happenin'. Sorry."

She didn't look so cute or mad now. Just disappointed. "Why not?"

I rubbed the side of my face.

My little jitterbug. I coined the name when she was four. She'd been playin' in the park, while me and Sandra lounged on a bench, when she spotted a big ol' beetle. She waddled right up to it, picked it up, and let it crawl onto her hand. Then she stomped her little way over to us and called out, "Mama, Mama, look what I found!"

I'll never forget the look on Sandra's face. It was as if someone had tied a weight to the bottom of her chin, and it dragged her mouth open like some old cartoon.

Then her scream came. She hopped, skipped, and jumped right on back. And then she shooed it away. I just laughed and laughed, my wide chest vibratin'. I went right up to Casey, hugged her, picked her up, and she showed me her new friend Mr. Bug, till Mr. Bug flew away.

When she went to sleep that night, all cocooned up under the blankets, I told her, "You're my little jitterbug." And she was just that—my little jitterbug.

But that night, the night of her twelfth birthday, as I stood next to her, I realized somethin' had changed. Her legs nearly stuck outta her blanket. Her bed, already built tiny for a tiny room, looked like it was made for someone half her size. The unicorns taped to the walls coulda easily belonged to someone else's daughter. Casey didn't even look at them no more.

Twelve years old. Twelve years since she was that tiny six-pound baby I held in my arms.

Since the day I started workin', I learned seasons jump into the next, and days disappear in the blink of the eye. Every year, the clock ticks faster and faster, addin' up to a decade in no time at all. Despite all that, it seemed I'd tricked myself into thinkin' that Casey would always remain that tiny baby, but as she lay above her covers, she wasn't lookin' little at all, and she sure as hell wasn't gettin' any littler. Every day, she'd been becomin' less jitterbug and more jitterbutterfly. How hadn't I noticed?

Maybe my eyes were just closed.

I shook my head. "Casey, I know from personal experience a dog is a bad idea. You just gotta trust me on this one."

"So," she said with a higher-pitched voice, "you had a dog?"

"That ain't what I said. I never had one. A friend got a dog, that's all, and it didn't turn out good."

"Did it bite you?"

"No, it didn't *bite* me." I smiled, then laughed. Not a fun laugh, but an exhausted, exasperated laugh. At least I found a laugh again. "No, Casey, it just turned out badly. Real bad. Now, baby girl, will you just go to sleep?"

She tussled around. "Okay, I'll go to sleep. Just think about it. Please?"

"Okay." I nodded. "I'll think bout it. Good night."

"Good night."

I cut the lights and walked outta the room. How stubborn that girl had become.

"She's all-in on that dog, Sand."

Sandra was hidin' out at the other side of the bed, while I stared up at the ceilin'. Sleep didn't want me—I'd been awake for the last thirty minutes. That dog talk had screwed up everythin'.

"Forrest, I was almost asleep," she grumbled as she stuck a pillow over her head.

"Sorry, but this is kinda important. She ain't givin' this battle up. She been talkin' bout it for weeks, maybe this entire summer."

I could hear her squirmin' around, tryin' to get comfy, but not findin' a position. She's a cuddler at heart, but after our fight, there were no cuddles to be had. Honest, cuddles had kinda been dryin' up over the past few years.

"Maybe it wouldn't be the worst idea. My folks got a dog when I started middle school, and it turned out fine. You remember him? Scooter?"

Turned out *fine*. When she don't wanna see somethin', she finds every way to avoid it, but when you make a mistake, she catches it every time.

I hung out over at her place nearly every day senior year, and each and every time, without fail, Scooter was hidin', gone real scared in some corner. On occasion, he'd pee on the carpet, the poor bastard. Only Mrs. Mama June of the June family would take him out. Mr. Daddy June was far too "busy," and the June children far too lazy.

See, they never resolved the real dilemma. The issue was they had this eleven-year-old cat, Jingles, that dominated him. You can't blame Jingles too much. When you're queen of your castle, you're gonna stake your claim when a challenger approaches. From the very first day Scooter arrived, she hissed at him, and he ran away like a fool, despite bein' three, maybe four, times her size.

In the end, she outlived him by six years.

"I don't know, honey. I ain't sure Scooter was so pleased with the situation."

She rolled over and pushed on my stomach to perch up and gave me a mean look. "What's that supposed to mean? What wouldn't Scooter be pleased about?"

I very nearly had an aneurysm that instant. She was gonna go sharp over Scooter? Everythin' seemed to make her go nuts those days. I just didn't get it, didn't get nothin' that was goin' on. I'm best at seein' what's right in fronta me. Predictin' the future, fightin' over the past, or readin' people's minds, that ain't never been me. I ain't good at fightin' endless wars of words. In a battle like that, every man is gonna bungle eventually.

I came up with the best answer I could, given the circumstances. "I just mean... what I was sayin' was... it's just, I don't know how happy he was. You remember how much he fought with Jingles? It simply wasn't a good situation, that's all."

She looked at me for another second before pushin' back down, jigglin' my stomach. "I guess you're right. They did fight a lot. I wish they could've stuck around a little longer so Casey could've met them."

I exhaled. One bullet dodged.

Unfortunately, she then said, "But we don't have a cat. Our dog would have no one to fight with."

"Baby," I said more carefully, "I need you to side with me on this one. Didn't you say you wanted me to paint the house? I still gotta buy the paint. A dog would stretch our budget."

"I guess that's true." Lyin' beside each other, she let out one of her patented corner-of-the-mouth smiles. She poked at my belly. "Maybe if you cut down a little on the snacks, we could save up for a dog."

I grumbled and turned over. Listen, I knew I was fat, I *know* I'm fat. It'd been buildin' up over the past couple years. It don't take much—some good beer, occasional loungin', more than one cheeseburger—but don't confuse yourself. I wasn't, and will never be, Macy fat. I just had a little chub going on, a little mass accumulation. Nothin' to rally the troops over. "Alright," I said, "I'm goin' to sleep."

She scoffed. "Come on now, don't get grumpy over that. When did you become so sensitive?"

I opened my mouth to spit more bull, but then stayed quiet. I remember wonderin': *Why ain't I never allowed to be sensitive?*

She picked up on my silence. "Fine. Be that way."

I buried my face in the sheets, tryin' go to sleep. It musta been twenty-seven days. Maybe twenty-eight. Not our longest empty stretch that year, mind you. The last time had only come around cause Casey had a sleepover, and in the lonely house,

Sandra started gettin' emotional and cryin' bout us still bein' stuck on one kid and wanted to try again. And try we did. Can't say I lasted too long. Ain't too proud of it, but who can blame a man when he's so out of practice?

See, our dry spell was a twofold problem. For starters, I got that slight weight problem, like I mentioned. But more importantly, each time we got hot and heavy, and Sand didn't get pregnant, her disappointment ticked up. Over the years, it'd been a problem, but somethin' bout Casey gettin' older had made it worse. The situation didn't make me happy neither, but by that summer, it'd reached a boilin' point for her.

At that point, I didn't know if she was just gonna give up and I'd never get laid again, or if she was gonna get so frustrated after another failed pregnancy that she'd go ahead and grab a knife and slice my dick off. Either was a possibility.

That ain't a good situation for no one.

A few times over the years, she'd mentioned she wanted to see a doc for herself, and that I oughta go check to see if I'd been firin' blanks. Each time, I told her it ain't worth the outta-pocket cost.

No way in hell was I goin' to no doc. Given how hard Casey's birthin' was, fertility seemed to be one of the rare problems that couldn't be twisted to be my fault.

We talked bout doin' some of those fancy lab, clone, vitro, fertilizer, tube, super-baby things, but after some research, we found that also runs us into a money problem, big time. Anyhow, we kept bargainin' with ourselves. "We're young parents," we'd say. "We have time."

Well, now our first kid was twelve, and there ain't a parent out there who wants a twelve-year age gap between their kids.

Sandra musta picked up on the sound of gears turnin' in my head, cause she made one last remark that night. "Forrest, is something going on?"

"What?" I mumbled.

"When your daddy came today, he was acting a little strange. Is something wrong with your mama? Is it getting worse?"

"No, that ain't it. He just wanted us to come over tomorrow. Wanted to watch the 'Skins."

"Oh. Okay," she said. Then, after a long pause, she added, "And Forrest?"

"Hmm?"

"I'm going to see a doctor on Monday. I want to know our options and what's been going on. With me. We're running out of time."

I had a sudden urge to remind her how much that would cost, how we didn't have insurance, how everythin' would be alright, how we'd cook up a little brother for Casey in no time, and how all four of us would play ball, run in the grass, and breathe easy forever.

But I only tell things true. So instead I said, "Okay. Good night."

CHAPTER 4

M e and the old man found ourselves sunk into the couch. It'd melted me in, first by butt, then by back, till I was a puddle drippin' over its soft, busted-up cushions. It was only proper—me and the couch were well-acquainted, friendly neighbors for just over thirty years.

We were back in my old home, Daddy's near-beachfront property. He was a lucky one, buyin' durin' the good market, back when this country still looked out for guys like us, but I guess I shouldn't complain. The beach kept me sane as a child. The waves will always listen to you.

We were watchin' the game while the girls—Sandra and Mama and Casey—hung out in the dinin' room. The 'Skins were lookin' miserable, per usual. Right before the half, our corner had slugged a receiver, and by the end of the third, they were losin' to the Patriots by twenty-two. Even in the preseason, they were losers.

Kinda spoke to the whole issue, I remember thinkin'. Like how South Virginia's gotta suckle at our nation's capital's shadows just to watch the pros, and even then they were talkin' bout erasin' the team's historic name. With every passin' year, the South was just migratin', retreatin', disappearin'. Soon it would all be gone, everythin' forgotten. The people gone, replaced with folks on the TV: pretty California girls or New York artsy guys with big square glasses or lyin' politicians. No one humble, no one with worn hands. No one real. Like they were just tryin' to wash everythin' away, brush the little people away, make it like we were never here. That's the worst thing you can do to a person—make everyone forget you.

But despite it all, I still remembered.

So, me and the old man watched the game in silence, as was tradition. The game spoke for each of us, and it ain't said nothin' good. Eventually, Casey came in durin' the fourth quarter and asked, "Can I go outside? I want to walk on the beach."

I lazily pointed to the door. "Sure."

After she left and the screen door shut behind her, Daddy finally stirred. He squirmed onto the edge of the couch and halfway glanced at me. "Forrest, maybe ya oughta tell Sand to watch Casey, and ya and yer mama can have that talk."

I waved him off. "Whatcha buggin' me for? I'm watchin' the game."

"Forrest, this ain't no joke. Yer mama wants to talk with ya."

Typically, the old man's got three different faces: flat, flatter, and angry. But when I looked at him, it wasn't none of those. His mask had cracked along its edges in a way that only happened once in a blue moon, revealin' the shockin' fact that a real, breathin' man lived underneath it. He was perturbed.

It got me nervous.

"Okay, fine. I'll get up, I'll get up."

Mama had been sick for a while. Stage two throat cancer had become stage three, and then sorta meandered there. When we'd found out, she joked bout it. She'd said, "Forrest, the only reason I got throat cancer is to remind you to quit smokin'. If I got better too quick, you'd just go right back at it."

That was what we did as a family, we joked. Everythin' became a joke, and anything else was left unsaid. Made life simpler that way. Anyhow, it was a good joke, and she was right. It did get me to quit.

I pushed myself up, rollin' my whole body off the couch, and I slogged my way to the dinin' room. "Sand," I said, "can you watch Casey? She just went outside."

Sandra shook her head. "Why don't you watch her? I'm comfy. Your mama and I were just having a great discussion about the *third* time you wet the bed."

My mama laughed, and I grinned for the first time in a while. Her laughs come out perfect. Never shrill, never suspicious, only warm. Genuine clouds of comfort. They hit you on the side of your head, make you think it's all gonna be fine. I just wish she coulda found a wig that looked closer to her natural hair. She always had nice hair.

Mama said, "It's okay, honey. The boy's offerin' some quality time for his old mama."

"Well, if that's it, I won't separate the two of you," Sandra said as she got up. She shot me an inquisitive look, then left the room.

When we were finally alone, Mama smiled at me. "What's wrong, baby?"

All good mamas got a sixth sense like that, knowin' when you're grumpy, or cloudy, or just gray. But in a strange way, I had my own sixth sense in that moment, like I knew what she was gonna say.

Maybe it was the way she didn't quite perfectly meet my eyes, or the fact her voice quivered, or that the old man was actin' so strange, but my gut told me somethin' new was comin', or rather, a return of the old.

"Ain't nothin' wrong, Mama," I said. "Daddy said you wanted to tell me somethin'."

"Yes, Forrest. I've got two, maybe three months, at best."

"Shit," I managed. That news alone made my head swirl, but it didn't come as no surprise. She'd been doin' crappy for a long time. Still crushed my heart. However, my thoughts remained mostly on another topic. Her tellin' me so plainly how sick she was only made me more certain of what was comin'.

"It's been a long time, too long, since you two little idiots were runnin' around this house, playin' tag, breakin' my lamps, and givin' your daddy heartburn." She snickered, laughin' at an image I couldn't see. "Forrest, it's time to bring him home."

"Mama," I choked on my words, "if he wanted to come back, he woulda already. He ain't comin' back."

I didn't wanna hear her say his name, cause I thought I'd cry, but at the same time, I wanted to hear it more than anything.

She started tearin' up too. "You might be right, baby, but there ain't no more time for waitin', no more time to pretend. You gotta find him."

She rose, her whole body shudderin' at the ordeal. She turned to her sink, bent down, set the water loud and high, and began to wash her hands.

Facin' away from me, she said, "I need both my babies back here. It's time to tell him to come back home. Find Bryan."

CHAPTER 5

I'm sorry that I ain't been fully honest with you on the nature of this story, but I didn't wanna start with the bad stuff. Hittin' Macy seemed like more fun. Maybe it'll all come out in time as we go along and get more comfortable with each other. Or maybe it won't.

For now, I'll tell you the simple facts. You've earned it, listenin' to me ramble for this long.

My brother left home when I was sixteen and he was seventeen. He didn't come back.

Ain't nothin' special. Just the stone of life turnin' per usual.

I LAID my arms across the table and rested my head on them and listened to my heart ache.

Bryan.

For sixteen years, she hadn't uttered the name. For sixteen years, it sat in silence, stewin' in my head, left dead in our old home.

Bryan.

For sixteen years, everyone else's eyes remained closed and their ears blocked.

Bryan.

No more, Mama'd finally decided. She'd taken her stand.

Bryan.

I spoke first. "Mama, I ain't seen him, and we ain't spoken neither. It's been too long. I don't know where he is. Whatcha want me to do? How do you expect me to find him?"

"I don't know!" she yelled.

I flinched. Mama was always the queen of composure—hadn't never before seen her respond the way she did then: rattled, with the wear on her all too apparent. She swayed her arms and stumbled back onto her chair. "I don't know," she repeated and bent her head low.

We ain't touchy-feely folk, us Wilcox clan, but I went over to her and put my hand on her shoulder. "I get it. I'm sorry you're gettin' sicker. You know I am. But you know if he wanted to see us, he woulda by now. And if I could find him, I would, but he's long gone."

"We haven't tried."

That got me a little agitated. "Well, it wasn't exactly our job to try."

She looked up, her eyes pink and red and puffy. "Boy, he's your brother."

"All I'm sayin' is we both know this battle didn't start with us. Talk to your man in the other room. If you want someone to find Bryan, it should be him."

Shakin' her head, she said, "Don't you talk about your father that way."

"Whose fault is it, then? Ain't like *I* got him to leave."

"Hush now." She raised her hand. "This ain't the time for this kinda talk, none of this blamin' game. There ain't time for it."

She sighed and tried to resume her normal disposition with

a weak smile. "You're gonna find your brother, and that's final. You're gonna bring him back here, at least for a little bit, so I can see my boys together again at last. Maybe he has a special lady friend. Wouldn't that be a nice bonus? A cool sister-in-law? Now, do you wanna fix somethin' with me? We can get it ready for dinner."

My hair suddenly got all kinda itchy, and I scratched, hard. A big hot wave of sweat fell down on my body. It wasn't feelin' right, nothin' bout this was right. Somethin' had been freed from a cage in my chest and began to rustle around, bumpin' against things that oughta stay buried. Memories work like that, I've found. One day they're blockaded at the end of a river, but then the next day, somethin' nudges the dam inside your heart, and everythin' rumbles loose.

It wasn't the right time for any of this. Nothin' was happening at the right time. Without anyone noticin', everyone had gotten older: Casey, Sandra, Daddy, Mama, me.

I was only thirty-one. I shoulda been jumpin' around, makin' money, runnin' with a son, but instead I was gettin' fat and gettin' stuck on old thoughts.

I stood up and said plain as day, "Mama, I'm sorry. I love you, but I ain't doin' none of that." Then I turned to the door and left.

CHAPTER 6

Next mornin', after walkin' out on Mama, I woke up at six a.m. I always wake up round then. Somethin' bout havin' a kid reprograms your brain, I reckon. Your sub-brain learns it's always got work to do, at all points of time, cause there ain't no break for a parent. Or maybe it's just the screams of a baby smackin' the back of your head, still echoin' even years after they stopped needin' diaper changes, that wakes you up.

After my talk with Mama, Sandra'd tried to ask me what happened, why we needed to leave my parents' so quick. I didn't tell her. Said it didn't matter. Usually in the mornin', I'd stay in bed with her and listen to her breathe while starin' at the ceilin', tryin' to fall back to sleep. That mornin', though, I wanted to move.

I rolled outta bed and walked to our porch in boxers, my hairy chest free to see the world. I just needed some air, and the broken-down AC in the house wasn't cuttin' it.

Outside was muggy and hot. School's eve, my ass. Summer was never gonna end. May as well been a jungle out there.

But you know what? When the hot air rolled down my

stomach and a small wind tousled my hair, for the first time in what felt like weeks, I could just stand still. I could just stay in my own head and think whatever I wanted to think. I chose to think of nothin' at all. Always the best option.

It felt good, it felt right, not thinkin' of nothin'. I forgot bout the 'Skins, Sandra's doctor appointment, Mama's words, Casey's dog, and even the fact that my truck was busted up. But despite my best effort, somethin' managed to creep into my empty head and wake me up, hard. I headed back into the house and went down to the basement.

It wasn't much of a basement, more of an underground closet, stacked with our crap from good and not-so-good times. On one side was Casey's old toys, on the other Sandra's old clothes, and in the smallest corner, my old junk.

I tiptoed over and kicked around some stupid fishin' rods that I never used to gain access to some boxes hidden at the bottom of my pile. After pushin' through them, I found what I was lookin' for—the brown shoe box marked with a hole in its corner. I lifted it up and threw the top off.

Inside was a single folded letter. Careful as all hell, I opened it up and read it once again, as I had every year for the last sixteen years.

Hi Forrest,

Hope things have calmed some and you're doing all right. It's been a good trip for me. After I left, I started driving and I didn't stop, not for a whole day. Eventually, I had to park and sleep, and then I started driving again. America's a beaut. She's got it all. Mountains, trees, and clean skies, the whole shebang.

I'm looking for a place to make my stand, somewhere as far away from Virginia as possible. I'd recommend the same to you.

Come join me. There's nothing there for us (but you should finish school first).

For now, I'm staying in this crappy little hostel in Phoenix for a couple weeks working at a cafe while I save up gas money. I think I'll settle in one of these hot states at this rate. They're nice places. Cali, Texas, maybe. The weather's pretty good, and the girls aren't bad neither. I met this stone-cold fox the other day. I think she thought I was pretty good-looking too.

Anyways, Forrest, I just wrote to make sure you were still alive, I guess. I'm sorry I had to leave you with the heat, but I couldn't stay. You know that.

I'll be here for two more weeks before I'll move on again. Send me a letter, let me know how you're doing.

See you soon,
Bryan
1412 Cerrillos Rd, Santa Fe, NM 87505

After I was done readin', I folded it up, slid it into my pocket in case I wanted to give it to Mama later, and tiptoed back up the stairs. Then I went to the bathroom and took a long shower.

CHAPTER 7

"Aye, Forrest, what happened to your ride?"

That was how Luis greeted me.

I popped open my door and hopped out. "Nothin'. Just got in a little bump, that's all."

"Ah." He walked over to me with a smile. "You want me to take a look at it? I think we can order a new bumper, no problem."

"No, Luis. It's fine. She rides good."

He rubbed his chin while starin' at the truck's exposed radiator. "Well, Forrest, if you say so." Then he went back into the shop.

Luis had always been an interestin' case. More than a handful of times, he'd described how he'd gone to school to be a doctor back home, but things got messy in Venezuela, so he escaped with his family. They were gonna go to Colombia, but after a series of shenanigans, the legality of which I've never been quite certain of, they ended up in Miami. Now he's a "citizen" and has four kids.

But to be fair to him, he was the hardest workin' guy in the shop. Harder workin' than me—most of the time, anywho—

harder workin' than the old man, and definitely harder workin' than Andy. He happened to also be paid the least in the shop.

When Daddy started havin' me run payroll and I found out, I asked him how Luis could possibly be makin' less than Andy. "Andy's a bum, and Luis has been around for three more years than him," I said.

The old man shrugged and told me Andy had asked for more money, and we needed him, and Luis hadn't asked for nothin'. You give that dinosaur an inch, he'll take a marathon's miles every time.

I followed Luis into the shop and avoided lookin' into the glass of the office, where I knew the old man woulda been since seven a.m., glued to a computer screen. In recent months, he'd been examinin' website options and got this nerdy, pimply lookin' kid from the local high school to help build it. Afterward, every Monday mornin', he checked it out to see our reviews on "the Googler."

Gotta admit, the site ain't bad. It's got this car with big eyes and a smile, and it says underneath: *Wilcox Auto Will Have You on Your Way in No Time!* And in smaller words underneath that, it reads: *A Family Business Since 1977!* I find that part hilarious.

I spent the mornin' mostly loungin'. We had a car come by that needed an inspection, and someone who wanted an oil change, but Luis took care of it. It was a mornin' for sittin' by the AC, watchin' other people work.

Durin' one real deep lull, I sat with Luis, and we shot the shit. "Hey, Luis," I said, "why'd you have four kids?"

"Huh? What do you mean?"

"I mean, why'd you want four kids? Why not one or three or six or somethin'?"

"Six kids? That's way too many."

I rocked back in this old crappy chair we had in the garage

and sighed. "That ain't what I'm sayin'. I mean, like, how'd you know four was the right place to stop?"

"I don't know."

"Just answer the damn question."

Luis rubbed his chin, as Luis does. "It just felt right. Two girls, two boys. Everyone's got a friend."

Fuckin' Luis. "You know, Luis, just shut up."

And shut up he did. We sat in silence and let the heat stew.

A coupla minutes later, there was a knock from the office, and the old man poked his face in fronta the glass. He wagged his finger at me. I pretended to not notice, but then he banged on the glass, so I got up and walked in.

"Boy, what's gotten into ya?" he asked. "Ya puttin' on all this attitude all the sudden, just leavin' yer mama. I didn't raise ya like that."

I grunted.

"I'm too old for this nonsense." He pushed his chair forward and turned away from me. "So."

"So?"

He grunted.

We stayed quiet, listenin' to Andy plop around the garage, and Luis's rapid-fire Spanish conversation on the phone with his wife, till he said, "Ya know, ya was always the lazy one. Ain't wanna do this, ain't wanna do that. Every day that's what I'd hear. 'I don't wanna study. I don't wanna play ball. I don't wanna fix the car. Mama says we're gonna bake a cake.' Always complainin', every day."

I scoffed. "It's funny. I seem to remember it different. If I recall correct, I was the only one willin' to listen to you, for reasons I can't tell."

He waved a hand in the air. "Ya know, Forrest, at some point yer gonna needa grow up. Man up. That ain't the note I wanted to give this whole speech on, but I guess it is what it is. Fact is, I don't like it neither, but yer gonna listen to yer mama and do what she says."

"Yeah?" He got me laughin'. "Why's that? You're his father. Do your duty."

"Fuck off, Forrest."

I hadn't heard my Daddy cuss like that for as long as I could remember, so yeah, I shut up for a bit.

"Boy, yer his brother." Raisin' his arms above his head, he groaned. "Ya know why I've taken such an interest in these computer folk? It ain't just bout cashin' in. I've been lookin' for him on the Googler, but I can't find nothin'. Boy's gone and done changed his name, I suspect. Dropped the Wilcox name. I hate the work, but yer mama kept askin' and askin' and cries when I ain't searchin'. She thinks my hearin' is worse than it is. And I simply can't have that no more. I'm too old to figure all this out, and even if I could find him, I ain't talkin' to him, not till he apologizes. So yer gonna do the talkin', and yer gonna do the findin', and yer gonna bring him back here to see his mama, and that's final. And if yer mama asks ya why ya changed your damn mind, ya don't say a damn word bout me, cause she oughta know her boy cares enough bout her to find his brother. Ya understand me?"

I inhaled hard and scratched my arm. I was fixinta list some foolish items from our past, but the better part of me decided against it. I stewed over the last sixteen years, the days' slowness, the months' speed, how hot it was outside, how hot the drive would be. "How am I gonna find him? How am I gonna afford the trip?"

Daddy crossed his legs. "A man can't get rid of a name that easy. Ya always had more brains tucked away in that thick skull of yers. Start usin' them. As for money, I'll give ya my card."

All the sudden he had this green rectangle in his hand

pointin' at me, and I looked at him with wide eyes. That was how I knew he was serious. I took it and slid it into my pocket.

"Now don't be spendin' money ya don't needa spend. Cheap motels only, no snackin' around. I expect ya to be back here in two and a half weeks."

"Two and a half? That ain't a lotta time."

He shrugged. "Any more and ya'd be gettin' lazy." He paused, then added, "And yer mama's sick."

I shook my head to hide my tiny smile. The farthest I'd ever gone was Florida.

"Now go and get some work done," he said.

As I was walkin' out, I don't know what possessed me, but I felt like sendin' one more drill into the old man.

"Hey, you wanna know what Casey wanted for her birthday?"

"What?"

"A dog." I regretted sayin' it immediately.

He stared at me for a second before turnin' back around to face his desk.

I LEFT the shop at five sharp, and as I rode 464 with my window down and the sun burnin' the side of my face, I knew somethin' was different.

Coulda been that day, maybe somethin' in the sky, but I felt different. The air I breathed in hit me smoother. Brain turned easier. I guess when every day becomes so familiar, any disruption hits twice as hard and creates ripples twice as large.

Felt like the shortest commute I'd had in years, and when I saw my house in the distance, I wondered how I was gonna broach the subject with Sandra. She'd understand, I suspected. She'd always had a soft spot for Bryan. Everyone did.

Lucky for me, she was right in fronta the house when I arrived, waitin' with a big smile. I smiled back.

It all just felt perfect, you know? Sky, sun, smile—that combination of tiny little touches that put the picture together.

I hopped outta my car and practically skipped toward her. Imagine that, a grown-ass chubster downright skippin'. But I didn't care—I'd made my decision. I was gonna find Bryan.

But to my surprise, she spoke first. "I have great news, Forrest!"

"Yeah? That's nice. I got some good news myself."

I could tell she didn't expect that outta my mouth, with the way she paused. "You go first," I said with another smile.

"Okay." She exhaled a tiny bit before rattlin' off. "You remember our conversation from last night? How I said I was going to see a doc on the baby situation?"

I grunted.

"Well, I went in today, and I met Dr. Max. He checked everything out."

"*Everything*?"

She laughed—fakeish, kinda, if I'm bein' honest—and playfully said, "Shut up, Forrest. Point is, he said it all looks good. All the business. My uterus, my tubes, my hormone levels, blood pressure, all that jazz! He said it looks perfect, that I should have no problem getting pregnant. I might even have a good decade of fertility left. And Dr. Max is the best in the business. He's Dr. Max *Goldsmith*."

I rubbed my chin and murmured, "Those Jew doctors ain't never wrong." My gears started turnin'. "So..." I trailed off.

She grabbed my forearm and leaned in closer. "So we're good. Dr. Max did have one tiny recommendation, though."

My head started hurtin', and the heat suddenly became unbearable. My forehead was gettin' too hot, half from that bastard sun and half from the fireworks goin' on in my brain.

"Dr. Max recommended you get a urologist exam, just to make sure everything's all right. He said if there's an issue, it's likely resolvable."

I pulled back and let her arm drop off. "You know I ain't never been too good with words. Whatcha mean 'urologist?' You want someone to look at my dick or somethin'?"

She shook her head. "No, it's just to check—"

"So you're sayin' there's somethin' wrong with me? That's what you're sayin', ain't it?"

"No, Forrest." Her shoulders hunched over, and she slid her hands into those pathetic jelly-bean-sized pockets they put on woman pants. "This is our chance. We can have another kid, another baby. Think about that. I thought you'd be happy."

"No, no, no," I said as I stepped away from her, toward the house. I scratched my back. It was like a rash had suddenly hit, screamin' at me to scratch. "No, what you're sayin' is there's somethin' wrong with me. That's what I'm hearin' from what you're sayin'."

"Forrest..."

I spat onto the dirt. "What? What is it, then? What else you wanna say?"

She started poutin', lookin' at the ground. "What was your good news?" she asked quietly.

I puffed up my chest and inhaled hard. "I'm gonna find Bryan."

Then I walked toward the house and ripped the front door open. There, standin' right by the entrance, was Casey.

The girl stared at me like she expected me to say somethin'.

"What?" I asked.

"Who's Bryan?"

"Nobody." I walked in and dropped on the couch. God, my head felt nasty. Then I heard Casey's tiny footsteps' pitter-patter, and before I knew it, she was lingerin' right over me.

"That's not what it sounded like to me," she said.

I closed my eyes. "That so? What'd it sound like to you?"

She pushed my side a bit to try to make room for her to sit, but I didn't budge. "Casey, I ain't in the mood for none of your shenanigans."

"Shenanigans? What does that mean?"

I sighed. "Shenanigans? It's like silliness, foolishness, annoyingness. And I ain't here for it. Not right now."

"Okay." She went back to pushin' me. "I'll stop all shenanigans if you tell me who Bryan is."

You know that split second right before everythin' starts up? Like an engine. One second it's dead, but then you give it a little spark, and suddenly it's roarin' and alive? That was me. Somethin' inside got lit, and a heat flashed across my forehead. In less than a second, I swung my legs and sat up and opened my eyes wide. I spoke deep and strong, loud enough to make the entire couch shake, the whole room tremble. "Casey, stop this right now."

She pounced back and froze. Looked like the little fawn I'd hit a few years back in my old truck. Then she scampered off to her room.

Damnit. "Casey," I called out after her, but she didn't say nothin'. I fell back onto the couch, groanin' and rubbin' my head till I thought bout how Sandra could come in at any second. I let out one final groan, picked myself up, and went to her room.

I knocked.

No response.

I knocked again. "Casey!"

"Go away," she said behind the door.

Twelve-year-olds, man. Hot and cold twenty-four seven.

"Casey, I'm comin' in." I turned the knob, and she was sittin' on her bed, holdin' her legs, cryin'.

I walked up to give her a hug, but she turned away. I sighed and fell down onto a bright-blue beanbag sittin' beside her closet. Then I rolled over onto a pile of her dirty clothes. I waited like that, with my head sideways, pressed into a stinky pair of sweatpants, till she finally stopped bawlin', turned only a little teary and sniffly.

"Casey," I said without much enthusiasm, "I'm sorry."

She didn't say nothin'.

"I'm just tired, that's all. Today was a long day. I didn't mean to snap at you."

Still, she didn't say nothin'.

"Well?"

It felt like I had to wait a good minute till she finally spoke. "All I asked was 'who's Bryan?'"

I sighed again. "Yeah, you're right. That's all you said."

"Yeah, that's all I said." Again we had quiet, till she asked, "So... who is he?"

I rolled over, tumblin' down the pile of clothes, and landed on the floor, starin' at the ceilin'. "That's a good question," I grunted and squirmed. "I knew him once, can't say I know him now."

"What's that mean?"

I snorted a bit and stretched out, ended up doin' a sorta half snow angel on her floor. You oughta try it some time. Carpet ain't too bad for tired bones. "I don't know," I said. "It's just somethin' I felt like sayin', that's all. Somethin' that came to my mind."

As I crawled back up the beanbag, I saw Casey's big blue eyes, Sand's eyes, lookin' at me, so I sighed, then spoke straight. "Casey, just cause you asked nicely, I'll tell you the truth." I paused, long enough to juice the moment, before I said, "Bryan's my brother, my older brother."

"Woah, woah. Really?"

I nodded.

She started tappin' her fingers against her bed, tryin' to process the information, I guess. Kids are weird. One second sobbin', the next all calm. But you know, she's funny like that. Another kid woulda probably been jumpin' around at that point, but not Casey. She's a driller—she wants to know every detail when she's focused on somethin'.

"Does that mean I have an uncle?"

I nodded. "I suppose it does."

"Woah," she repeated. "Does this mean I have cousins?"

"Maybe, I don't know." I'd considered the idea myself from time to time, tryin' to picture a niece, maybe a nephew or two, but the picture always flowed outta my brain like sand through your hands. I couldn't imagine Bryan as nothin' but that seventeen-year-old hothead. Sometimes I wondered if he was thinkin' bout me.

"So where is he?"

"I don't know."

"What do you mean, 'you don't know'? How could you not know where your brother is?"

"Ain't too complicated. I don't know where he is." I grunted and then remembered the piece of paper burnin' a hole in my pocket. I yanked it out. "You'll like this. Have you ever seen a letter? You kids ain't got a need for it, I guess."

I crunched it up a bit and threw it at her. She missed the catch but then scooped it up.

"What's this? A letter from him?"

"Yeah, it's the last thing he wrote me."

She started readin' it aloud, like she was tellin' me a story, so I closed my eyes and listened.

"*Hope things have calmed some and you're doing all right. It's been a good trip for me...*"

She's good at things like that, readin', all that school stuff.

Could read at a fifth-grade level in third grade. Don't know where she got it from, but it's pretty incredible.

"*...Mountains, trees, and clean skies, the whole shebang...*"

I tried to picture it, him ridin' down America's roads, starin' at her scenery, but I couldn't. It was too foreign, too alien.

"*...For now, I'm staying in this crappy little hostel in Phoenix...*"

I opened my eyes and realized maybe I shouldn't have let her read it.

"*...and the girls aren't bad neither. I met this stone-cold fox the other day...*"

I got up and walked over. "Okay, okay, nice readin'. That's enough."

I grabbed it back as she finished, "*Send me a letter, let me know how you're doing.*"

Stuffin' it back into my pocket, I said, "Yeah. That's Bryan."

"Interesting..." She trailed off and went back to tappin' the bed. "Did you send him a letter?"

"What?"

"He said at the end, 'send me a letter.' Did you send him a letter? Maybe you could've figured out where he is."

"Yeah, well, he probably ain't there no more. He wouldn't get the mail there."

"That's not what I meant. I meant did you send him mail *before*, like when you got the letter."

I stretched my legs and walked to her door. "I'mma watch some TV, care to join?"

After some thinkin', she nodded. "Sure."

We went to the livin' room, and I had a look around for Sandra, but she was nowhere to be found.

CHAPTER 8

The sun was already down, the crickets yappin', and Casey corralled to bed (where she was probably hidin' out on her phone), when Sandra rolled through the front door with an H&M bag in hand. I eyed the woman down, expectin' some kinda explanation, but she didn't offer nothin'. Didn't even look at me.

"Where the hell you been?" I hollered. "Why didn't you respond to my texts? You can't just take off like that. I had to fix up somethin' for Casey, and she kept askin' where you were and if you could pick up dino nuggets. Did you read the text? Did you pick up the nuggets?"

She put the bag on the ground and crossed her arms. "No, I didn't pick up any nuggets. I had an evening out for myself. Seems like you do it plenty. Guess I felt like it was finally my turn. I did a little retail therapy, did some thinking, met up with my sister. What's the big deal?"

"I'm sorry I snapped at you, but I have a lot on my mind, and I still ain't goin' to no ball doctor."

She stopped for a second, then moved toward the kitchen. She acted different, seemed she walked a little taller, I reckon, with her neck higher and her back straighter. "So be it," she said.

So be it.

I plopped back onto my recliner. "We're gonna be fine. Everythin's gonna be fine."

She sat on a stool behind me, watchin' the muted baseball game with some teams neither of us cared bout, just somethin' to stare at. "I'll be fine," she said.

I twisted my neck and poked my head over the back ridge of the seat, lookin' at her with one eye. "Whatcha mean by that?"

She sipped her water. Man, I swear, between Bryan, the ball doctor, and that summer's heat, my brain was outta whack. While she gulped the liquid in our dark livin' room, the night hugged her and hid her from me, hid all her faults. Everyone looks better in the dark. I half wanted to cry and apologize, I half wanted to yell and fight, and I half wanted to just walk up to her and haul her off to bed.

But I did none of those things. I just waited for her answer. And I suppose that was always the problem.

"I mean what I said. I'll be fine. I mean, Forrest, till you get your business figured out, I'll be fine. Casey and I will be fine."

"Business figured out?"

She laughed. No, not even really a laugh, more a fake scoff, tryin' to drill me. "I tell you we have another chance at a kid and you start freaking out about getting a doc to look at your balls? What are you so worried about? It's not a big deal. And then you say you're looking for Bryan? What on earth are you talking about? Why are you worried about that screwup when we should be focusing on our own problems?"

"Hey." I sat up. Leanin' over the recliner, I growled, "Don't you say that."

She got up. "I'm going to bed. I'd advise you to stay here for the night and mull things over."

As she walked away, I couldn't believe my ears. This was the same girl who laughed like a drunk hyena when I prank-called Mrs. L and told her that her sprinkler system would be automatically reprogrammed if she didn't call my buddy Frank, who just so happened to have the same number as a "naughty" phone line. Where'd that girl gone? Who was this serious lady in my house?

"Mull. You usin' fancy words now?"

She didn't respond or shake her head. She simply closed the door to our bedroom and let it click behind her.

THAT NIGHT, I couldn't sleep good. Bein' on the couch didn't help none, obviously, but it was more than that. It was like my brain was pullin' me in all directions. I remember this one movie, or maybe it was a TV show. I don't know, it don't matter. Point is, on it, they had this guy strapped down and horses tied to each of his limbs. They were drawin' and quarterin' the poor bastard. And that night my damn head was the same—bastard was bein' drawn and quartered.

On one corner, I got tugged toward a wholesome family sight: Sandra and me makin' amends, embracin', maybe even workin' toward another kid.

But on the other corner of my imagination, I was gettin' pulled toward somethin' much more blurry, and with that blurriness, more excitin'. I saw Bryan, a road, a sun, and a car. I saw him on an endless drive. I saw his leavin' and his arrivin' and leavin' again. That night, on the couch, the vision I'd tried to find over all those years finally became clear.

I saw his car pass America's sights: her mountains, her rivers, her lakes. I saw him take it in, take in her glory. I saw him ridin' at seventeen with a grin on his face.

Then gradually, before I realized there was any change in my mind's eye, it was me I saw in the car, and me alone. I saw myself leavin', leavin' everythin' behind, drivin' to the unknown with no possessions except the clothes I wore. I drove with no weight, nothin' pullin' me down. Strange part was, I wasn't goin' in search of Bryan, or drivin' to somewhere in particular. I was just goin'. I was drivin' and drivin', and I couldn't see the end of the road, but it didn't matter, cause in the distance there could be anything. There was only me, the engine, the wind, the sun, and I was free.

Then my logical side pulled me back: I wanted to help Mama, but I knew the chance of findin' him was awful low. Didn't help neither that Sandra had reached a boilin' point. Leavin' might break her. And why should I look for him? Seemed Bryan hadn't been bothered enough to check his rearview mirror over all these years.

So that night, I twisted and turned on the couch, driftin' between my two heads, fallin' in and outta sleep, playin' with myself, stumblin' in and outta certainty, in and outta my decision.

But then, in the middle of the two roads, with my head rippin' apart, someone pulled me from my thoughts.

A little girl wandered outta her room in pajamas and with two sleepy eyes. She was headin' to the bathroom when she spotted me rustlin' awake and came over. "Daddy," she asked as she rubbed her eyes, "what are you doing on the couch?"

"Just takin' a nap. Go back to bed," I whispered.

"No. I need to use the bathroom." She began to walk away but then turned back. "When am I going to get to meet Uncle Bryan?"

With her bleary eyes fixated on me, I realized we both had the same question. And at that moment, after hearin' her say *Uncle Bryan*, my decision was made for me.

I said louder, "I'm gonna go look for him. I'm leavin' tomorrow. I mean today. I'm gonna drive, and I'm gonna find him."

She nodded, as if my early mornin' rambles made sense. "Can I come with you?"

I smiled and shook my head. "No. I don't know how long I'll be gone."

"I don't have school for another three weeks."

"Go to sleep, baby."

And she walked away, peed, and went to bed.

CHAPTER 9

I woke up sweatin'. In a panic. My body had me all wound up tight—my head rang and my hand went straight to grabbin' my heart.

Damn. I'm late for work.

I grunted while crackin' open the curled ball I'd found myself in, but then I fell off the couch and landed hard on the floor.

Shit. Wait. I ain't goin' to work. With my tailbone rattled, I pushed myself back up real slow, groanin' all the way. Then I checked the livin' room for Sandra, but she wasn't there. God, I remember my head felt like absolute garbage, just pure trash disposal on a loop. Shoulda mentioned it earlier, but I had more than a coupla beers the previous night while Sandra was out missin'.

With my dead head, I went to the kitchen to get some water, but a kid's laugh-scream floatin' through the air distracted me. I turned around and popped open the door to our backyard and squinted as the summer light hit me.

Outside, in the middle of the bright grass, under that damned perpetually hot sun, were Casey and Mary Anne sittin' on this crappy little bench we built for our backyard, while Sandra watched them from our crappy little patio.

I ran my hand through my hair to try to look halfway decent and sat beside her. As we watched the girls, she didn't say nothin', so I spoke first. "Last night was as strange as that one time a bat flew into your cousin Jerry's room and knocked over his lamp. You remember that?"

She shrugged. "I slept fine."

I grunted. "Alright, be like that." Casey was on her phone, and Mary Anne was on hers. Neither even looked at each other. Damn kids don't know how to play these days. "I thought bout what you said last night."

"And?" She had this small tell in her voice. A tiny waver that wasn't there before. My old man's trainin' gave me some skill at least, that attention to detail. That man could pick up a dozen unique problems based on different pitched engine-whirs. The night musta done her in too, I thought. She'd cooled off.

"I gotta find Bryan."

She raised her hands and her voice went higher, almost pleadin'. "But why now? Why now? Why didn't you look for him earlier? If he wanted to be found, he would've come back. Forrest, you're just distracting yourself. It's like that time you said you were gonna start boating and bought that silly little dinghy—"

"My mama's sick."

She stopped talkin', and I stopped talkin' too. Her shoulders bent in, like some kinda paralysis had hit her spine, a new kinda tension. "I know she's sick," she said. "She's been sick."

"Naw. She's real sick. Like sick, sick. Gotten sicker. She told me she wanted to see Bryan before, well, you know. She said that I had to find him."

Sandra started rubbin' the jeans over her thighs and stopped lookin' my way entirely. "Okay, okay, that's fine. Just do a Google search or something. People do this professionally."

Shakin' my head, I said, "Naw, there ain't time for that. I needa *see* him. I needa look at him in the eye and tell him man to man to come home for our mama. The old man's been tryin' to find him online, apparently, but he can't get a trace. Seems he's gone and changed his name, but I'll do my own research on the road and figure it out. Sand, Mama ain't seen him for fifteen years. She needs him back."

Sandra let out this exhale, this annoyin' noise that stretched out, looped back, and slapped me. "Sounds more like you want to join him."

The summer and the crickets and the children spoke for me.

She sighed. "I get it. I really do get it. I'd want to see my sister too, after that long. It's just that... this isn't the right time. Get someone else to look for him. Even when you're here, you're never really *here*. Do you get what I'm saying? Baby, this is our life. And the moment I tell you we have a shot at another kid, you go on and tell me—"

"This ain't bout that."

"I don't care what it's about. How long will you be gone? Two weeks? A month? Two months?"

"It'll only be three weeks, max."

"That's not the point!" she shrieked.

That got the girls' attention. For once, they weren't starin' at their damn phones. They looked up at us, tryin' to piece together what the hell was goin' on.

I waved at them. "How you doin', Mary Anne? You want some water?"

"That's okay, Mr. Wilcox. I think I'm good."

I smiled and nodded, till they finally went back to their little distraction rectangles.

Sandra began starin' at me again with that smooth heat she

had yesterday when she came home. "I told Barb I'd drop off Mary Anne at one. She's finishing up her morning shift at the 7-Eleven."

"Aight."

Sandra stood up and looked down upon me. Her shadow was long and dark. The woman really did seem like a 300-pound warrior at that moment. "When were you thinking of leaving?"

"I don't know. This afternoon? Maybe tomorrow mornin'?"

She spoke with one smooth, bold line. "Forrest, if you go on this trip, we may not be around when you get back."

"What?"

She turned to the girls. "Come on, Mary Anne, I'mma drop you off at your mom's." Then she quickly added, "Casey, you come too. We can go get ice cream after."

I did nothin', just stared at my shoes. You woulda thought I was a bitch or somethin' if you just saw me from the outside, frozen. But you oughta know—inside my head everythin' was steamin'. Her words ricocheted around my brain like a .50 slug, tore me up thick and draggy, violent as hell. She'd punched me, busted me right in the gut, with just a coupla words.

What the fuck? What the fuck was she talkin' bout? Sure, we'd had some fights, but "we may not be around when you get back"? What the fuck was that supposed to mean? Where'd that shit come from?

I wanted to yell, to scream, to cry, but instead, bein' so rattled, all I could muster was starin' at my shoes while the world moved around me. I couldn't do nothin' but watch Sandra enter the house, then watch Mary Anne follow her in. But just as Casey was bouta trail in after her, I managed a whisper. "Casey."

As I spoke, my mouth felt all cracked and dried and nasty. Mind you, I still hadn't showered or brushed my teeth or drank water, but it was more than that. All the energy in my body had been zapped out just by Sandra threatenin' that tiny glimpse of an end.

"Casey," I whispered again.

"What?" she asked back, matchin' my volume.

I managed a weak, forced smile. "You wanna go on a trip with me?"

"CASEY," Sandra yelled from the living room. "WE'RE GOING."

"What trip?" she asked.

"You wanna help me find Bryan, your uncle?"

Her big eyes grew ever bigger, and a sick grin spread across her face.

"Okay," I said. "Tell Mama you actually wanna stay home, that you don't feel so good."

She's a smart girl, and she had this shine in her eyes. She knew what was up, but she also didn't wanna get caught in a mouse trap. She started sayin', "But I feel fine—"

"That don't matter. You wanna come or not?"

"CASEY, COME ON," Sandra called again.

She peeked into the livin' room, then nodded at me, and I said, "Okay."

She ran into the livin' room, while I listened closely behind the door.

"Mama, actually, I'm going to stay. I don't feel so good."

Then I heard a sigh from Sandra. "Fine. Whatever. Let's go, Mary Anne. I'll be back in a half an hour."

After a couple seconds, I got up real slow, draggin' my head's weight up with me. If she was gonna threaten leavin', and worse even, takin' Casey, then I'd just haveta get equally dirty. I walked one step, two step, till I was back in tune with my body.

"Casey," I said, "find a week's worth of clothin' and whatever you need on a trip. We'll be out for around two weeks."

"Mama's not coming?" she asked, real nonchalant.

"No," I said. "She's gonna relax here while we go."

She put on this little face. "You know I'm not stupid, right? I'm twelve now."

I grunted. She wasn't wrong—she was twelve, after all. "Whatever. Just get ready. Quick."

We ran off, me to my room, her to hers. I grabbed seven T-shirts, and one nice collar-up in preparation for when I found Bryan, five pairs of jeans, and nine pairs of underwear. Then I ran to the bathroom, changed, brushed my teeth, and packed up a kit.

I went back down the hall, and there was Casey, already ready, with a big heavy duffel bag slung over her shoulder. "You got everythin'?" I asked. "A toothbrush? Toothpaste? Enough clothes?"

She nodded profusely. "Yes, I have everything."

"Do you want me to check?"

"No, I'm good."

"Fine. Let's go."

I led the way out, while her bag weighed her down. I grabbed it, swung it over my shoulder, and walked to my truck.

She stopped in fronta it, in fronta the gash from my incident with Macy and the oak, and asked, "We're going on the trip in the truck? Will it work the whole trip?"

"Yes, it'll work," I said in a hurry. "She's a good truck. Come on now, let's go."

Casey started to open up a back door when I said, "It's fine, Casey. You can sit in the front."

You shoulda seen her face. You woulda thought it was Christmas. She scrambled into the shotgun and buckled right up. I threw her bag and my suitcase into the back seats and went to the driver seat. I turned on the truck and began to pull the reverse, when she went, "Wait! Wait!"

I put the truck back in park. "What?"

She unbuckled and hollered, "Let me use the bathroom first!"

I groaned as she hopped outta the truck. While I waited, I checked my rearview mirror a few times, lookin' for incomin' trouble, till the girl finally came rumblin' back.

She climbed back in, looked at me with a determined face, and said, "Let's go!"

It was at that moment, when I looked into her proud eyes and considered her small bladder, that I decided I shoulda just driven away while she was on the commode.

CHAPTER 10

"We're goin' to the beach first," I said.

"Why?" she asked.

"Cause I wanna. It's gonna be a long trip."

The truth of the matter was, I wanted to feel the sand on my tiny toes and see the waves one more time before I'd haveta say goodbye to them, but I wasn't bouta tell her that.

I found us a nice little parkin' spot beside someone's big fancy blue house and grabbed her hand and ran us across the street. A car or two goin' twenty over zipped past us, nearly squished us, but we dodged them good.

The beach was two-thirds alive, with stay-at-home mamas and little boys and girls runnin' about, but no grown men, except me, I guess. As we pulled off our shoes and walked onto the sand, I looked at the families and wondered where the hell all the years went.

When we reached the ocean, Casey said, "Daddy?"

I grunted.

"Why did Bryan leave?"

I closed my eyes. The sun burned the back of my neck somethin' fierce while the cool water ran over my feet. My toes sunk slow into the wet sand, and I flexed each one, tryin' to curl the sand around them, make them feel good.

"I remember this one time when we, the whole family—me, Bryan, Grandmama and Papaw, and my grandparents—were all here, right on this here beach. While they lounged lazy, me and Bryan were buildin' this giant moat in the sand. We were gonna have this mighty ol' water system, on the scale no kid had ever before seen, and we were gonna stake out the land. Conquer it. Make it our own little plot of beach and cut out everybody else, cut out all those other ten-year-old punks on the beach, cut out our folks too. It'd be only us."

For a second, there was only me, my head, and the waves' whooshin'. You know those moments where it's like you done floated outta your body, and you're starin' back at yourself cause you've lost all focus so all that's left is your swimmin' head? No arms, no legs, no nothin'? Just alone with a memory? Thinkin' bout it now, you probably ain't got a clue what I'm talkin' bout. I barely do. This whole business has made me softer, I guess. All I can say is that was how I felt then.

But Casey brought me back to myself. She bumped against me, and I opened my eyes. "What happened?" she asked.

I bumped her back. "One of those ten-year-old punks kicked in our moat. It disappeared in seconds after it took hours to build." Then I laughed. "But Bryan kicked his ass."

After one last big breath in, one to put all the salt and sea goodness into my system, I asked, "You ready to go now?"

"I've been ready to go. Are *you* ready to go?"

"I don't know. I guess so."

After a few minutes or so back in the truck, I handed my phone to Casey and said, "Find '*Ain't No Day Like Today*' and play that."

She started scrollin'. "Who's it by?"

"What do you mean 'who's it by'? There's only one '*Ain't No Day Like Today*.' It's by Tyler Preston."

"You could've just said it's by Tyler Preston."

"Whatever. Just play the dang song."

"The Bluetooth isn't connected."

"Well, connect it, sugar."

Then finally:

Risin' like the sun in the east,

There we go. I leaned back into my chair and put one hand on the wheel.

she'll come back one day, I know,

This wouldn't be too bad, I thought. Just cruisin', relaxin', gettin' into a groove.

even though she's left with the wind

"Can I choose the next song?" Casey asked.

But I can't stay here—

"Uh, sure, but only the next one."

—wonderin' where she's gone—

"Traffic doesn't look good," she said. She was right—looked like there was another accident.

"That's okay."

—put the ol' engine to the test—

"We're in no rush." Was it too damn much to just listen to a song in peace?

But ain't no reason to be stressed
We just gonna head out west, yeah—

"How long will it take us to get to Uncle Bryan?"
"I have no idea, let's just listen to the song. Okay?"

'Cause ain't no day like today
The journey will be—

RING, RING, RING.
"You got a call, Daddy."
I put some edge in my voice. "I know. Who's it?"
RING.
She pulled the phone to her face. "It's Mama."
I grunted.
"Should I answer it?"
RING.
"No," I said real fast. "Just let it go to voicemail. I'll call her back later."

Casey let out a tiny chuckle. No, it wasn't even a chuckle, more of a chortle, that smart ass. "You're just going to get in more trouble," she said.

I glanced at her. Man, as a kid, I'd sit in my daddy's car, keep quiet, and pray I wouldn't get whooped like a redheaded stepchild when I got home. All these kids havin' a phone since the day they left the crib has rewired their brain, I swear. When I became a father, I decided if I had a son, he'd get a coupla smacks of the switch. Not as many as we got, though. Lucky for Casey, I'd never hit a girl.

"Whatever," I said, "just let it go to voicemail."

Finally, it stopped ringin', and the song picked up again.

and all my friends have go—

RING, RING, RING.

"Shit, just give it to me."

She handed the phone over, and I turned it off. "Thank God."

And just as quick as it came, my music had left. Casey filled the vacuum with this modern country noise from her phone. It wasn't bad, but it wasn't Tyler Preston. Country's gone all hip-hop and electronic and shit. I don't get it.

Unfortunately, in the middle of the third song, her phone started blastin' off too.

"It's Mama again."

I muttered some less-than-holy things under my breath.

"I'm going to answer it," she said.

"No, don't," I managed, but it was too late.

There were some loud noises from the phone before Casey said, "She wants to talk to you."

After a quick grunt, I stretched out and weakly took the phone. "What's up, honey? Can't really talk right now, I'm drivin'."

I remember this one teacher I had, Mr. Bentley. What a savage man. Whenever Mr. B would get frustrated, pushed to the edge of his sanity, he'd take a piece of chalk and find the worst angle to shred it against the chalkboard, creatin' this awful screech. Everyone's ears would *bleed*. It hurt, physically hurt, burnt all the way down your spine and made your insides turn.

You know what, though? It got the class to shut up.

And to my surprise, Sandra unlocked her harsh inner Mr. Bentley within that light sunny voice of hers, and shut up I did.

"Forrest... Forrest. Forrest! Dear Lord, Forrest, what on earth were you thinking? It's one thing to go on this crazy trip without even saying goodbye, just taking off, but don't tell me you're actually taking Casey with you? What in the Sam Hill are you thinking? She's twelve years old. She's got school in two weeks. What are you going to do if you can't find Bryan? How long will you stay out there? My Lord. We're going broke, and now you're going on this little adventure. Lord, I could just choke you, if your neck wasn't so dang pudgy. Forrest, I know I sound like a nagging biscuit, but you know I'm right. Oh my Lord."

I waited till I was sure she was done talkin'. "It's three weeks, actually."

"What?"

I swallowed. "She goes back to school in three weeks."

"No, she goes back to school in seventeen days." The line went quiet, and for a while I only heard her breaths, tiny puffs of anxiety. "Forrest," she finally said, "just come home, just drop off Casey, and we'll talk about this. I don't want you to just go out and wander around. What'll happen if you can't find Bryan? Or what if he doesn't want to come home? Look, I get that he's your brother. Bryan is—was—a good guy, but that doesn't mean you can just take off."

When Sandra gets quiet, you know it's gotten real. Her words blew through my brain with some backbone, but in the end left no mark. Naw, my anger boiled her plea all away, boiled it right into the air and out the truck's window.

I pulled the phone close to my mouth and lowered my voice as much as I could, till it became a growl. "You said, and I quote, 'We may not be around when you get back.' What the hell was that, Sand? No, I reckon things been quiet for too long. I've been quiet for too long." I raised my voice. "Casey, you wanna find your uncle, right?"

She gave me this unsure half-held-prisoner, half-excited nod, but it was a nod nonetheless.

"The girl wants to find her uncle. It's only natural."

"I swear, Forrest, I'm gonna frickin' scr—"

I threw the phone out the window.

Bye. Bye.

"HEY," Casey hollered. "You just threw my phone out the window!"

"Yes, I did."

I glanced at her next to me. From the half I could see, her mouth was wide open and at least one eye was stuck in a lock.

"It's okay, Casey. Look, you can have my phone." I tossed my phone at her. "It's two generations ahead, bigger screen, faster, everythin' better. All yours."

She started fidgetin' with it. "Are you serious?"

"Hundred percent," I said as I accelerated—at last there was a break in the traffic. "I don't want it. I don't want it at all. All yours. Just turn it on airplane mode for an hour or so, for me. Your mama needs time to cool down. Then you can text all your friends."

Reluctantly, she shushed and focused on the phone. As it began to glow, she looked up at me like she wanted to say somethin', but the words didn't wanna come out. After the third glance, I asked, "What?"

"Nothing," she muttered. But then she asked, "What's your password?"

"2-0-0-4."

She made a sound somewhere between a squeak and a grunt.

CHAPTER 11

The day Casey was born, it rained by the bucketful, fulla cow-sized droplets. First day of rain that month, in fact. It'd been a dry summer in general, with too many long, hot days, but I kept it wet enough—had plenty of beer and some golf with old high school friends before they all disappeared into their own lives.

Man, what a good summer. That was the first summer after me and Sandra got married. Even workin' at Daddy's shop wasn't too bad back then. And I acted like I was the hottest shit to bless this planet.

"Keep your head high," my mama always told me, and back then I still listened: neck up, chest out, standin' tall and proud.

Though, on the day of the birth, my head was bent against the rain. I pulled Sandra along through the downpour, and when we reached my car, Sandra—high off pregnancy hormones—cried as we drove. She said it was rainin' somethin' fierce cause the Big Man upstairs wasn't happy. Said He was gonna ruin the delivery.

I remember bouncin' her comment off my shoulder and flippin' it around. I was wittier back then, or maybe I'd just become a master of deflection after Bryan left. I told her, "No, God himself is cryin' cause he'll haveta wait a hundred years to hang with Casey in heaven, after she's born and has walked the earth." I was a poet too, I reckon. That was back when my words still stuck, rather than peeled off and fell to everyone's feet like shit drippin' down the wall.

When we parked at the hospital, Sandra really started flippin' out. She was a tiny woman, which just made her belly all the more big. We ran the short distance from the parkin' lot to the hospital, and her hair and shirt and pants ended up soaked, while she screamed and raved like a madwoman. It was a miracle she didn't slip and fall.

It wasn't a smooth situation, not at all.

We finally managed to get to the doctor, and that was when things went from bad to worse. Sandra screamed, the nurses hollered at her to keep pushin', and I stood silent like some dumb lamppost. All the while, out the window, it seemed the Big Man wasn't done tauntin' her. Lightnin' and thunder hit, the whole shebang.

Patter, patter, push, push, CRACK, push, PUSH, patter, patter, PUSH, CRACK. The whole night.

Casey was stubborn, stubborn as all hell. She'd grown too used to her little cave, I guess, and had no interest in leavin' anytime soon.

The docs were debatin' a C-section, while Sandra screamed. A coupla times, I played messenger to the crew waitin' outside the delivery room as the hours dragged on. Everybody— Sandra's parents and her sister and my parents and two cousins —had decided they wanted to be around for the big show.

It was a blessin' Sandra had asked them to stay outta the delivery room. If I had to hear all their nonsense durin' the birth, I woulda asked the doctor to gimme a C-section as well, only don't zip mine back up.

The hours felt long... one down... another up at bat... while I just stood there, watchin', waitin', bein' generally useless. At one point, I was bouta fall asleep, sink over from the exhaustion drownin' my brain. But then it happened.

"*Push*," the doc yelled again, and scream Sandra did, and lightnin' struck hard, and thunder roared loud, and in one great dramatic slippery moment, out came this *thing*.

You know how in the TV shows after the birth the kid is already this cute baby, fully ready to be a chubby-cheeked bastard and spend its days beggin' for attention? Reality ain't like that. Instead, you get this slimy, yellowish, old-man-lookin', drownin'-rat creature. They more fishlike than human for a good while. But you know what else? That ugliness didn't matter.

That second between after Casey came out and when she started cryin', I couldn't hear nothin'—not my heart, not the nurse, not even Sandra's painful screams meltin' away into tears of joy. Naw, in that second, the world froze, and that little ugly baby became the center of it.

It was just her. It was just her.

But after her scrawny head squirmed, and she screamed and her tears poured, things began to move again. A cork I didn't know I had became unscrewed. Everythin' started to rumble: My arms shuddered, my chest shook, and my eyes got a little more than wet. I had to will my whole body into stillness to be able to cut the cord. I was worried I'd screw somethin' up, cause I couldn't see nothin' straight.

I reckon the rain was just an announcement, an announcement that the world had changed.

When we presented her to our families, I thought bout how I hadn't cried in so many years. Baskin' in the warm glow with everybody felt real good, but still there was a hint of somethin' bitter. A tiny, almost microscopic drop of disappointment hit my brain. I remembered the last time I was caught cryin'.

It made me wish Bryan coulda been there to see the little girl.

Enough of that sentimental crap, though.

Casey was lyin' on the seat, head pressed against the window, sun shinin' on her hair.

"Casey," I whispered as I poked her awake. Nothin'.

I pushed her again. "Casey."

She didn't budge but said, "What? Are we there yet?"

That got a good laugh outta me. "Baby, you've been sleepin' for two hours. We ain't even outta Virginia yet. I wanted to take a quick stop. We're at Humpback Rock."

Finally, she stirred and glanced out the window as I parked. "What's a humpback rock?" she asked.

"It's not a rock. It's *the* Humpback Rock. We're near Waynesboro and we're goin' hikin'."

She pushed herself up and raised an eyebrow. "Since when do we hike?"

I grabbed my suitcase from the back and pulled out two plastic water bottles, then chugged half of one down. "Since now. Why not? I thought on it while we were drivin' up here. It'll be a good way to kickstart things."

She took the water and began to open the door, but then turned around and asked, "Is this about you and Mama fighting?"

"What? No. Sorry, Casey, but that's some kinda new-level stupid comment. Ain't I allowed to just spend some quality time with my daughter in the great outdoors? Is there somethin' wrong with that?"

Reluctantly, she shook her head. "I guess not."

I grunted and opened the door, and the raw pollen and crisp grass hit me all at once. "God, Casey, do you feel that?

That pure breeze? That's what life's bout! Nature. Just good atmosphere."

Unfortunately for Casey, she started sneezin' up a storm. Allergy bug got her good. Me, on the other hand? I sucked in the air, and my lungs thanked me. I thanked the Lord above for no exhaust pipes for one day.

We began our trek up a small trail with a low slope. Humpback ain't too bad, I thought. Sun felt good, body felt right.

"Ain't this nice, Casey? Just you and me and the mountain?"

"Sure," she said with a sneeze. "I just wish I—*achoo*—could get a signal here." She kept tappin' on my phone—well, her new phone—while we walked up.

"Don't worry bout that. Just enjoy the nature." I pointed at the clean sky, the nice scenery. "Look at that. Everythin's gonna be alright. This is how this country's meant to be."

And you know what? I was genuinely enjoyin' myself. Till bout five minutes in, when my sweat beads finished makin' their trek from the tip of my upper back down to the bottom of my ass crack.

"Casey," I stammered as two teenage kids passed us up on the trail. Breathin' heavy, I bent over and grabbed my knees. "Lemme take a minute here." I leaned against a boulder.

She laughed, then sneezed again. "We just started. Up your endurance, Daddy."

"When... you're... my age... you'll... under... stand," I puffed out. "Okay... Let's go." We started up again, and the mountain took on a nasty incline transition, hittin' my knees hard. Damn, that bitch was tall. Soon, I slowed down once more, and Casey got ahead of me. She leaned against a rock and looked back, waitin' for me.

"We can go back," she shouted.

"No!" I wheezed. "It's fine." When I finally caught up to her, I leaned up against a tree trunk and started slippin' down till I fell down on my caboose and just sat there, on the dirt, tryin' to catch my breath.

"Seriously, we can go back."

I waved her off. "No... it's fine..." I said with a cough. "Just a minute." I took three minutes, and when we finally set off again, I slowed to a crawl almost immediately.

Eventually, as I crept forward, Casey stopped. I got a little ahead of her before I stopped too. "What's... wrong?"

"Daddy, what are we doing here?"

Leanin' against my knees, I panted a bit till I caught my breath. "Whatcha mean?" I asked. "We're on a hike."

"We never do hikes."

I grinned. "Gotta start somewhere."

She didn't think it was funny. She frowned and crossed her arms. "Why are we on a hike? We only left this morning, and we're already going so slowly."

Luckily, her shadow covered me a bit, so I could cool off. "We got plenty... of... time. It's not like... we're in... a rush." Then I caught my breath. "Look, I wanted to go on a hike, okay? Is there somethin' wrong with that?"

She sighed. "No. But—" Then she looked away.

"But what?"

"But we left to find Uncle Bryan, and you're already dilly-dallying."

I raised an eyebrow. "Dilly-dallyin'?"

"You know what I mean. If we're going to find him, we need to keep going."

You know, as she stood above me, she looked kinda funny. A day ago, I was puttin' her to sleep, now she had the nerve to gimme the business. Kids ain't never really dumb, just a little inexperienced and a lot curious, but I wasn't even sure how kiddie this cocky girl really was. I barely knew this Casey.

I groaned and grunted and pushed myself back up. "Okay, honey. You win. Let's go back to the car."

We clambered downhill on the trail, back to the parkin' lot—her smooth and steady, me like a crippled, hot, sweaty donkey. Only half an hour in, and my shirt had become drenched.

I almost considered tellin' her why I took her on that dang hike. How I'd once hiked that entire mountain and how us boys practically ran the whole way and the sun shined bright on us, back when I was her age, back when there was no bullshit, back when my family was still whole.

I decided against it.

Instead, I said, "We'll go on a hike a different time."

"Sure. When we get a signal again, I'm going to start looking up where Uncle Bryan might be, some clues or something."

"I reckon he's in the Southwest."

She looked at me like I was brick dumb. "I know, I read his letter. But that's not enough. We're going to need an address, or at least a city. Some lead." She kicked a rock. "I've read enough mystery books to know he'll probably be where we least expect him."

I rubbed my chin. "I don't know bout that. Bryan was never the trickiest type or much of a recluse. He mighta changed his name or somethin', but he ain't hidin' out there, if that's what you think. He ain't a hider. Wouldn't hide from us. And he always wanted to be a cowboy as a kid."

"That's good." She nodded. "Clues."

As we walked down the hill, an epiphany hit me—Casey was more excited than I was. "Casey," I said, "we might not be able to find him."

She shrugged. "I think we will. Besides, I need to find out if I have any cousins."

I laughed. The idea of little Bryans runnin' around. Talk bout a storm.

Finally, we reached the bottom of the hill and spotted the truck. There Casey made one last comment. "And, Daddy, you're not old." I almost smiled, but then she finished with, "You're just fat. That's why you can't hike."

Middle schoolers say the damnedest things.

CHAPTER 12

I drove hard after the hike. No music for me. The phone had died while we got outta the mountains, and Casey realized she forgot her car charger, or any charger. I scolded her before I realized I forgot a charger too. Radio was also still broke. I shoulda fixed that one before the trip, but I'd been too lazy to get a new one forever. Not that it mattered to Casey—she'd fallen asleep a couple minutes into the drive.

We started runnin' down 81, past Roanoke, past Lexington, past tiny shacks that looked like they were outta the fifties. Little places labeled names like "Al's Grocery Store" or "Bobby's Garage." Some of them flew old battle flags—quality cotton with red and white and blue—only with lines that formed an X rather than stripes. This one small hut of a home had a sign that showed the proud words: *God, Guns, & Guts Made America Free.*

Those small towns, I knew that was where the real Americans still lived—good, hardworkin' folk—but as we passed the dust and broken-down cars and bad roads, I realized they were disappearin' real fast. Quicker than ever. Made me wonder: *What would happen if I just picked one of them towns and hid out? Would I disappear too?*

After a couple bathroom breaks and more of Casey sleepin', we reached Blacksburg, all the way on the other side of the Commonwealth, and although it was seven, it was still bright as hell, so I got a good full look at the fine Virginia Polytechnic Institute and State University.

I pushed Casey. "Casey, wake up."

Stirrin', she mumbled, "I'm awake. What is it?"

"We're at Virginia Tech, check it."

She got up and stared out the window, lookin' bored. "So what?"

"If you keep your grades up, study hard, you might could go to a place like this. College's good for you."

"Why didn't you go, then?"

I didn't answer. "Don'tcha wanna study science or math or somethin'? You're so good at that stuff."

"What about English?"

I grunted. "English might not get you paid like you'll wanna be."

We cruised down N Main Street, and it wasn't the prettiest place. It wasn't that it was horrible, just that it was more of the same. Too in between a city and a town. And there ain't no beach in Blacksburg, and too many young people dressed foolishly down the street. Good football, though.

"You see any interestin' grub? We can get whatever you want. Granddaddy's payin'."

She pointed out the window. "Joe's Diner looks fine."

I considered it some more, and my words came back to me: *Granddaddy's payin'*. "Naw," I said, "actually, let's find a hotel. We can get some fancy hotel food."

She didn't complain.

.   .   .

AFTER DRIVIN' a little further on, I found us a nice Marriott Inn. They told me it'd be $150 for the night, and normally I'd balk at that, but it wasn't my money, so I paid up. I asked them where their restaurant was, but they said they didn't have one, which didn't sit right with me cause I had this whole vision of showin' Casey a good time, with some fancy-lookin' waiters and waitresses, but I guess that's only in the movies. I ain't been in too many hotels, to be honest. Even after the weddin', me and Sandra took a "discount honeymoon," which is to say we hid away in our apartment and went at it like rabbits. The last time I'd stayed at a hotel musta been when I was a kid, down in Florida.

They did, however, have room service, which suited Casey just fine. We settled up, ordered a hamburger for me and some chicken tenders and fries for her, and made do with the space. Then we brushed our teeth and washed our faces. I took the pull-out couch, and she took bed. It was 9:23 p.m. when I cut off the lights.

It took her only five minutes to say, "Daddy."

"What?"

"I'm not tired."

"Course you're not tired, you been nappin' all day. I'm tired. I had to drive all day."

"I guess you're right." She went quiet for a bit, but then I could hear her rustlin' around, rockin' back and forth.

"What? What's it? Why you squirmin'?"

"It's just..." She trailed off. "It's just the covers are really tight, that's all."

"Well, loosen them. They'll redo them. It's their job."

"Okay." She tugged at the bed, then lay back down. "That didn't help. I'm still not tired."

I grunted. "Get tired. Count sheep."

"What?"

"Ain't you heard that before? Never mind, just go to sleep."

She went quiet, but I started rustlin' too. After a solid twenty minutes, I said, "I can't sleep neither. You wanna watch TV or somethin'?

"Sure." She grabbed the remote from the counter and turned it on to some kinda kid nonsense, but I didn't complain none. Though I had to lurch over my cot to see the screen. She saw my struggle and asked, "You want to sit on the bed?"

"No." After I said that, I realized it'd been a coupla years since me, her, and Sandra had last curled up together in the same bed. Maybe it was when she was eight, maybe nine. She was convinced there was a monster in her closest rustlin' around. We told her to essentially shut it and go to sleep, till she harassed me into checkin' it out. I tiptoed in and crouched down to point out there was no monster, just her wild imagination.

Then a massive rat jumped out right at my face.

That got a wild scream from me, a good number of tears from her, and earned aplenty of snuggles. Damn, that little kid was warm—all little kids are bundles of friendly heat packs. I guess you never realize the last time you snuggle with your daughter actually is the last time.

"Watch for a bit, then turn it off and go to sleep," I said as I closed my eyes.

"Okay, but Daddy?"

"Yes?" I asked in an annoyed tone.

"I know you don't like talking about it, but tomorrow can you tell me more about Uncle Bryan?"

I didn't say nothin', till I asked, "Why?"

"I want to search him up. I need some details if I'm going to find him."

I sighed. "Fine. Just go to sleep. Tomorrow we hit the road hard."

"Okay, but first things first, we need to buy a phone charger. I still need to text my friends my new number."

I'd almost forgotten that I gave her my phone. I groaned internally and said, "Fine. Now go to sleep." And at some point, we both did.

CHAPTER 13

Turns out, once you start relyin' on a phone, it becomes hard to rely on anything else.

"You sure you saw a sign for Walmart on the road?" I asked.

"Yes," she said.

So I took the exit, started roamin' down some local roads, but we only found some green no-man's-land called Sulphur Springs, so we went left, right, left again, back out, in a giant fuckin' circle, then back onto the highway.

"I knew there was no Walmart," I muttered.

We drove some more, and the F-150 got low on gas (she ain't the most efficient), but luckily we spotted a 7-Eleven.

"Okay," I said, "we'll get your phone charger, and I'll get my gas."

We parked, I handed her a ten, and told her to get the wire while I filled up. Leanin' against Ms. Reliable, I tried to create a mental map of the States, figure out where we were goin', but I had no clue. Already I'd gone the farthest west I'd ever been.

"Blessed day we're having, isn't it?"

I turned to my right and saw a forty-somethin'-year-old

smart-ass-lookin' bald guy fillin' up his big-ass luxury SUV. "Amen, sir. It is. I reckon it is," I said.

I thought that'd be the end of it, but then he smiled and nodded at my truck. "Got in a dustup there?"

"What?" I rubbed the part where my bumper shoulda been. "Ah, this? Ain't nothin'."

The man made this annoyin' little snicker. "My second-oldest son, Jeremy, just busted up the car we got him for graduation. Cost me a good ten grand."

"That's a shame." *Where was Casey with the damn charger, and how long was the truck gonna take to fill?*

The man went on. "You got any other kids? I noticed your daughter."

I respected his Southern hospitality, don't get me wrong, I'm well acquainted, but at a gas station? Naw, fillin' your gas means quiet time. Everybody knows that. *Everybody*, I thought. But that guy, Mr. Sunshine on my bald spot, proved me wrong. "Just the one," I said.

"Ah, I see."

See what? I wanted to ask, but before I could say somethin', he said, "I have four. Three boys, one girl."

The truck filled up, thank God. I pulled out the pump and said "Four! Bless your heart" as Casey finally emerged from the shop. I yelled, "Come on, Casey, let's go."

She yelled back, "The car jack charger costs fifteen dollars."

Goddammit. I pulled out my wallet and rifled around for the old man's card.

"You running low there, buddy?" the guy went off. "I can spare a five."

I growled, "I think we're alright." Then I turned to Casey. "I'm comin'."

I followed her into the 7-Eleven, where a bored-lookin' Black kid—who had his pants too low for my taste—manned the front counter. She pointed out the charger, and I reached for my daddy's card.

"You were talking to that guy?" she asked me.

"Don't get me started."

But speak of the devil, Mr. Friendly walked in.

He waved. "Just looking for a snack before going back to the wife." He journeyed to the back of the store.

After I handed the card over, I nudged Casey and whispered, "Casey, go out and kick that guy's car or somethin'."

"What?" she asked, just a hair too loud. "What are you on about?"

The guy found his jerky and headed to the front, so I let the issue slide. "Nothin'. Don't worry bout it," I muttered.

Then the kid behind the counter said, "Sir, this card's not working."

That put a good shock on me. "What?"

"The card didn't work."

"Seriously, I can help with that five if you need a little pocket change," Mr. Hairless-rat-lookin'-ass went off.

I waved him off with some aggression and said between my teeth, "It's fine."

I took my daddy's credit card back and pulled out my debit card and handed it over and did some mental math while a certain heat itched my neck. I never shoulda got that joint account with Sandra. After all those medical visits, I was thinkin' there could be a good chance we'd be hit with an overdraft. Real problem was that we got rid of all the credit cards after the debt got over $20,000. We shoulda just let it climb to $30K.

Fortunately, it didn't matter, cause the debit card went through, and the kid handed us the new charger. I grabbed Casey's arm and said, "Let's go."

I guess I pulled a little too hard, cause she flinched and cried, "Ow!"

I let go and stopped. Everybody stared at me.

"Sorry. Let's go now. We're leavin'." I marched out, and Casey followed me real slow, too slow.

When we finally got in the car, she plugged in the phone and asked, "What was all that about?"

"What are you referrin' to, specifically?"

She kept pressin' on the phone, tryin' to get it to go back on. "Your whole freak-out in the store."

"I didn't freak out."

"You kind of did."

"Casey, don't start in with me. I'd know if I'd freaked out, as you say, and I can explicitly say I did not freak out. I just know when someone ain't showin' you proper respect."

The phone finally started glowin', so she didn't say nothin' more. But after around a minute, after I got us back on I-81, she said, "Uh, Daddy?"

I snapped, "What's it?"

"The phone's going off."

"Whatcha mean it's goin' off?" I turned to her and saw the screen floodin' with messages.

She looked down. "A lot of them are from Mama, and she's using some... um..."

"What? Whatcha mean, 'some... um...'?"

"Well, let me just read you one: *Lord have mercy. Forrest, I swear I'm fixin to beat your—*"

"Gimme the phone, Casey."

"It's okay. I'll respond to her."

"NO, CASEY, GIVE ME THE PHONE RIGHT NOW." That shook her all up. She handed it over.

I grabbed it and thumbed around, barely lookin' at the screen. "You shouldn't text while driving," the girl mumbled.

"Just hush up for once," I said. I felt a little bad bout that, so I said, "Don't worry. I ain't textin'."

I kept glancin' up at the road, but it was plumb empty, so I dug back into the little device. First I deleted my texts with Sandra. Didn't even really read what she'd written, but I saw some nasty words for sure. Then I dug in the settins, lookin' for a way to block her, but I couldn't find nothin'.

I think I started to worry Casey, considerin' I wasn't fully lookin' at the road and all, cause she asked, "What are you trying to do?"

"I'm tryin' to block a number," I said in between tappin' and glancin' up the road.

"Mama's number? I can do it."

"What? What are you talkin' bout? I ain't tryin' to block your mama's number."

I finally found the little page where you block numbers, and I was bouta finish up, when Casey said, "It's fine, just give it to me."

"No, I got it." But then she reached her grubby little hand out at me, and as I was tryin' to push it away, while clickin' the block button, I didn't even see the bicycle to my right.

My brain told me: *Fu*— Then I clipped the bike and sent a kid flyin'.

CHAPTER 14

"Fuck, fuck, fuck," I said as I pulled over. Then I told Casey, "Stay in the damn car."

I ran out to the kid's bike by the side of the road. The impact had bent the front wheel from an O to an L and snapped the gear cables. Wrecked. Luckily, the backpack next to it had fallen off and avoided the crash. I glanced around, lookin' for the kid, and realized he'd rolled down the hill beside the road's edge. I hustled down the grass after him, into the trees, when I lost my balance and tumbled down. I bumped my head, cut my elbows, got grass all over my pants, but eventually landed next to him.

He was so short, shorter than me even, Chinese-lookin' with slanty eyes, well, not actually that slanty, to be honest, but I didn't even care none, or think that much of it, cause all I could think bout was how happy I was that they were open. I grabbed him by his shoulders and shook him. "Son, you alright?"

He was rattled, no doubtin' that, and didn't say nothin'. I worried I got him brain-dead and all, the kinda thing you hear on the news and see in the papers, but then he twitched his arms and legs and everythin', and I breathed a sigh of relief.

Slowly, he opened his mouth like it took the effort of a damn drawbridge risin' at the moment of an awful surrender. Wincin', he said, "I think so, but my foot... My left foot really hurts."

I poked down on his quad. "Here?"

"No."

Then his shin. "Here?"

"No."

Then his ankle.

"No."

His foot.

"No."

Big toe.

"No."

Finally, I reached the last possible culprit. The pinky toe. And that was when he started howlin'—the moment I touched the smallest piggy of all of them.

The kid got clipped by a F-150—two and a half tons of steel —and all that got banged up was his pinky toe. Honest, there was an argument he oughta been thankin' me there, for barely touchin' him and all, but I wasn't prepared to make it.

I helped him up, practically draggin' him up to the top of the hill, where Casey waited for us. I perched him up next to his bike, and he reached for the mangled metal mess. "My bike..."

"Yeah, sorry, buddy. She's a goner."

He closed his eyes and did a starfish on the ground, stretchin' like a fool. I waited for him to say somethin', anything, but he seemed beat. With some displeasure, I asked, "You goin' somewhere?"

He inhaled and pushed himself up, hoppin' on his right foot. "I was biking out west."

I studied him harder. He was a young, thin fella, twenty tops. Had a T-shirt with some band I ain't never heard of before, and he had a tiny stud piercin' in his left earlobe.

"Well," I said, maybe with more than a little reluctance. "We're goin' out in that general direction as well. You want a lift?" I was halfway hopin' he'd say, "Hell no, I'm going home," and we'd all be on our merry ways, but instead he kicked his broken bike down the hill with his good foot, grabbed his backpack, and managed a smile for me.

He said, "I guess this is a sign." Then he trudged over, reached for the back door of the truck, and said "Hi" to Casey, who said "Hi" back. She helped him limp into the back, then closed the door.

I gave her a glance. She gave me a shrug. She also added, "I blocked Mama for you, but I think it's a bad idea."

That whole day was startin' to feel like the beginnin' of an aneurysm.

CHAPTER 15

I drove on, not sayin' much, and Casey didn't say nothin' neither. Just buried her face in the phone. The whole situation was far too awkward. The kid kept on squirmin' in the back, tryin' to lie down, but it seemed he couldn't get no comfort.

The scenery was nice, at least. Passin' by some jumbo-sized trees and clean green on all sides and some rocks. Casey liked it some—I could tell cause after a while, she stared at the earth rather than the screen.

After nothin' was said for a good twenty minutes, I felt like I had to take control of the situation. "So, you a Chinese or somethin'?"

Casey shot me this glance like I just cursed at him, but I ain't done nothin' of the sort, so I just shrugged it off.

I watched him in my rearview mirror. He rumbled again before he sat up and took a big exhale then made a big smile. "No, I'm from New Jersey."

"But where you from, from?"

"Daddy," Casey began, but the kid in the back waved it off and laughed at her.

"It's okay. I get it a lot. I have Vietnamese blood in me. My mom's from Wisconsin, though."

"So you a mixed breed or somethin'?"

The girl clearly didn't like that, cause she nudged my leg, but Shorty only laughed again.

"Something like that," he said as he stretched out and seemed to finally get comfortable. "What about you? Where are you from?"

"Well," I began, "I was born and raised in Virginia, and the Wilcoxes have lived here a long time. My daddy's daddy was born here, and his daddy was born here, and so forth, till you hit the beginnin' of Jamestown. We ain't sure if they came from England or Scotland or one of those fancy cold Nordic places, but we're fairly certain it's good ol' Europe for us. Maybe a tiny smidge of Cherokee too."

"So that's where we are?" he asked. "Virginia?"

I shot him a look in the mirror. "Course we're in Virginia. Well, now we're headin' into Tennessee. I ain't never been there before, but I hear it's nice. Where'd you think we were?"

He scratched his head and cracked his neck, like a cat do wakin' up. "I wasn't sure. I started biking from West Virginia, going down, planning to go out west to California, but I wasn't quite sure where I was."

I grunted. Next to me, Casey had finally started to cool off a bit. No more foot jabs from her. Instead, she found the courage to speak to our new stranger. "So what's your name?"

"Tom. Yours?"

"Casey."

And I mumbled out, "Forrest."

Tom started tellin' us all bout him, his whole life story. How he was originally born in Maryland, but his parents moved to New Jersey when he was three. How his older sister just finished law school but couldn't find a job yet. How he'd just finished his freshman year at West Virginia University. How he liked cats more than dogs, unless the dog was a small fluffy one, which got Casey talkin' dogs, which pissed me off. Then some story bout his roommate's sister's cousin, which I couldn't follow none, till I finally cut him off and said, "Son, why were you drivin' a bike out here? Why were you bikin' out west?"

"That's a complicated story."

"We got time."

He touched the side of his head. "I guess you're right. First things first, though, do you guys have any snacks?"

I thought to myself, maybe this Vietnamese kid's a natural-born storyteller, or maybe just a snacker. I pointed to my bag and told him to grab a granola bar, which he started chewin' on quite loudly.

Casey watched him chew and asked, "When are we going to stop for lunch?"

"Soon." My belly wasn't too calm neither, but it was always grumblin'.

Between his chews, he began. "It was my first day at WVU, and I was starting to get a feel of myself. I don't quite mesh with the kids there. They're all white, kind of large and blocky, a little more country than me, but I made that my advantage. To be unique in a pile of boring people. I think any freshman feels the same way, just trying to find their place on campus. Well, everybody except my terrible roommate, Matt. All he did was sulk and play video games all night, but that's beside the point.

"I was feeling good about everything, and that's when I went to my second-ever class at college: Film Appreciation."

"They teach that at school? Why don'tcha just go to the movies?"

"Yeah, they do. It's an elective. Just one credit. I'm studying aerospace engineering, mostly. Anyways, I was heading to the class, and I'd already made one friend in my dorm who was in the class. This dude named Gary. When I first met him, the initial thing I wondered was: Who names their kid Gary? How do you look at a little baby and decide their name is Gary? He wasn't even actually a Gabriel. Kind of a whack name, and I told him as much when we became closer, but Gary turned out to be a pretty cool guy, actually, so I sat next to him.

"We were chilling, but then about a minute before the lecture, I looked past Gary's big head and realized there was this girl sitting next to him. Being my friendly self, I said hi to her, and when she turned to me, I thought to myself: *college rocks.*"

"She good lookin'?"

"No, Mr. Forrest," Tom said, shakin' his head, "she was *beautiful.* We'll call her Eve. Anyways, we started whispering a little bit throughout the lecture in between Gary, and by the end of it, I could tell she was a cool one. She was from Lewisburg, a small-ass—excuse me—a small town with only 4,000 people, but she wasn't... she isn't a hick or anything. She's smart, sophisticated. She's a big reader. I told her that she should get lunch with me and Gary sometime, and she smiled a teensy bit. I think she was just happy to have a friend.

"However, when class finished up and we stood up, I realized how long she was. She was thin, beautiful, but *tall.* She was about a half head taller than me, to be honest about it. I didn't think much of it at the time, and we made our parting. Walking back to dorms with Gary, he asked me what I thought of her, and I said she was pretty cool.

"The months rolled by, and we all became better friends—me and Gary and Eve—and we gained a few others along the way. It's like I said, being a little different helped me, made people interested in me. It's crazy, some of those West Virginians had never met an Asian person before.

"Then one day, Gary asked me casually if I was in love with Eve, and that's when it all began. I told him he was crazy, but all the sudden it was as if a switch had flipped inside my head, and all I could think about was her. I tried to forget it, to ignore the issue, but I had no luck. I saw her eyes in the back of my head when I went to sleep, and the memory of her laugh hit me during the most boring classes.

"Meanwhile, I started eyeing myself harder than I ever had in the mirror. How short I was, how skinny I was. I got uneasy, and whenever I saw her, I just became more crazy and more doubtful. My friends sensed that I'd gotten all tense, and asked me what was up, but then my anxiety spread to include them too. All the sudden, I thought I was only the token Asian kid to them, the short jokester, an idiot or something, I guess. I don't know. Anyways, that's how some months went by, and I texted Eve more and more, but really I was just annoying her.

"By the end of this last semester, my mind had become all scrambled up. I couldn't sleep right. I tried to take these stupid testosterone pills to gain some strength, some height, or something, but all they did was make my piss smell weird. I even considered bleaching my skin or something crazy.

"I think Eve had started avoiding me, but I saw her around plenty anyways, if only on the street. We didn't have any real conversations. It came to a head when Gary told me he was going to ask her out. That broke me. I asked him how he could do that. He told me it seemed I hadn't done anything about the issue, and that we weren't really close anymore.

"For the next week, my head hurt, so I sent a few dumb memes to Eve, which she didn't respond to, while I kept staring at myself in the mirror. Finally, when my head was going to blow up, and I couldn't take anything more, I asked her to get lunch with me, lunch back at our old spot. I waited a day for a response, and then she finally agreed.

"She showed up, looking good as ever, and all I could think about was how stupid I was. We made small talk while I over-thought every single word I said. When we circled back to the subject of baby hamsters for a third time, she finally broke and asked, 'What the hell are you talking about?'

"I spit out, 'I'm in love with you.'

"She sighed and said, 'I know.'

"She didn't say anything, so I was like, 'So?' Honestly, she cringed, I cringed, we all cringed. Then she said, 'Sorry, Tom.'

"We finished our food, and I waved bye to her, then she said bye to me. And as she walked away, I had this out-of-body moment. I re-experienced the day I met her, and remembered how easy everything felt. How we talked, how I said what I wanted to say, how I did what I wanted to do, how easily we became friends. But somehow I'd become this cold, awkward idiot. I'd lost myself. Doubted myself too hard.

"So I finished my last final, left, and started biking."

The car went silent after that, outside of the wheels rollin', the AC blowin', and the engine hummin'. I didn't know what the hell to make of it, so I said, "That sucks."

Casey agreed, "Yeah."

Tom didn't respond, just let the truck's sounds take over, but I felt obliged to ask, "That said, what does that have anything to do with the bike ride?"

"Huh?" Tom said.

"It's like this," I began, "I'd never date a really fat woman, no offense to them, just maybe a moderately chubby one. It's like the same thing with your Eve—she just wanted someone a little taller, maybe someone a little whiter. Ain't nothin' to take personal."

I could sense that wasn't the response Tom wanted, cause he went back to squirmin' in the back of the car, so I continued, "I guess I just don't get what that all had to do with a bike ride across the States."

Tom sighed. "Mr. Forrest, it has everything to do with it."

He didn't say nothin' after that, just stared out the window, watchin' trees pass by, so I decided to let it be. Both of us runnin' from painful matters both inside and outside our two sides, I suppose. The brain and the world can be real unkind to the heart.

CHAPTER 16

We'd already passed Knoxville, gettin' closer to Nashville, when Casey regained control of the music. It was this horrible bop, repetitive, same damn thing over and over and over and over again. Reminded me of goin' to work. Wake up—painful sound—wake up—painful sound—then somehow it ends... till a new painful song sneaks up on you. The worst part was, Tom backed her up. The boy straight up bobbed his head and everythin'.

Finally, I broke. "Casey," I wailed. "Shut it off."

She paused the music. "What?"

"No more music right now. I can't hear myself breathe. We're makin' a stop." I was runnin' low on gas, and I needed to make a call anyways, but mostly I needed some air. I turned right toward an exit, and then toward a golden arch.

"Time for some Mickey D's." I didn't hear any complaints, so I pulled in.

As Casey and Tom scuttled out, I said, "Casey, gimme the phone."

"I thought it was my phone?"

So difficult, that girl. "It is, but I needa call Papaw and

Grandmama. I'll give it right back." Then I handed her my debit card. "Here, you and Tom can order lunch."

Tom jumped in, "It's all right, I can pay my own way."

I almost said "No, I broke your toe," but then I decided against it and let them be on their way, but when Casey was almost gone, I yelled outta the car, "Casey, get me a double cheeseburger!" Then I added, "And fries." She gave me a thumbs-up, and they went in.

I fell back into my seat. Finally, I could relax. No more music. No kids.

I scrolled through my phone. Seemed she hadn't wasted any time makin' it hers. Two messages to Mary Anne, four to Kat, just exchangin' new numbers, talkin' nonsense bout the trip, how we picked up a guy... and quite the chat with Lil Pete.

Yes, in fact, he'd gotten the full rundown. Was very interestin'. He'd gotten notice on how: *My dad acts kind of crazy sometimes.* Huh, yes, real crazy. And another one: *I thought he killed him...* That one was *very* interestin'.

I didn't wanna let my cheeseburger get cold, so I called my old man.

"Huh, who's there?" he started. "This is Mr. Wilcox of Wilcox Auto."

"Daddy, I know you have a new phone. I helped you set it up. I know you have caller ID. It's me."

"Forrest, what's happened? What's goin' on?"

What's goin' on? He told me to go on this damn chase. "What do you think's goin' on? I'm in Tennessee. I'm lookin' for Bryan."

"I mean Sandra just called me. She was cryin', sayin' ya took Casey?"

Ah, shit. I rubbed the back of my head. "Yeah, she wanted to go."

"She wanted to go?"

"Yeah, she wanted some bondin' time."

"Forrest, that's not what I—"

"I called cause your card ain't workin'. It rejected me this mornin'."

He went quiet, then grunted. "What on earth were ya buyin' to get my card blocked?"

Damn idiots, all of them goddamn idiots. "That's not how it works. It's cause it ain't used to the activity outta Virginia. Just call the company and get it fixed. I'm gonna go broke if I gotta pay it all outta hand."

"Go broke? Ya ain't been savin' money good."

"Daddy, just get it fixed."

"Fine," he agreed, "but you needa call Sandra and explain yerself."

"Okay, I will. Is Mama there?"

He paused for a second. "Yeah, but she's restin'."

"Well, can I talk to her?"

"Naw, let yer mama rest, she ain't feelin' good."

"I wanna speak to her. Does she know I went out to find Bryan?"

"Yeah, yeah, I done told her. Honest, though, Forrest, I'm havin' second thoughts bout this whole trip you're on—"

"Okay, fine, whatever. Please get the card workin'. I gotta go. Bye." I slammed the screen on the red button, but didn't get no satisfaction. These new phones annoy me so much—all screen, no tactile.

Inside of the Mickey D, Tom and Casey had gotten a table and were chattin' up a storm, but when I sat down, they went quiet real fast. I didn't care anyhow. I stretched, Casey handed me my card back, and I took a big bite of the double cheese-burger. And you know what? Absolutely. Fuckin'. Delicious.

Between bites, I handed the phone back to Casey and garbled my words. "Lotta texts to Lil Pete, I see."

"Hey," she spat out, "you were looking at my text messages?"

"Just a glance."

Tom added, "That isn't cool, Forrest."

I slowly turned to him. Kid was eatin' a salad at Mickey D's. I didn't give him no killer eye, can't do that after I broke his toe, but I still gave him a stink eye. "Mind your own business."

"No, he's right," Casey said.

"Whatever," I muttered. *He's right. What the hell did right even mean*? Who decided what was right? Only the Lord himself, and even He made a questionable play or two, at least based on what I'd seen so far on planet Earth.

While we all munched, we listened to the families around us. One goober had a meetin' to go to, one oldie didn't like his burger, and one woman had lost control of her toddler. That kid ran the show—howlin', cryin', actin' a fool. He screamed so loud how he wanted more chicken nuggets, but his mama told him he'd already finished them, but he wasn't havin' it. The kid jumped, hollered, then threw half his fries across the floor.

I laughed a real honest laugh, good belly laugh.

Casey asked, "What is it?"

Slyly pointin' to the kid, I said, "If I talked like that, my daddy woulda given me a whoopin'. Woulda been no hesitation too. He woulda done it right here, right in fronta everyone. You kids think you're so smart, but you ain't got no life wisdom."

I gulped down another chunk of the burger. "Lucky for me, and for my behind's sake, most of the time, I was the quiet child. Bryan didn't much like the whoopins neither, but he took them on the regular. He was no crier, though, don't get mixed up bout that. He'd take them standin' and strong. Thing is, he was a talker, never had a filter on him, and that's what got him into trouble."

That sure got the two interested, but only Tom asked me a question. "Who's Bryan?"

I grunted into a grin. "He's my brother."

That cheeseburger got me goin', I swear. Good food just gets blood flowin' all around, makes it easier to talk.

"There was this one time we were in Florida. Disney World. We'd just waited for two hours to ride Splash Mountain, and if you know anything bout Splash Mountain, you'd know they got all these scary robot critters, and they got some mighty water drops."

I pointed out the kid again. "I was bout his age, maybe six, seven."

"You never took me to Disney World," Casey said.

After another big bite, I smiled. "Not yet." Like we could afford that.

"Anyhow, we were goin' on this ride, goin' up and up and up, and all these robot critters started singin' at us, and to be honest, the whole thing freaked me out. I remember this one chipmunk, starin' at me, twitchin'. I reckon its machinery was broke. It kept twitchin', and between that guy and the first drop, I got really freaked out. I started cryin' and everythin'.

"Our car was me and Bryan in the front and my old man in the back. Mama don't like rollercoasters much, so she sat out, and as I'm bawlin', Bryan's havin' a great time, a real thrill of it. He liked the bumps and everythin', but that didn't calm me much. I'm cryin' and cryin', and we ain't even halfway through yet when Daddy takes his hand and slaps down hard on my shoulder.

"He went off, 'What ya cryin' bout, boy? Stop yer cryin' before I give ya somethin' to cry bout.' Vacations always gets folks runnin' high emotion, both good and bad. So I tried to stiffen up and regain control of myself, but Splash Mountain takes this turn, you see, and it gets all creepy. When the robot sparrows came out tauntin' us, and we climbed up and up, gettin' ready for the drop, I started bawlin', just drownin' in tears. Bryan took my hand and tried to calm me down some. He said,

'Look, Forrest, it ain't that bad,' but the old man hated the whole thing.

"He screamed at me, 'Forrest, ya stop cryin' right now!' but that wasn't gonna change a thing. So as we're nearin' the top, he starts slappin' me on the back of my head, tryin' to get me to ease up, but it didn't work, and it hurt a little, to be honest.

"At some point, Bryan lost it. He gave Daddy the killer eye and started yellin' at him, 'Stop hittin' Forrest! You ain't helpin' anything, you dumbass!'

"You can bet he didn't like that." I laughed, took another bite, and continued.

"So the real interestin' thing bout these rides is that they take your picture durin' the craziest point, and you can buy it at the end. Outside, Mama was waitin' for it to pop up, and right when we met with her after the ride, it showed on the screen. Gave her quite the sight. On it, while we were plummetin' unreal fast, you can see lil me with my eyes wide open and screamin', the old man's hand across Bryan's face, and Bryan lookin' angry as all hell.

"Mama asked, 'What happened?' but none of us said a thing. Instead, I was wipin' my eyes, Daddy was lookin' mighty suspicious, and Bryan had a big ol' red welt on his cheek. Finally, Bryan spoke up and said, 'Nothin'.'"

I took another bite. "It was a great trip." Then I laughed one final thick laugh, loud as the waterfall's crash we flew down all those years ago. How we flew.

But Tom looked at me kinda funny. Wide-mouth funny. Looked to me he was a bit of a softie. "That's horrible."

"Whatcha mean?" I asked. "That's just family. And a little discipline. Like I said, cause of that, we didn't grow up to be that kid cryin' bout runnin' outta chicken nuggets."

Casey asked the more rational question, "Did you guys buy the picture?"

I smiled and shook my head. "Naw, wish we had. After we all cooled off a bit, Mama had a big laugh on the situation and almost went back to pick it up, but those things are crazy overpriced. Costs an arm and a leg just to get a picture. Profiteerin' off memories, that's all it is."

Then she asked, "When will you take me to Disney World?"

I took a final bite and stood up. "Y'all ready for the road?"

CHAPTER 17

A fter three piss breaks, a coupla duels on the road, and one bad bumpy highway, another day was almost gone. We'd cut our way through Tennessee, all the way to Memphis. It ain't a bad part of the country, I must say. Down I-40, you got fields, water, the whole lot. I hadn't quite reached the full picture I'd imagined for Bryan, but I could feel myself gettin' closer, and that was what kept my foot locked down on the pedal.

It was a good day for Casey too. She'd been googlin' all kindsa things, lookin' for a "trace," as she described it. And her music choices had been gettin' better. I directed her to some oldies, and some she even liked.

The only real problem was Tom. For the rest of the ride, he'd been slinkin' in the back, either fallin' asleep or starin' out the window. More than once, I had a mind to ask when he planned on makin' his exit, but it didn't seem my place and all, considerin' his lack of mobility was sorta my fault. Occasionally, he'd strike up a conversation with Casey, and they seemed to get along alright, but I couldn't follow a damn word. Their heads were up in the internet, babblin' techno nonsense they'd both seen. Unlike them, my feet were—still are—on the earth. And he kept tellin' her all bout WVU, gettin' her hyped up on college. Seemed to me he was just a showy type, tryin' to impress her with all the books he read, tests he took, but I saw through that. He didn't have a single ounce of street smarts.

Tryin' to be smooth bout it, around eight p.m., just when the sun was startin' to rest and the moon was comin' out to play, I said, "So, Tom, what's your plan?"

He pushed himself up and finally sat up straight. "My plan?"

"Yeah, like where you gonna go? Whatcha gonna do?"

"I don't have a plan. That's the whole point. I just wanted to go." The question musta put him off balance, cause he spun it right back at me. "What's your plan? What are you doing out here?"

I wasn't gonna answer him, but he asked honest, no sneer, no bullshit. "You've gotten bits and pieces, I'm sure. We're gonna find my brother, Bryan. Casey's uncle."

"Yeah, I got that part," he said. "But, like, what happened? Like why do you need to go 'find' him? Where is he?"

"We dunno where he is, that's the problem."

"Yeah, but why did he leave?"

"Don't worry bout it."

"Well, that information seems kind of important if you're going to find him."

"It's family matters."

"But you haven't told me either," added Casey.

"Is there something I could do to help?"

"No." My knuckles were white.

"What about contacting my uncle? He's in HR, but he does background checks, I think."

"That's alright."

"You sure?"

"This ain't *none* of your goddamn business."

Everyone shut up. He went dead silent. Casey shut up too.

Noisy Chink. And just like that, a good day of drivin' was ruined. All that beautiful Tennessee grass melted away, forgotten cause of another stupid angry heat of mine. I hated that, God I fuckin' hated that.

I kept drivin', with no one sayin' nothin', but eventually it hit late, and I was exhausted. I spotted a sign for a motel and turned in. "We're gonna pack in for the night." Puttin' a little edge on the situation, I parked, turned around, and asked, "So, Tom, whatcha gonna do?"

That got him goin'. He twitched ever so slightly, started really swallowin' his words. "Well... I can buy a new bike... and just keep biking... I guess." He spoke like he had a gun on his forehead, and that forced me to look around. Dark night. Secluded road. Two strangers.

Kid made me feel like a retard.

When you're the scary one in a situation, you ain't never realize it, unless you tryin' to be scary on purpose, I guess. Naw, instead I had just waltzed my way into completely spookin' him, and by the looks of her, Casey too.

"No," I grunted. "You ain't gonna buy a new bike. You'll just take the damn sofa."

ANOTHER NIGHT, another hotel, another fat payment on my debit card. Déjà fuckin' vu. As we walked up to the room, I said to Casey, "Casey, gimme the phone, I needa call Papaw."

She called him for me and put it against her head, so I grabbed the phone from her. "Daddy, you there?"

"This is Mr. Wilcox, who am I speakin' to?"

"You've gotta stop doin' that."

"Forrest? What's this bout? We just talked earlier today."

"The card! The damn card! I asked you to fix the card."

We reached the room, so I ushered the two inside while I stayed outside and closed the door, then walked down the hall.

"Don't raise yer voice at me," he grumbled. Then for a bit, all I could hear was his chewin' on a thick wad of gum, slimin' it across his mouth. Finally, he said, "I called them up. Whatcha wastin' my hard-earned money on?"

"Whatcha mean? I paid for a hotel for me and Casey. Maybe a lunch. I'm out here cause you told me to go."

"Yeah, I did say go, cause yer mama wanted you to, but why ya spendin' money on these nice fancy hotels? I ain't made of diamonds."

"It wasn't that fancy." I leaned against the hallway, tryin' to keep it all in. "Daddy, I'm with Casey, and we're in a shitty motel right now. Don'tcha want her to have a safe place to stay?"

"Yeah, but I never told ya to bring her." He sighed, and again I heard his age come through—wispy and weak. "Listen," he said real slow, "maybe ya oughta just come home. Yer mama's not doin' so hot. Sorry to her, but I reckon this was a stupid idea."

I couldn't believe my ears. The most stubborn man east of the Mississippi tellin' me to give up. "What you hollerin' bout? We're already almost through Tennessee."

"But have ya got any idea where yer gonna end up? Where yer final stop is? Why in God's name we gotta do all this for that damn boy?"

I ain't had nothin' to say, so I didn't say nothin'. Just listened to him sigh again.

"Forrest, I'll pay ya back after the trip on what merits payment. Just keep yer receipts. But finish up quick, ya hear? And if ya can't find him, give up. It's okay. Yer mama will understand."

I thought back to all those years ago when she was sittin' by the porch, waitin', lookin' out to the road. How she'd waited and waited for hours and hours, waited till the sun was long set and the moon was high in the sky. Waited for everythin' to be alright. Waited for the car to come back. Then came the moment—the moment when she realized he wasn't comin' back. How her eyes went wild and red, how her tears refused to stop. And how I cried alone.

There was only one direction to go.

"She might understand, but this is what she *wants*. I'm gonna find him. And I'll save your damn receipts."

I hung up and smacked the wall so loud I'm sure the sound went through every flimsy two-inch piece of plaster in our ugly yellow piece-of-crap motel. I marched back up to our room, fumbled around with the keys, and when I opened it, I saw that Viet Cong piece-of-crap kid far too close to Casey, with both of them sittin' on the one bed next to each other, lookin' at his phone, playin' a video.

"Ay!" I hollered. "You sleep on the couch."

He shot up and waved his hands a bit. "I can sleep in the car, if you'd prefer that."

I rubbed my eyes. "No, you ain't gonna sleep in the damn car. Just pull out the couch." Lookin' around, I realized there was no second bed. I coulda sworn they said there was two beds.

Casey asked, "Should we ask for a cot?"

Scratchin' my hair, I could feel dirt under my fingernails. Everythin' had gotten all sweaty and nasty durin' the drive. "No." I sighed. "I'll sleep on the floor."

CHAPTER 18

You gotta look at all these billboards and wonder what the hell we doin'. Big, bulky rectangle things pointin' outta the ground, stuck there, watchin' people go by, tryin' to sell their shit that ain't nobody buyin'. They done bastardized the roads. Somehow even cruisin' got commercialized.

We were passin' one on the edge of Arkansas. Looked like a dumb elementary schooler's poster-board project with squiggly lines and too much color. Will's Windows. Had a fat old white guy with a goofy smile and a thumbs-up next to this hot young babe. First thing I wondered was how old-ass Will got his whole arm wrapped behind this poor fine girl. Didn't even wanna imagine where his hand was at. Will's Windows wasn't what I saw when I imagined Bryan ridin' through the open terrain. Where were the mountains, the rivers? Well, we had some rivers, a few mountains, but honest to God, there were more billboards on the road than anything else.

I wanted to make a joke bout it—ask everyone if they thought Will could still get it up—but the kids were dead silent, sittin' with their phones. The truck rattlin' against the wind was the only sound, my only companion. It felt too strange, that quiet. Got me feelin' lonesome. Awful lonesome. Lookin' into Will's girl's eyes, I realized Sandra woulda never let things get that quiet. She woulda been pointin' out everythin', all the little signs and grass and trees and people. We woulda made five more stops and taken plenty pictures. Probably shoulda taken some pictures for her, I realized.

Those last few days had been the longest we'd been apart since we got married. I missed her mightily.

Then someone finally said somethin'.

"Where are we?" Casey asked.

"Didn't you see the sign?" I gestured out to the window at some lush trees and wide open fields and more billboards.

She rubbed her eyes and stretched her gangly arms. "No. What sign?"

"We in Ark-Kansas, baby."

From the back I heard, "I think it's pronounced Ar-kan-saw, with a W."

"I know, was just makin' a joke. Sorry, we ain't all scholars like you." Dumbass kid.

"Daddy, how far are we from the West?"

"Far enough. Go look it up on the phone."

I zoned out a bit from that moment on. You must think Sand is a mean ol' bitch the way I've been describin' her and all, but she ain't nothin' close to the sort. That was just my rattle brain talkin', my screwy perspective. Naw, truth is, she's got a good heart.

When we were young, she knew just what to do, what to say, to get me outta my shell. Sometimes when we were all alone together, and she'd go on talkin' 'bout her girlfriends or what movies we oughta see, I'd just stare at her wall. I remember it was white and grainy like dirty eggshells. It wasn't cause I didn't wanna listen to her, not even cause I was bored. Honest, I ain't sure why I did it, but I'd just stare at the wall. Like I told you before, it was my moody year, and I'd stare at the wall and forget everythin' except how bad I felt. I'd wonder when Bryan would roll back into town. I'd plan out every word I'd say to him. I'd wonder what he'd say.

Mind you, I did this all in my head. I stayed strict quiet. But Sand always had a way of feelin' out the situation. She's good like that. She'd stop her rattlin', go up to me, and gimme this heavy hug. Her hugs were somethin' to behold, real amazin', given she was so tiny. Her wrap was strong—she could hold all of me, despite how big boned I was. She could make me forget everythin' bout Bryan, forget that he even left, and make it just me and her. Somehow, she could read my mind when I stared at walls, I reckon. That's the only explanation.

"Daddy? Daddy?"

I shook myself outta my head. "What?"

"I found something."

Tom perked up from the back. "What'd you find?"

That shoulda been my line.

"Well, I'd been googling 'Bryan Wilcox' and couldn't find anything useful. It turns out there's a lot of Bryans. Then I started spelling it all kinds of ways. 'Brian Wilcox,' 'Bryan Wilsox,' 'Bryan Wiltox.' That didn't work either. Then I added Bryan Wilcox plus Arizona, because he said he was in Arizona. I tried that with a bunch of different names, but those didn't work either. So then I added Bryan Wilcox plus Arizona plus different dates—"

I slapped the side of the wheel. "Out with it, honey."

"The last thing I googled was: Brian Wilcox Arizona Phoenix 2001, and that's when I found this."

"Found wh—"

She went ahead and started readin', cut me off entirely. I couldn't complain. My anticipatory ass was nearly hoppin' off the seat.

"*April 12, 2001 Phoenix Nation Archive: FOUR-MAN BRAWL BREAKS OUT IN DOWNTOWN PHOENIX OUTSIDE STEVE'S DINER*

Four men were arrested after a free-for-all brawl broke out in the parking lot outside Steve's Diner in Downtown Phoenix.

At 8:25 p.m., police responded to a call from diner patrons about a fight brewing outside the diner, according to a statement from the Phoenix Police Department. Once they arrived at the scene, they found two men tumbling on the ground, while a third man threw various kitchen utensils at another, unarmed man.

'It was ridiculous,' said Steven Brown, owner of Steve's Diner. 'Two of my waiters got into a dispute with a couple of our more-than-intoxicated customers who were yelling, and things just spiraled.'

One customer on scene at the time of the incident, Ms. Paula Hernández, told Arizona National, 'Two customers were complaining about their food, quite loudly, then started shouting at other patrons. At some point, their waiter just didn't like it. He pulled another coworker into the argument, then they took their fight outside. Just silly young men, that's all.'

Other witnesses described a chaotic scene where one of the combatants screamed, 'I hope you like this burger!' before jumping into the fight.

According to the Phoenix Police Department, no serious injuries were sustained, and the men's fight was promptly broken up after the police's arrival. Only two participants, Billy Wilcox and Adam Isiah, waiters at Steve's Diner, were charged with disturbance of the peace after instigating an argument with the police that they were in the right to 'smack those sonsabitches up.'

When Phoenix Nation asked Steven Brown the status of his waiters, he said, 'Well, they sure aren't working here anymore.'"

I started laughin'. No, that ain't right. I began to choke, howl. I swerved through traffic, scarin' the hell outta the kids, but I couldn't stop—I had the jitterbug in me. Blood felt right again, heart hit right again. I cackled, like some kinda witch, till my eyes got all watery and I could barely see the road.

"What are you laughing about?" Casey and Tom asked me.

I rubbed my eyes, tryin' to calm down some, but I knew there was no chance of that. "What do y'all mean? It's him! It's him! That's Bryan."

"How do you know?" Casey asked.

Between my chuckles, I stammered, "Read that line again for me, honey."

"What line? Four men were arrested after—"

"No. You know which line."

She took a second to figure it out, but eventually she got it. She's a smart girl. She said, "I hope you like this burger!"

Well, that got me goin' all over again. Laughin' for a good minute. I couldn't remember when I'd last laughed that hard. Well, actually, I could, but it'd been a good while. So I'm laughin' and laughin', till the laughs finally died out, and all I was left with was feelin' good.

Then Tom repeated, "How do you know it's your brother?"

"Boy," I asked, "did you listen to Casey? To that article? Bryan's got a head of steel, argument-hungry. I can hear his voice in those words. I can see it all. He probably went ahead and tried to convince the police officers that they shoulda helped him beat up the ol' drunkie.

"'Billy.' A silly name suits him. Casey, bless you, baby, for findin' him. Bless your heart. We're goin' to Arizona. We're goin' to Phoenix!"

I reached out to her. "Gimme the phone, baby. I'm gonna tell your mama."

CHAPTER 19

Casey got the phone all set up for me, unblocked Sand and everythin'. I was nervous-excited. I knew she'd be mad, but I needed to tell her the news. I needed her to know. We were goin' to Arizona. We were gonna find him.

Casey said, "I'm going to call her."

I nodded but didn't say nothin' cause my throat had gotten all scratchy. As I reached over to take the phone, my hand shook a little bit. Couldn't tell you why I was so nervous—whether it was finally talkin' to her again or just thinkin' 'bout Bryan—but nervous I was.

It took two stressful rings before I heard her voice. Lucky for me, it was soft. "Hello? Forrest?" She spoke at almost a whisper, like she couldn't even believe it was me.

"Honey." I knew I needed to start sweet. "I know you're probably a little upset—"

"Is Casey okay?" Her voice made me confused. Just wasn't what I expected. Guess I thought there'd be a little more sharpness, a little more vigor. Naw, rather, it seemed she could barely keep herself together, too much gloominess bubblin'.

Then she started to cry. I pulled the phone back, as if her

tears were gonna hit my ears, cause that's how close it felt. She went ahead and started sobbin' and sobbin', a bit of wailin' even. Sandra's never been a major hard-ass, but I can't call her a complete softy neither. I hadn't heard her cry that hard since her last miscarriage.

She fought through the tears and bawled like a wounded animal. "Is... Casey... okay?"

"Yes!" I said. "She's fine, she's right next to me. What's wrong?"

That didn't help much. In fact, I think the tears just came stronger. "What's... wrong?" She sniffed. "What's wrong? What do you think's wrong? What's wrong with you?" And just like that, the weepy faucet had closed. "Forrest, how can you ask me what's wrong? You've been gone for days."

"Yeah, I told you, we were gonna find Bryan—"

"You haven't called for days. You haven't even texted. Casey hasn't either."

"Yeah, well, you were yellin' at me and all, and I threw her phone out the wi—"

"I don't know if you're crazy or just stupid!"

Well, that sure didn't feel good. I shut my muzzle while she sniffed up her final few tears, then spoke clear. "Forrest, this can't continue. Just... just come home. Come home right now. You have no idea how worried I've been. How scared. Come home, and we'll talk. Please."

And just like that, all my excitement of Casey's discovery had been wiped out. I looked out the window, then at my dash, while one sweet-ass Corvette zipped by. The sun on the left side of my face felt hotter than ever. I flexed my fingers against the wheel. Then I took a big breath. "Sand. We found Bryan."

She stayed silent for so long that I thought the call dropped. I was bouta say somethin' when she finally asked, "Is he there with you? With Casey?"

"Naw. Not yet, anyways."

She sprang on me. "Then how can you say you found him? Usually finding someone involves finding someone."

"Well," I said real slow, "we know where he is. We're headin' there, and then we're gonna find him. In fact, Casey's the one who found the clue."

"Clue?" I guess Sand's got multiple super powers. Mind reader in youth, buzz killer in adulthood. My elation snuffed out in a single word, with a single tone. "What do you think you are, a detective? Some kind of investigator? Forrest, you fix cars."

With heat risin', I tried to make my stand. "Naw, I don't think I'm an investigator or nothin'. It's just that we know where he is now—"

"Forrest. I almost called the police. You haven't called for days. I had no idea if my daughter was dead or alive. And you're out here talking about clues."

I glanced up at my rearview mirror. That slanty-eyed fuck was leanin' up on the edge of his seat.

She continued, "So where do you think he is? Where did your clue lead you?"

"Arizona. Phoenix," I mumbled.

"Phoenix? Huh, okay. How old is this clue? Three years? Five years?"

I didn't say nothin'.

"How do you know he's still there? How do you know he didn't leave? How do you know he's still alive?"

"HEY!" I yelled. "Don'tcha talk like that. Don'tcha say somethin' like that."

"Well, Forrest, I guess I just don't know what else to say."

We got into a stalemate. I noticed how much my chest hurt all the sudden. My head too. Shit felt like it was gonna break, snap like some twig. Too much pressure or somethin'. I could hardly breathe.

"Just put Casey on the phone."

I happily obliged and tossed the phone over to Casey while tryin' to puff air in.

I stared straight ahead, just feelin' all kinda woozy, feelin' like the heat finally got to me. I looked right down the road, down at the white lines goin' on and on forever. I wanted to just *go*. Get gone. Go on, go, go, go straight forever. Ride till no one else was around me, alone again. To drive free again, like when I first got my car, when I was young. I wanted to be like Bryan, how I saw him. Drivin' forever. I wanted my freedom.

That got me calmed some, to the point I could listen to Casey. She spoke quiet, havin' pressed herself in a corner in the car. "No, Mama. It's fine. It's fine!" It went on like this for a bit, till she finally handed the phone back to me.

"She wants to talk to you again," she said.

I gripped the phone with a limp hand. "'Ello?"

"How much longer do you think you'll be out there?"

"I dunno. A week? Maybe longer?"

Her sigh was so loud it seemed to blow air through the speakers. She just wasn't havin' none of me. "Okay, Forrest. Okay. Go to Arizona. Play detective. Go find Bryan."

I was bouta say "great," when she burst back in. "But if you cut off me from Casey again, I swear, I will never forgive you."

In fronta me, the road became a gray fog, ready to swallow me. How could she not get it? How could she not fuckin' get it? Ain't a man supposed to make his family whole? That was all I was tryin' to do. Why was she tryin' to break it apart?

My nostrils flared, and my body hardened, became some kinda rock starin' out the window, till, after waitin' for me to say somethin', she finally hung up. I tossed the phone at Casey's lap and mumbled, "Here you go."

I drove on, tryin' to focus on the road and only the road—

white line, white line, white line, white line—but somewhere in my chaotic mind, an annoyin' voice pulled me out.

"What'd you say?" I asked.

Tom repeated himself, "So what happened?"

My car started sputterin' all the sudden. Made this tiny shrill shakin' sound somewhere below my dash, like it was upset at me too.

I rolled down my window and spit out some high-velocity saliva, sent it flyin' with the breeze. "Whatcha say?"

Clearly the boy did not jive with the tone of my voice, cause all the sudden he got sensitive on the issue. He crossed his arms. "Nothing."

I spat again, this time a big old mean ball of stick. I hadn't realized it prior, but it'd been growin' in my mouth, ready to come out. "Naw," I said. "I thought you said somethin'."

Casey hopped in. "Just chill, Daddy. Calm down."

Calm down?

"I am calm. I am supreme Mr. Calm," I said. "You kids don't know nothin' bout calm. I'm the calmest of the Wilcoxes, calmest of all. Well, maybe outside your grandmama." I pressed on the gas. Sixty to sixty-five.

"Y'all don't think I'm calm? You oughta've seen the fights Dad used to brew up with Bryan." Sixty-five to seventy-five.

"They used to get into mighty shouty matches! Ol' man nearly wanted to exorcise his ass." Seventy-five to eighty-five.

"It'd get physical, beyond physical. You don't even know. It damn near turned into a battle of will. Hell, it reached biblical proportions." Eighty-five to ninety-five.

"And guess who was the calmest of the bunch while they were fightin' and Mama was cryin'? The one who kept things cool? The peacekeeper? Yours truly!" Ninety-five to 105.

"So don't you ever say 'chill out' at me, young lady."

"Daddy!" she cried.

I glanced down at the speedometer. I'd hit 110.

Outside, the world zipped by. All them trees, rocks, they didn't even look like themselves, instead they was just blurs. There for a second, gone the next. One tiny-ass sports car was lucky he was in the right lane. We woulda crushed him otherwise. Then it became a dot behind me. Everythin' was goin' by, all of it gone. Gone, gone, gone. It all was runnin' and runnin', runnin' away from me. It was all too fuckin' fast. Everythin' was goin' too damn fast.

"DADDY!"

When she shouted, I realized how clammy my hands had gotten and how fast my heart was goin' and how strong the wind in fronta us was blowin' against the car. Slowly, I lifted my foot off the pedal.

My fingers were damn near twitchin', barely able to hold the wheel straight, like a teenager first learnin' how to drive. The whirrin' didn't help neither—the buzz under the dash had just gotten louder and louder.

So with shaky hands, I tried to regain control, doin' my best, when I heard somethin' go *POP*! Well, that threw me entirely off. I turned the wheel slightly too fast, which pushed us over into the next lane. That got the car next to me swervin'. Everythin' was comin' to an end, all comin' into one, collapsin' into a split second.

I'm gonna crash. I'm gonna crash. I'm gonna die, we're all gonna die, this be the end, end of everythin'. My heart and stomach did backflips. *My life is gonna amount to a bug gettin' squished on the side of the road.*

Then the car next to me—a little Honda—got control and went straight, and started honkin' all the sudden.

HONK!

HONK!

That's what he sounded like.

HONK!

HONK!

And God knows, that took me back. The sound transported me to Macy's chubby cheeks. Fury and frustration overtook fear, which thankfully helped me regain control of the wheel.

I angled us back into the lane and resumed goin' straight.

As I drove on, you woulda thought someone died. The kids looked petrified, like they'd seen the devil's image and he'd done a little dance. All the light in their eyes had been sucked out, and any color turned to gray. They clutched the sides of their seats as if they were out boatin'.

"So," I said, "that was a little scary."

Casey mumbled somethin' under her breath, but Tom took a different approach. He sat right up, finally found his courage, and said straight, "ARE YOU CRAZY?"

"What's that? I couldn't hear you."

"Were you trying to kill us? What's wrong with you?"

There it was again—*What's wrong with you?* Seemed like I was gettin' that a lot recently. Everyone was lookin' to bite off a piece of me.

Tryin' to laugh it off, I said, "We just got a little fast, that's all. Y'all were distractin' me."

"No," the boy said, "that's not what happened."

"Oh? What happened, then?"

"You're manic or something. I don't know. But all the time I've been here, been in this car, it's been you screaming, getting angry, or doing something dangerous."

"Am I screamin' right now?" I asked. "Seems to me you're the only one gettin' heated here."

"Listen to yourself—just the other day you were yelling at your dad on the phone, now you snapped at your wife."

"Is that any of your business?"

"Then you go ahead and drive so fast you nearly kill your daughter."

"HEY." That was it. I turned to the right lane, then slowed down on the shoulder, then reached a stop. "Get out."

He got all confused, lookin' at me with those white-Chinese eyes. "What?"

"I said get out."

"Daddy," Casey jumped in. "We're in the middle of the highway. Tom was just trying to be nice."

"Get out," I repeated. "Get out, get out, get out."

Slowly, but surely, he got the message. He began to squirm in the back and collect his junk.

"Daddy, stop this," said Casey.

"No, no," Tom said, "it's all right. It's time for me to go. I can tell when I've outstayed my welcome." He swung his backpack over his shoulder. "Casey, it was great to meet you." Then he opened up the door. "Forrest, thanks for the ride. I hope you find your brother. I really do. And I hope that when you find him, he's actually happy to see you."

He slammed the door, and I began goin' down the road once again.

That's when I realized that poppin' sound had stopped buzzin'. In fact, it'd gone beyond quiet. There was no sound at all.

I put my hand in fronta the fan and groaned. "I think the AC's broke."

CHAPTER 20

Lettin' the mood sink in, I rolled down the windows and breathed for a while. There was enough to keep me distracted, enough beauty around: the blue sky, the smooth road, the grass stretchin' across the distance. Looked like somethin' cosmic, with every single thing shinin' under the sun. I tried to feel good again, tried to smile, tried to remember we were gonna find Bryan. But I couldn't help but sense the little tickin' time bomb next to me. So I finally said, "He talked too much."

That broke the situation. It started as a sniffle, then a single tear, then it multiplied into a million, till she was bawlin' just like her mama. "He didn't do anything wrong!" she whimpered.

I shook my head. "Naw. He didn't do much wrong. But he didn't do much right neither."

"He was nice. And smart. That's why you hated him. You're just jealous."

"I ain't jealous," I said. "I just know a smartass when I see one. He thought he knew what was best for you."

She pulled the seat back and turned over to lie down. She didn't even wanna look at me. "Oh, and you do?"

"I'm your father."

I'm your father.

You know how some words just slip you into another time, another place? Like you were livin' your life in the today, but then your head hands you a little image of somethin' you'd forgotten, but then you realize you'd always remembered it, and it was just hidden away, hidden close at hand? That was what happened to me, at least.

"Case," I said, "lemme tell you a story. It's a good one. It involves your uncle."

She didn't respond, only sniffled, so I took it as a truce.

"There was this cold, a real cold, a winter, and you know it don't get that cold back home, but this was a serious situation. Trust me, it woulda even made a Yankee cold. I ain't felt nothin' like it before or since. I was only a little tyke then, probably four or five, so I barely remember nothin', but this, this I remember clear. You see, what made it so special was the *snow*."

I knew that'd be a magic word for her. It'd only come around a couple times in her life, and only one time real big, but without fail, each and every snowfall, her eyes opened so wide I coulda sworn the rapture had begun.

"Snow?" she grumbled.

"Mm," I agreed. "Snow." Now I had her attention.

"Mid-Feb, I believe it was. It was the worst storm since 1892, if I ain't mistaken. You woulda never believed it. The snow came down by the brick. It came down till my old man's backyard had snow stacked as high as my shoulders. It came down till not a soul could go to work. Course, that meant there was no school neither.

"I remember wakin' up that day to Bryan's hollerin'. He yelled, 'Forrest! Forrest! Get up! There's no school.' Well, I may have not started school yet, I can't really remember, but I remember Bryan was real excited, and that rubbed off on me some.

"We got dressed as fast as we could and ran outside and just started goin' all kinda crazy. Snow angels, snowman, the whole lot. Mama made us breakfast while Daddy stayed glued to the boob tube. Then Bryan got this wild idea—"

I slammed the brake a bit and smashed the horn as some bozo cut us off. "What a damn asshole. You see these people, Casey? I guess there's some drivers out here even worse than the ones back home."

She sighed. Then she asked, "What was Bryan's idea?"

I smiled this dumb smile, cause I knew I'd caught her. "Well, Bryan's always one with an adventure in his back pocket. You know that big hill a couple minutes from Papaw's house? The one that goes straight down?"

She nodded. "The big hill."

"Yeah, that's right, the big hill. So Bryan got this bright idea: We were gonna beat the big hill. He ran inside, while little me fumbled around in the snow. See, we had no sleds, cause what's the point with how little snow comes around and they're expensive as all hell, but Bryan figured out a trick. Daddy had these big ol' boxes in the basement from some car parts that got shipped around. Bryan grabbed two, crunched them down, ran back outside, handed me one, and we started on our way.

"I reckon the old man had caught wind of the mission, cause he opened up the door and yelled, 'Boys, stay near the house!' Well, Bryan didn't much like that, cause instead he yelled to me, 'Let's go, Forrest!'"

I laughed. "Lotta his stories go that way. He just knew how to make somethin' happen, you know? He could turn detention into recess. Just that kinda guy."

"I wish I had met him." She said it soft, and it hit real.

I pushed her shoulder a little. "Don't worry. You'll see him soon enough."

"Finish the story."

"Okay, missy, you got it. So, we start runnin', boltin' for the hill, and behind me I'm hearin' Daddy just goin' crazy, gettin' angry, but you see, the snow was pretty thick, and he was a good ways away, so we turned the corner long before he could catch up, not that he cared enough to run after us anyhow.

"We got away from the house, but since Bryan was a little bigger than me—he's always been—he got away faster. And that's when the snow started really comin' again.

"See, the issue was the cardboard had gotten all wet, and I was too little to really push it around much, so it mostly just dragged snow. After a minute, I realized Bryan was gone, and I couldn't see the house neither. Everythin' was all so buried and white, and I was so small, I didn't know where I was at all.

"Not gonna lie to you—remember, I was a little tyke—I started cryin' and panickin' and goin' in circles. I don't even know how long passed, but I got real cold. I remember that much. It don't snow much back home, so we were sorely unprepared. All I had was some stupid thin jacket. My little nose, my little hands, my little ears all froze up—you coulda taken a chisel and chipped a bit off, I'm certain.

"So there I am, scared outta my little-kid mind. Eventually I got so cold and tired I just fell on my bum and sat while my cold tears just made me feel even colder. I don't think I quite understood my troubles, but I coulda gone right there and died. It's true."

Casey was damn near at the edge of her seat. "What happened?"

"Well," I said, "I got all tired, and right before I closed my eyes, I heard a faraway voice: 'FORREST!' Then another, 'Forrest!'

"I pushed myself up and started wavin' my arms. I couldn't see them, but I knew they were there. I yelled back, 'I'm here! I'm here!' But they musta been too far away, or my voice was too weak or somethin' cause they didn't come toward me. In fact, their shoutin' grew dimmer and dimmer till I almost couldn't hear them. In my final moment of desperation, I grabbed that damp cardboard Bryan had given me. It took all my tiny-boy strength, but I managed to lift it above my head and wag it around, above the snow.

"I waited some long, gruelin' seconds, almost givin' up, nearly droppin' the darn thing. But in the midst of the storm, I heard, 'He's there, Daddy! He's there!'

"I dropped the cardboard and tried to climb above the snow with my last bit of energy. There I saw a glimpse of Bryan grabbin' the old man's hand and runnin' toward me. True enough, Bryan had gone ahead and lost me in our trek, but he also was the one who found me again. Well, Daddy broke from him, cause he had the longer stride, and came dashin'. In a few seconds, he was all over me, and he yanked my arm up, snatchin' me up whole. He yelled, 'Listen to me next time, boy! I'm yer father!'"

I exhaled, then grunted. "Yep. And that's the story."

"That's it?" she asked.

"Whatcha mean, 'that's it?' Don'tcha see the point? We needed to listen to our father. He was right. We shoulda stayed by the house. People should listen to their fathers."

She fell back into her seat and went straight back to sulkin'. "I don't think that's the point at all," she mumbled.

"Oh? Then enlighten me, oh wise one. Explain it to me so even I, Mr. Dumb Brick, can understand."

She rolled her eyes. "You're such a drama queen."

Me, the drama queen? I wanted to say *look in the mirror,*

honey, but even my pea-sized brain could tell that'd be unwise. So I shut up.

"Papaw shouldn't have let you get that far away," she said. "You were five years old. He should've been outside with you guys. He could've helped you make snow angels or a snowman, or something."

I wanted to argue with her more, but I realized I ain't had nothin' to say.

CHAPTER 21

The ride to Oklahoma got all kinda delirious. After the AC broke, we had to roll down all the windows till the truck became a wind tunnel and blew our hair plumb crazy. Even that didn't help much, cause the road was still hot as hell. My pasty face got turned into a mean red, burnt all over. Sandra called Casey five, maybe six times, makin' sure she had a toothbrush and all that shit, like I ain't had no common sense. In truth, she probably sensed Casey was a little upset bout Tom over the phone, but Casey didn't say nothin' bout him. She's a smart girl, like I said. Still, I felt a little bad, so after a couple hours of no talk, I asked, "You excited for school?"

She nudged her head up but didn't turn around to face me. "I guess."

I guess. I guess. I guess I gotta guess. "You excited to see all your school friends again?"

"I don't know."

"Whatcha mean, 'you don't know'?"

"I don't know if Kat is going to stay friends with me and Mary Anne. She has another group of friends at school."

"Oh. Well, it'd be her loss." I'd forgotten all bout middle-school politics. Those kids can be real sharks. "What bout Lil Pete?"

"What about him? And why do you call him Lil?"

"I just mean is he gonna stay friends with you and Mary Anne."

"Yeah," she said, all annoyed. "Why wouldn't he stay friends with us?"

I put my hand out the window, tryin' to get some air back in my body. "Course he would. I was just askin'. Seventh grade's got a lot goin' on."

She curled up some more, watchin' the landscape go by. "It'll be fine. I wonder what grade my cousins are in?"

"Your cousins?"

"Yeah, Uncle Bryan's kids."

I grunted. "Case, we don't know if Bryan had any kids. We don't even know if he's married."

"I know, but I got a feeling."

The girl had a feelin'. For whatever reason, I didn't like that kinda talk on Bryan. Got me all nervous. "Anyhow," I said, "look, bout earlier today, I just wanted to say—"

"Daddy, just stop. I already got a stomach cramp, this isn't helping."

"I wanted to say it shouldn't have gone down like that, but it did, and I wanna make it up to you."

She stopped talkin', but I could tell her gears got turnin', and before I realized my mistake, she asked, "We can get a dog?"

Damnit all. "I'll think bout it," was all I could say. Then I continued, "But the actual surprise is we're gonna get fancy."

"Fancy?"

"Yeah, we're gonna get fancy." I took Exit 159B toward Oklahoma City. "Look up a nice hotel. Four stars, at least. And it better have a pool. No, no, it better have a *jacuzzi*."

"What's a jacuzzi?"

. . .

I FIGURED the trip had already made us broke, so what was the harm of goin' a little more in the red? I'd make my old man pay it off anyhow. Casey did some internet research and found a fancy-soundin' establishment, *The Sirwin* (ooh-la-la). It had everythin' rich people could ask for: a lavish art restaurant, a bar, an indoor pool and jacuzzi, a gym, and big rooms. We didn't need much other than the room and jacuzzi, but the rest were nice to have. When we got closer, I saw the hotel was as huge as a hippo and that got Casey all kinda excited. A good change of pace.

"How tall do you think that is?" she asked.

"I don't know, baby." See, back home, most of everythin's flat. There's aplenty of stuff, but it stays pretty simple, close to the ground. But *The Sirwin* was different. It had these fancy curves, looked all classic, with a pretty roof and big round doors at its base, like a castle straight outta a movie.

We parked and when we got inside, this receptionist with a big black mustache was dressed fancy too, full tux, nice tie. He said, "Sir, madam, welcome to *The Sirwin*."

Some folks know how to treat a guest.

Turned out to be $200 for the night. First, I tried my old man's credit card again. Still didn't work. Then I crossed my fingers when I gave him the debit card, and by the grace of the good Lord himself, that worked. We had our hotel.

Casey got real excited and said she wanted to get some ice cream, cause she'd seen their dessert menu online. I told her fine, but after that, we had to get our bubble on. That said, it was a good call by her. Turned out they had this ginormous ice cream machine right in their bar. I got a double hot fudge sundae. It was delicious as Mama's desserts on Easter Sunday.

After we got to the room and settled in, I said, "Time to get bubbly."

She seemed excited, and it was good to get her back in a

good mood after all the stress of the day, but then she stopped and said, "We don't have bathing suits."

Shit. She was right, but I didn't wanna lose the momentum, and honestly I wanted to check the tub myself, so I just went with it. "That don't matter," I said. "You can wear a shirt and your shorts. Just pick shorts you don't care bout if they get wet. I'll wear some shorts too, ain't no thing."

She nodded, got changed, and started practically buzzin' with energy. I changed after, then hollered, "Let's hit the jacuzzi!"

The hot tub was mighty special. Shiny with clean silver on the edges and water deep enough that you could just melt your whole body in. And the best part? It was empty—no one else in sight. Yeah, me and Casey looked kinda dorky—me with my basketball shorts and fat hairy chest, and her with her white volleyball shorts and unicorn T-shirt. But you know what? That didn't matter. I didn't care one bit.

I turned the dial to put the bubbles all the way up and touched the water. "Man, Casey, that's hot."

"Is it supposed to be that hot?"

"Yeah," I said as I slipped one foot in, "that's the point. It warms you all up, makes you feel right." I slid in and let out the biggest grunt I had the entire trip. All stored tension just slipped outta my body, got absorbed right with the heat.

Casey came in slower, but once her leg got halfway in, the water splashed the bottom of her shirt and shorts. She pushed herself back up and sat on the edge with her legs danglin' inside the tub.

"Too hot for you?"

"No, I just don't want to get my clothes all wet."

I shrugged. "Suit yourself." It took a while, but I reckon even she got pretty comfortable too, just relaxin' with big bubbles burstin' up on her toes. It was a good scene, no doubt. She mighta even said a "Thanks, Daddy" but that part I cannot recall.

However, the next parts I can.

We were talkin' somethin' stupid. Maybe I was describin' to her what makes a good cake versus a bad cake, I don't know, but I do know we were havin' a swell time when these kids emerged in the pool deck.

Maybe I shouldn't call them kids—they were probably twenty-somethins—but the three of them came in lookin' like foolish brats. One had his blond hair all curled up, the other had to be six foot six, at least, and the last one could barely walk straight—he was all wobbles. Each with their swimmin' trunks and big biceps and six packs.

They approached the jacuzzi, and the tall one asked, "Can we hop in?"

He smelled like heavy vodka, but it wasn't like I was bouta say no and get in a fight and ruin the tub, so I just grunted, and me and Casey scooted over. One by one, they climbed in, till me and Casey were outnumbered, and the pool stunk of pure alcohol.

"So," the wobbly one burped, "are you two on your honey-moon or something?"

"What did you just say?" I burst out.

The blond one waved his hands at the wobbly-word-slurrin' bastard. "Sorry about that. My friend here is very drunk."

"Yes," the tall one added with a laugh, "just ignore him."

I almost felt like takin' my foot and shovin' it up where the light don't shine, but I held it in. I leaned back, tryin' to just let the bubbles heat me up.

They all started gigglin' like a pack of morons. "So," the tall one said, "what brings you two to Oklahoma?"

Casey probably sensed my steam risin', cause before I could

talk, she said, "We're looking for my uncle. What are you guys doing here?"

The blond one said, "We're on summer break from OSU. You guys ever watch lacrosse?"

"Yeah," the very drunk wobbler said, "we're DI Lacrosse."

"We play for OSU," the tall one added. "We're here for vacation. We've been driving all across the Southwest. Where's your uncle?"

I didn't like any of them, but the tall one specifically rubbed me the wrong way. The blond one was just a vain moron, and the wobbler a drunk idiot. But the tall one, now, he was too friendly. He was lookin' down at us like we were some hicks, just cause we didn't bring bathin' suits. I could tell—it was in his eyes.

"We're not sure where he is. We're looking for him," Casey said.

The wobbler jumped in. "How'd you lose him? Did he take the wrong route?"

"No, it's not like that."

"Then how is it like?" the blond one asked.

All the sudden, they all were lookin' at me, expectin' me to say somethin'. Casey, the blond one, the tall one, and the wobbly one, all starin' at me, expectin' me to clear up the situation.

"We're just lookin' for him, that's all." I crossed my arms and fell deeper into the tub. It wasn't feelin' hot enough no more.

The drunk one said, "I was looking for my sister this one time when she was hiding from our parents, and it took me half a day to find her. It turned out she was at the mall."

"Yeah," the blond one added, "if you haven't been able to find him, why do you think he wants to be found?"

Suddenly, I felt a tiny kick on my shoulder from Casey under the water. I assumed she was tryin' to calm me down, but she oughta known it wasn't gonna work. "What business do you have talkin' like that?" I asked. She kicked me again, and again.

"Daddy?" she whispered in my ear.

I waved her off.

"I don't think he meant any harm," the tall one said. "I'm sure you'll be able to find him. What's your names, anyway?"

"Forrest," I said, real stern.

Casey took a good three seconds to come up with an answer, but she didn't respond to their question. Instead she mumbled, "Daddy, did you bring a towel?"

Slowly, I turned to face her. Her knees were shiverin' by my head. She looked terrified, all big-eyed, scared as hell. "What's wrong, Case?"

Then I saw somethin' I ain't never seen before. Right in the middle of her shorts, right by the jacuzzi's edge, and right in fronta my face, was this great big dark-brown stain. "Oh my Lord," I exclaimed. "Did you just shit yourself?"

Then the bastards started breakin' out in laughter.

"What the *fuck is that?*" the blond one spat out.

"Holy crap," the drunk one slurred. "Is that *blood*?"

Casey's face turned bright red. Then she got up and dashed away.

"Oh my God," the drunk one continued. "I think she just had her period!"

The tall one, for all his pleasantries, was the first to clamber outta the jacuzzi. "Dude, I think some dripped into the water. That's just nasty."

Next, the blond one followed, who just kept shakin' his head.

Finally, the drunk one stumbled and laughed and laughed and laughed. His friends tried to pull him outta the water, but he wouldn't budge, too stuck in his stupor, probably pissin' in the water.

Eventually, I said, "You best be shuttin' up right now." I

waded my way through the tub, grabbed him by the neck, and shoved him out.

"Woah, woah," his friends called out, but I wouldn't have it. I practically choked him while I pushed him back. Then I tucked my hand under his back and threw him halfway up the jacuzzi's ledge.

"Shit," he cried out. I'd scratched his back against the tub's side.

"Shut up," I said as I gave him one final shove. Crawlin' on all fours, he finally scrambled his ass outta there.

As they walked away, the blond one called out, "Screw you, you crazy hicks." Then even the tall one started laughin', while the drunk one went back to wobblin'.

My blood was boilin' at such a rate I could barely see the world in fronta me. Everythin' was red. I wanted to smash their skulls in, watch them bleed. It's scary to say, but that's the truth. My brain cooked up a plan instantly: How I'd find them and kick their asses, get my vengeance, glorious retribution. All I could think bout was how dare they laugh at my family, my pride.

That was, till I remembered Casey was AWOL.

CHAPTER 22

After I grabbed a towel from a stand by the pool, I went to the ladies bathroom in the lobby and knocked three times. No response. Pushin' the door open without lookin', I called out, "Case?"

Just heard a groan. Sounded like a Wilcox groan if I ever heard one. "Casey, I brought you a towel. Now, I'm bouta come in, so you better have your clothes on." I waited another second, then pushed my way in.

Above the pretty and bright and shiny marble bathroom floor of *The Sirwin,* Casey stood shiverin', even with all that left-over jacuzzi heat. I reckon she just got a little unnerved, that was all.

Comin' down from her shorts was this trail of dark red—really a brown. Never realized blood could get that dark. It wasn't that bad. Really, it wasn't. Some people woulda never even noticed. Now, that said, there was a bit more brownish-crimson on her shorts than I woulda preferred. It was hard for me to evaluate that stuff, seein' as I got different plumbin' myself, but it seemed to be a little heavier load than the norm. That flow wasn't quite just a trickle. The white teeny-weeny volleyball shorts weren't the best plan neither. All in all, it really wasn't a good scene, so I tried to lighten it up.

Forcin' a smile, I said, "Nice move, Case. You got those sons-abitches to take an early departure."

She didn't respond, just looked at me with a strained face.

"Come on." I handed over the towel, and she snatched it, then covered herself completely, wrappin' her lower region in a cocoon.

"Look, baby, we'll get you new shorts."

I don't know if that made her feel any better, cause her face didn't change at all.

We hurried up the elevator and went to the room. There, Casey made a dash for her suitcase, then headed straight to the bathroom.

I sat on the couch to take a breather. My fatherly instincts were kickin' in, tellin' me I couldn't let this whole night be a bust. This was supposed to cool her down, after all. Sighin', I thought how it was just my luck that of all nights that girl had to become a woman, it was this one.

She didn't say nothin' from the bathroom, so I just hollered a weak, "It's alright, honey."

From the bathroom, she said loud and clear, "Daddy, just shut up. Please."

Well, I didn't like that ugliness at all, but considerin' the circumstances, I wasn't gonna say much more. I waited around, but after a minute, a good idea came to me. "Gimme a second, honey. I'm gonna go downstairs and talk to the hotel folk."

I stood up, and of course my—Casey's—phone started goin' off. She'd left it next to the bed to charge. I peeked over. Sandra. I grunted. I didn't wanna pick it up much at all, but considerin' our recent spat and the night's dilemma, I felt I had no other choice. "Sand?"

"Forrest? Put Casey on the phone."

I peeked at the locked door and lowered my voice. "I don't think this is a good time right now."

"What? What do you mean, 'not a good time right now'?"

"The girl's gone on the rag," I whispered.

"What?"

"I mean, she's gone on the crimson tide."

"What? Oh my Lord, speak up. I cannot hear you. What on earth are you talking about?"

"Casey just had her first period." I surprised myself at my volume, so I quieted myself and repeated, "Casey just had her first period."

"Oh Lord."

"It's fine. I'm handlin' it."

"Put me on the phone with her."

"She's hidin' out in the bathroom," I explained. "Don't worry, I'll handle it. I'm gonna go get some feminine materials."

"Forrest—"

"It's fine, Sand. I'll call you back in a bit." Then I hung up and threw on a shirt. I said to the bathroom door, "Hang tight, Casey. I'll be right back."

There wasn't much of a response besides somethin' between a groan and a pout.

After a quick sprint to the elevator, I found myself back in the lobby. It was empty besides its nice setup with crystal chandeliers and fancy chairs, and the late-night receptionist with his big black mustache. But none of those fixins impressed me no more. I just wanted to get Casey to stop bein' so upset.

I went up to big mustache man and said, "Hey, buddy."

In his fancy voice, he greeted me, "Hello, sir."

"Yeah..." I can't say his talkin' didn't tickle me at all—he spoke real polite—but it wasn't the time for it. "My daughter's havin' a situation, and I need your assistance."

"Oh?" he asked. "What kind of situation is she having?"

I grunted. "She's havin' her period. Y'all got lady pads or somethin'?"

At that moment, I heard a familiar, annoyin' snicker behind me. I didn't even wanna turn, cause I already knew the suspects, but I felt obliged. Exitin' the elevator and walkin' through the lobby were the three lacrosse sonsabitches, and this time they had backup with them, two girls. The tall one headed up to me while the other four lingered back. They had changed—cleaned up all nice with the boys in their polos and the girls in some slutty dresses. Made me feel a little dumb in my shorts, which were still a tad wet.

The tall one flashed his perfect teeth. "Hey, man," he started in, "everything turned out all right?"

Meanwhile, mustache man completely misread the situation and blurted out, "We don't carry sanitary napkins here, sorry. But I think you can buy some from the 7-Eleven down the street, most likely."

Well, that got a good laugh outta everybody but me. The bystander crew snickered a bit, while the tall one just kept on smilin', like he couldn't do nothin' else. "Hey, man," he said, "sorry about my friends earlier. They're just too drunk. Should I ask the girls if they can help out your daughter?"

I didn't say nothin' at first. I just squared up and stared at him straight. I'd seen his kind before. Sharp eyes, big muscles, good-lookin' face, easy attitude. He was too proud, too cocky, thought a smile or a laugh could get him anywhere. Honest, his confidence reminded me of Bryan a little, at least Bryan at seventeen. Difference was Bryan at least had gotten some good discipline along the way to help mold him, developed him a good heart. This kid was just pure cotton candy. A spoiled brat.

"No thanks," I said. "We're good."

He shrugged. "Okay, well, have a good night, then." And he started to walk away.

For some reason, I didn't like his shrug. Maybe it was too far back, like he was throwin' somethin' over his shoulder, looked fake, insultin'. Pompous. I don't know. All I remember is that things started goin' in slow motion. I shouted, "Hey!"

I walked up to him and grabbed him by the shoulder. "What business you got talkin' to me like that?"

He whipped around, finally showin' some real emotion in the whites of his eyes, somethin' besides just cool indifference. "Excuse me?"

"You heard me."

All the sudden, his two buddies—the blond and the wobbler —grouped up next to him, while the girls hung back. The boys seemed to have sobered up pretty good, if I say so myself.

Behind me I heard Mr. Mustache say, "Sir, I'm going to need to call security."

He was still callin' me "sir" even then. After a long, long three seconds, I pulled my hand off of the kid. I tried to think bout what Bryan would do. The answer wasn't too hard to figure: He woulda smashed him right in the face.

But I just didn't have it in me. I didn't feel good at all.

The boys eyed me down, then they left with their girls, probably to drink some more.

I glanced around the hotel. All the lights suddenly felt too bright, too much. I didn't like them at all. I didn't like the gold paint on the roof or the big paintins on the walls. I didn't like gettin' called "sir." I didn't even like the jacuzzi. It all made me sick as a dog. Nothin' there felt right for me, and I just wanted to go.

I returned to Mr. Mustache. "Is there any way we could get a refund?"

"A refund?"

Finally, he'd given up on the whole "sir" act.

"If we leave now, can we get a refund?"

He shook his head. "Sorry, once a guest begins their stay, the transaction is complete."

I got all frustrated, so I kicked his desk a little. "Can you make an exception? My little girl is havin' an emergency."

"Sorry, no exceptions," he said. "And if you will, please back up."

That was when I realized I'd gotten right up in his face. Walkin' away, I said, "Fine, have it your way. No refund."

I dashed up the stairs—I was too angry to wait for the elevator—opened the door, and said, "Casey, come on. We're leavin'."

CHAPTER 23

First I grabbed a fluffy pillow from the bed and stuffed it into my bag—my neck had been hurtin' the whole drive. Then I grabbed some clean clothes and knocked on the bathroom door. "Casey, did you hear me? I said we're leavin'."

The door just barely creaked open. "Why?"

"Cause this place ain't right. Wrap up your business. We're headin' out. Don't worry, we'll pick up the proper toiletries in just a bit."

"Daddy, I don't want to go. It's almost nighttime."

"Baby," I said with a little sigh, "don'tcha wanna find Uncle Bryan? We gotta keep movin'. You can sleep in the car."

"Yeah," she said with just the tiniest bit of doubt sprinkled in her voice, "but we can look for him tomorrow."

"Sorry, honey." I got up real close to the bathroom door, so she could hear me better. "We're just runnin' behind schedule, and I don't think this hotel is all that great anyhow. Too stuck up. Listen, just grab a towel. We'll get you the proper materials in a bit, like I said."

She came outta the bathroom holdin' a towel and wearin'

some fresh clothes. "I don't need a whole towel," she said in a kinda unsure tone.

"Good." I smiled at her. "Just take it anyway, might could come in handy." I hopped in the bathroom and took a quick piss. Over the stream, I yelled, "Get your stuff ready!" Then I changed and grabbed two more towels, just a coupla keepsakes for the road.

Sittin' on one of the queen beds, the girl simply didn't look like herself. All dazed, confused, tired, the whole lot. At least she had all her stuff packed up. I took my bag and said, "Alright, you ready, kid?"

Slowly, she followed me out the door.

ON OUR FINAL walk through the lobby, only Mr. Mustache, the front desk man, remained. When we left out through *The Sirwin's* big fancy doors, I flipped him the bird.

The days seemed to last forever that summer, but every night's gotta come eventually, and for us it was comin' right then. It wasn't even that warm, not without no sunshine and with a little wind attackin' our sides. We hustled to the truck in the hotel's parkin'. Man, Casey was walkin' so slow. I remember I called to her, "Casey, come on, hurry up. Let's hit the road."

We clambered into the truck, and when I saw the fresh leather car seats I got only a coupla months ago, I told her, "Hey, just put the towel over the seat, baby doll."

Listen, can't say it was the best thing to say, but you try gettin' blood outta leather.

Still, she didn't respond, just complied like a robot. Then I drove us down the street to that 7-Eleven and parked. "Come on, Casey, we'll go into the store real quick and then hit the road."

She slid down into the seat even more than she already had,

almost slippin' through her seatbelt and fallin' onto the truck's floor. "No, I'll just stay here," she mumbled.

She looked so miserable that there was no sense in arguin' with her. "Fine."

I barreled my way into the store and glanced around, searchin' for some curious products. I couldn't find nothin', mostly cause I didn't know where to look. I turned around, aimin' to ask the employee at the front where the pads were at, and that was when I realized that the cashier was the damn near most beautiful woman I'd seen in a long time.

I approached her, now all awkward and nervous-like, and said, "Ma'am."

"Yes?" she asked. She did this little double blink with her eyes, and that got me all dead inside. She had these gorgeous eyes and a crazy body. She was probably twenty-five, twenty-four, maybe. Hopefully not too much younger, for my sake. It ain't good to judge a book by its cover, but this lady shouldn'ta been workin' at a convenience store, naw. She shoulda been a model.

Given the circumstances, I didn't know how to say what I had to say. My brain just hopped to different places. I asked, "You from around here?"

She nodded. "Yes, born and raised in OKC."

"Ah, you like it?"

She shrugged. "It's okay. It's what I know."

"Huh, I guess that makes sense."

Lookin' at her, somethin' inside me moved. I thought bout how I had an upset girl in my car, an angry wife at home, a shitty job with my old man, and a mama who was dyin'. Thought that I might never even be able to find Bryan, that maybe those boys in the tub were right. Just for a second, I wondered what life would be like if I just took this young lady into my life and ran away, ran away onto another road. Just ran till I reached the end of the world. Maybe we'd go north, all the way to the polar bears. Or south, to the beaches of Argentina. Goin' west didn't seem to be turnin' out so great. No one needed me anyways.

But then she broke my illusion. "So what were you looking for?"

I shook myself and said sheepishly, "I needa buy some lady's pads."

She laughed a little, then pointed me down a coupla aisles, and I found some pink packages that looked to be made of good cotton. Didn't come cheap neither.

Headin' back to the truck, I heard a faint sound. I walked slower, listenin'—thought it mighta been trouble—but as I got closer to the truck, I realized it was Casey. I ran up, swung open the door, and shouted, "You alright?"

She was just on the phone, cryin' and all, talkin' to Sandra. She said, "No, no, it's fine, it's fine."

I slid into my seat, closed the door, and stared out my window toward the night sky. It was real beautiful in the summer.

After I waited for a bit and she finally finished her conversation, I slid the 7-Eleven bag over to her. "Uh... just slide one of these puppies in your underwear, and you'll be all good." Wasn't like I had any experience.

She looked at me all confused.

"Oh yeah," I said. "I'll leave you to your privacy for a bit." I hopped back outta the car and wandered down the street while the wind blew past me. Starin' into the dark, I just couldn't get the girl-from-the-shop's face outta my head—had it imprinted in my skull. Lord, she was beautiful. But after a good five minutes, I clambered back into the truck and asked, "All good, then?"

I didn't get much of a response outside a slight puff of sound, which I took as agreement. We set off, and after drivin' for a good hour and half, Casey fell fast asleep, while I was gettin' pretty tired myself. I took an exit and found a mall parkin' lot. I put my seat all the way down and watched my little girl flinch in her dreams, while I tried to fall asleep. She was real beautiful too.

I realized then that sometimes a girl really just does need her mama.

I realize now that night, I acted the most shameful I ever have in my life.

CHAPTER 24

The highway plays funny tricks on your eyes. You don't know what's been passed and what's ahead—at some point time just blurs together, once you get tired enough. Down I-40, we cruised across the top hat of Texas, passin' nowhere towns like Erick, Alanreed, and Groom, where everythin' just seemed like dirt, grass, or telephone lines.

Interestin' enough, there were a few wind-turbine-type gizmos that caught me by surprise. Big white giants in the distance, with three long thin arms. Texas never struck me as the kinda place to get all frilly with their power, but what did I know —I'd never been before.

So we drove on. We stopped in Amarillo to get a quick bite and piss in, but me and Casey didn't talk much. She was quiet that whole mornin', in fact, outside of a quick chat with Sandra and some textin' with her friends. Basically, she didn't wanna talk to me none, except to tell me we had to buy some headphones so she could listen to her music. I told her she could listen on the car, but she said she needed headphones. Fine, I said.

While we drove on and on and on, the sun beat us down.

Honest, felt the Big Man upstairs was torturin' us. It got unbearable at times. Unholy, even. Remember, our AC was broke. Down under the dry Texas heat, it got to the hundreds, and I sweated like a dog.

Then we passed Vega, Adrian, and Boise, ghost towns on the edge of the world. Vega looked to have maybe two good restaurants at best, Adrian just a school and two churches, but Boise ain't had nothin' at all. We passed by an old sign for it: *Boise*, and I peeked out my window, but there was nothin' there. Only empty, dead land. And those turbines over yonder. Old dirt set against future wind.

Kinda got me all depressed, if I'm bein' honest. I wanted to know where the mountains and lakes were that I'd imagined for Bryan's journey. Those Texas lands dried up my spirit, made me feel like I was meltin'. Still, there was one reliable friend to keep me company if Casey wasn't gonna talk to me none: good ol' billboards.

There were a couple borin' ones—the usual suspects:

Help me help you sue someone... Buy our damn insurance before you crash your car... Our burgers taste the best and probably won't make you too fat... But every once in a while, there was a gem.

Standin' stranded in the middle of no-man's land, taller than a tower, was this big and bright sign. It hailed down on me like some beacon. On it, one giant cartoon bowlin' ball rolled into some pins. It read: CHECK OUT BARRY'S BOWLING! ONLY 5 MILES AWAY!

After rereadin' it a coupla times, I glanced around. All I saw was a whole lotta nothin'. The sign defied physics, defied explanation. It had no business bein' there. But still, there it stood.

That got me all sentimental. Laughin' a bit, I started in, "You know, your uncle Bryan was an odd one. Always found a way to get himself into trouble, no doubtin' that."

I waited for her to pester me with one of her trillion questions, but nothin' came, so I kept talkin'. "I had to be thirteen, fourteen, maybe. I remember he was a junior, while I was a freshman. There wasn't much to it, day to day—I just kept my head low, chewed my gum, took my notes sometimes, you know how it goes. But Bryan was always popular. He's got a good attitude to things, relaxed bout everythin'. Both the teachers and the students liked him, just that kinda guy." Still nothin' from her.

"It helped too he played some ball, free safety. He was no pushover neither. He was good, *real* good. The 757 feared him. He had a quick step and a long reach, coulda battled with the pros, college, at least, I swear.

"Anyhow, it was gonna be his year. He was gonna start, probably was one of the best five people on the team, no lie. He was gonna ball! And, well, lookin' at him, I wanted to ball too. How could I not? I'd dabbled a little in Pee Wee, then Youth—nothin' too serious—but I'd say I could hang, at least compared to my contemporaries, especially this one tiny Black kid, Timmy.

"Timmy and I'd played together a good amount throughout the years, and I could always rely on Timmy to make me look a little smoother than I probably was. Timmy just had some fundamental issues: He couldn't catch a ball to save his life, couldn't throw one, and couldn't hit no one well neither. Every game, his old man would be sittin' in the sidelines, hollerin' at him. 'Son, don't you be playin' soft now!' or 'What the hell was that?'

"I don't think Timmy liked the game much neither. As we got older, he didn't grow too big. Stayed string-bean skinny and didn't get much taller, no muscle neither. Not a good combo. I always thought bein' that small was impossible for the darker race. And he always had this pencil mustache—looked like a pedo.

"Anyways, we was sorta friendly, but goin' into high school, I didn't want nothin' to do with him. He just wasn't the kinda kid you want in your circle, followin' you around. Didn't seem to be a good look for fourteen-year-old me. Didn't know why he'd always taken a likin' to me. Always wondered why he couldn't make more friends of the same shade, if you catch my drift."

Casey glanced away. I tried to ignore it.

"So imagine my surprise, when on the day of tryouts, who trotted up but Timmy! I went up to him and asked, 'Timmy, what the heck you doin' here?' Not in a mean way or nothin'. I was just shocked, that's all. I assumed he was gonna quit for sure. Blue Lakes ain't no pushover team. Timmy looked at me all shy-like and said, 'My daddy asked me to just try out. I've been gettin' better lately.' *Better?* I remember thinkin'. *Better at what?* He could sorta run, but had no chance in hell to be a runnin' back. A breeze could blow him over. And he could barely jump over a pile of dog shit. Again, I ain't tryin' to be mean or nothin', just givin' you the facts. So when Coach and some of the upper-classmen came out to watch, I knew it wasn't gonna end well.

"We ran some drills—honest, I missed some catches and tackles—but Timmy? Man, Timmy was the worst. It wouldn'ta been so bad if he wasn't so bad. But he was. It got to the point of misery. He was so nervous he tripped up on some cone routes, got lapped by everybody in runs, just stuck out like a sore thumb. And Coach tore him up. He'd scream, 'Run, son, run!' and eventually the seniors caught on. 'Run, boy, run! Run, boy, run!' they'd scream at him. Just not a good day for little Timmy. But at least it eventually finished, and he got to go home.

"In the end, it turned out neither of us made the team. Shocker of my life. I was devastated, whiny for weeks, but I reckon Timmy was secretly relieved, outside of his daddy's fury. Little did he know the only thing worse than bein' the worst player on the football team is not bein' on the football team at all.

"See, ain't nobody was gonna make fun of me cause I was Bryan's brother, but Timmy? Naw, Timmy was screwed. Beyond Timmy's lack of athleticism and general coordination and bein' one of seven Blacks in Blue Lakes, he had the reputation of bein' a little queer. He just wasn't set up right for that time. He'd do better today. Too quiet, too nervous, too into the books. Caught some nasty rumors, couldn't shake them off.

"So a coupla days after tryouts, Timmy took a beatin'. A mean beatin'. See, at lunch the poor bastard accidentally spilled his milk all over Henry Bell's shoes, one of the senior line-backers and a well-known hothead. I didn't see it happen, not many did, but apparently after it happened, Henry acted instinc-tually. He cracked him, instantly.

"The story spread like wildfire around the freshmen, but I didn't believe a lick of it—just thought it was another ploy, another rumor—but the proof was in the puddin'. Next time I saw Timmy, he had a big ol' bandage wrapped around his head and a fat welt for a left eye. Told me the doc said it'd take a week for him to be able to see fully again. Henry didn't get in no trouble neither—no way in hell was Timmy gonna snitch on him after that. Ain't like anyone woulda helped him anyhow, with him bein', well, you know. Honest, though, seemed he had taken it well, didn't get no teeth knocked out or nothin'.

"And that coulda been that. Honest, shoulda been that, but I got too excited by the whole ordeal. After I found out everythin', I ran home hollerin' and told Bryan all the details: how Henry had gotten Timmy good, how Timmy was all beat up, how Timmy really had to work on his hand-eye coordination. You can imagine my surprise when Bryan was mighty interested. Asked me all kindsa questions: Timmy's background, the inci-dent, what Henry was doin', so I gave him what I just told you. And I thought that was that. Turns out, I didn't know Bryan near as well as I thought."

I giggle-grunted there a bit. It was strange to look back. Man, high school's just a weird time, ain't it?

"Anyhow," I said, "I thought that was that, and for a bit, it was. Timmy was healin' up alright, and it seemed like Henry was gonna leave him alone. But like I said, your uncle Bryan always had to stick out."

Grimacin', I remembered that day. "At some point around lunch, Timmy came up to me, which I didn't like much, cause I was startin' to make some good friends, but I listened to him anyhow. He told me, 'Your brother told Henry off. They're gonna brawl after school.' I remember thinkin': *Oh God, that moron.*

"All day, I tried to find him. Ran around, wantin' to tell him not to do nothin' stupid, but I couldn't find him nowhere. I think he'd cut class. Soon, 3:30 rolls around, and a good helpin' of people, myself included, are rushin' to Noah's Hill. Noah's Hill was off school property, so the teachers couldn't do nothin'. It'd become a sorta grounds for settlin' disputes.

"So we were all waitin', Henry pacin', lookin' all jacked and flexin', and I remember wonderin': *Where the hell is Bryan?* Well, there's one feature I oughta mention bout Noah's Hill: It has a great view of the parkin' lot.

"See, Bryan had figured out Henry's one weakness. Thing is —Henry wanted to brawl. Henry loved to brawl. Didn't matter to him if he lost. Even if Bryan gave him a good beatin', as long as he did at least some counter damage, he'd be happy. Henry's assumption was they'd tough it out and go back to the field, cool as ever. I don't think Henry understood Bryan very well—Bryan thinks bigger—but Bryan understood Henry.

"Bryan knew Henry loved his '97 Chevy Malibu. Honest, I never could see what the big deal was. It's just an ugly box, and it's got tons of issues—bad timin' chain, bad fuel pump, bad ignition switch, but that's beside the point. Point is, Henry loved nothin' more than cruisin' with his window rolled down, mullet hair flyin' on the way to school. And Bryan knew it.

"This is the part that gets really ridiculous." I started laughin', I couldn't help it. "So we're all standin' on Noah, and someone hollers, pointin' down at the parkin' lot, '*Is that Bryan?*' We all turned around, and sure enough, there was Bryan. He was holdin' a mop, and I was like, *Oh God, no, don't bust up the car.* I panicked for a second, thinkin' he couldn't possibly be that dumb. Lucky for me, he wasn't. No, see, he had this big white bucket beside his foot, like a janitor's bucket. But there was somethin' inside, sure enough. Somethin' brown and mushy.

"So he walks up to the car, holdin' the bucket and the mop. Then, right in fronta it, he turns around and smiles at the crowd and gives a big ol' thumbs-up." I started dyin' laughin' again. "So he takes the mop, dips it in the bucket, and it drags out a whole buncha wet shit. To this day, I don't know where he got all that shit from, but it was a whole lotta it. Wasn't human shit, I can tell you that much. And, simply put, he starts moppin' down Henry's car. Got every angle of it, didn't let nothin' up, and Henry started yellin'." Chokin' on my laughs, I sputtered, "Henry hollered, '*Not my car! Not the car!*'

"He ran down and pushed Bryan off it, but the damage was done. He'd gotten it everywhere: on the dash, under the wheels. I think he'd even snuck a bit of it under the hood. We all could smell it from the hill. Ain't no way Henry was gonna get that smell out no time soon. As for Bryan? Well, Bryan just walked off whistlin' like it was no big deal."

In the truck, I kept on laughin' and laughin', till I finally could calm down a bit and managed to rub the tears from my eyes. Just rememberin' it was almost too much. I managed to say, "They kicked him off the team for that. I remember I ran home, took ahold of him, and yelled that he was stupid. It wasn't worth it at all. Asked how could he do that for Timmy. For Timmy! But he just shrugged it off, said, 'I'd do it for anyone. Ain't no thing,' and smiled and asked Mama what was for dinner. Man, what an alien."

I laughed again. "You shoulda seen your granddaddy's face. I swear, his head damn near exploded."

Pretty good story, right? I thought so. I expected her to say somethin', anything, but there was nothin'. No response. Pure silence from her.

Instead, the quiet snuck back up, with only a steady stream of wind and engine spinnin' around us. I hadn't expected that, that sudden quiet. Somehow, it got me thinkin' more bout Sandra, the story, the time, and Bryan, the kinda guy he was. It messed me up. Can't explain it. Honest, all I know is bein' right back in my head after a classic story made me think of all the years that'd passed since then. Got me worried. Awful worried. Worried that everythin' I was doin' was wrong, that Sandra and my old man were right, that I shoulda just taken us home, that we were never gonna find Bryan, that I'd wasted all this time and money, that Mama was gonna die, that I was just a big fuckin' idiot. Got myself all kinda caught up, I swear. I thought I might just have a breakdown right there—felt like I needed to slam the brakes or scream out the window or honk the horn or bang my fist against the dash or drink some liquor or call an ambulance or shoot somebody or drive off a cliff or lie down or call the old man or call Mama or crash the truck, just do somethin' before every little thing turned into a piece of cr—

But, at last, she laughed.

It was the tiniest, itsy-bitsy, teeny-weeny chuckle I ever damn heard. If you weren't listenin', you may have as well missed it. Barely under her breath, almost passive-aggressive, even. But you know what? At that moment, nothin' coulda been better. Tasted like sugar.

"Y'all were so stupid," she said.

"Yeah, I guess we were." I laughed and took a deep breath. Then I whispered, "I'm sorry."

She nodded once. "We'll want to stop at Phoenix's police headquarters. I did some research. They should have Bryan's arrest record and maybe his address."

And like that, we had somewhere to be.

CHAPTER 25

I t took the whole dang day of ridin', but we got in Phoenix at 10:36 p.m., with the sun set and the stars out. I thanked the Lord—we'd been sweatin' like dogs. Casey's hair was stuck all over her face, with strands glued onto her nose, while I could feel my boys hangin' like they was on the gallows.

But we didn't care one bit. No, not one bit.

Durin' the ride, I told Casey more bout Bryan—how he once broke his arm, then responded by breakin' this kid's nose, and it got her a little excited again. She asked me a zillion questions like she would when she was younger and would drive me plumb crazy: "What's in Phoenix?" "Are we close to Disneyland?" "What do you think Uncle Bryan is doing?"

I shrugged and shrugged and shrugged. "I dunno," I'd say. But inside, I was feelin' the same way, with a kinda energy pumpin' up my blubbery guts. We were closin' in.

New Mexico hadn't been much to sneeze at. Just more dry sun keepin' us hot as hell, almost burnin', even. I chugged five waters down like there was no tomorrow. But, man, Arizona finally had what I'd been imaginin' this whole time. Ridin' on I-40, we got all kinda parks that looked mighty fine with big trees and plateaus and all that, but that was nothin' compared to when we reached the Apache National Forest.

Only a coupla hours from Phoenix, it was a sight to behold: You could see the mountains, the trees, the water, all wrapped together like heaven on earth. The heat didn't even feel that bad then, not with the wind and the air bein' so fresh. Sky looked aqua, is that it? Marine blue. Coulda been the sea itself driftin' up in the sky. Truly a marvel, through and through. And what made it all the more magical? Bryan had ridden on that road and seen those sights.

Funny enough, though—made me a little hungry for home.

Casey liked it too. She said, "Daddy, we should come back to visit this place sometime after we find Uncle Bryan. We could go hiking."

I smiled to myself then. Kids bounce back more easy than adults, I guess. The mountains helped her forget my previous stumble.

As we rolled through, gettin' closer and closer to Phoenix, the green turned back into brown, back into the flatlands, then back into man's land. In the distance, it looked like a nice enough town. Like any other, really, with a few big buildins and long stretches of road, but I'll tell you what—at that moment, it coulda damn well been Disneyland.

Bout five minutes away, Casey's phone went off. I assumed it was Sandra—she'd been callin' her throughout the day but didn't wanna talk to me none.

Casey said hello, then handed the phone over. "It's Papaw."

I grabbed the phone. "What's up?"

"Forrest? What happened to yer phone? Why'd Casey have it?"

I rubbed my eyes. "We've been over this, I lost it."

"Is that right?"

"Yes, that's what I told you before."

Soundin' all snarky, he said, "Well, I'm *sorry* for askin'."

I sighed. "How's the shop? How's Luis? How's Andy?"

"They're fine, the shop's doin' good. Been slow. Didn't need ya around."

I waited for a follow-up, but none came. "So... why the call?"

"Forrest, I wanted to tell ya... I think... I really think y'all oughta come home now. I know I told ya to go, but I changed my mind. I want what's best for yer mama. That means y'all comin' home."

"Why? What happened?"

He groaned deep, almost a heave even. Then a grunt followed. "Yer mama's not doin' so hot. Doc says it's gettin' worse faster than expected. Like some kinda super tumor. Said she did pretty well, but it ain't good no more."

Again, I waited for any kinda follow-up, but that damn ogre of a man ain't had nothin' to fuckin' say. "Well, spit it out. How long?"

"Coupla weeks, max. Probably less."

Under my breath I muttered, "Goddammit."

A long silence followed, longer than any of the previous ones. Once again, I could hear everythin': the wind, the engine, and Casey's little breathin' as she snooped in on the conversation.

"Put Mama on the phone," I said.

"She's asleep."

"I don't care, just put her on the phone."

"I ain't gonna do that, Forrest. If ya wanted to talk to her, ya shoulda called. If ya wanna see her, ya oughta just come back home. I want her to have at least one of her sons in the house."

I started breathin' heavy. I couldn't take it, not at all. "Daddy," I managed to say, "I'm close. We're close to findin' Bryan. Mama wanted to see him. Bringin' him back is the least I can do. Then we'll come back, we'll come back real fast."

Another fuckin' grunt from him. Imagine the most annoyin', disrespectful, contemptuous sound you ever damn heard. Like someone pissin' on you to wake you up, then murderin' you, then pissin' on your grave.

"Forrest, I ain't gonna tell ya again. Ya listenin'? That boy left and didn't come back. Clear as day, he don't wanna be found. What kinda man leaves their family? I know yer mama done got sentimental, and we both wanted to help, but there ain't time for that no more. If ya don't turn round right now, I'm worried you'll break yer mama's heart, and you'll end up regrettin' it till the day ya die. Actually, ya best regret it, cause I ain't payin' a dime for this damn luxury vacation getaway. Ya hear me now?"

Lookin' out into the pink horizon, where that big and golden eye sank watchin' me, I didn't know if the Lord was tellin' me to listen to my old man or to press harder on the gas. Guess we all gotta come to our own conclusions on the matters of the heart.

"I'll call Mama tomorrow," I said. "We're gonna find Bryan, and I'mma bring him home." Then I hung up.

Casey's big blue eyes drilled into me, could feel them probin' the side of my big head. Whole mood in the car had shifted around, changed in under two minutes. I handed her the phone back.

"We almost there?" I asked.

She pulled up the map and said, "Yeah." Then she played with her feet a bit and watched the world fly by out the window. "What happened?"

"Nothin' you needa worry your pretty little head over. Where should we get a hotel? We'll wanna hit up the police department first thing in the mornin'."

She did a little searchin'. "Central City. It's right by their office."

I hummed and tapped the side of the car. Then I said real quiet, "Okay, you got it, jitterbug."

CHAPTER 26

When I woke at six sharp, Casey was still sleepin' below the ugly yellow motel blankets. It wasn't all that bad, though—the place was nice and cheap, the beds were comfy enough, and I didn't even see a single cockroach. Only downer was the shower. It had somebody else's hair sittin' around when I soaped up that mornin'. Still a good deal for forty bucks if you ask me.

After I dried off and got dressed, the girl was still sleepin'. She looked so at peace. Tiny breathin', curled up like a little ball of joy, brown hair strewn out. Reminded me of another kid I'd watched sleepin' for so many years. They had the same shade of hair. I was always the early riser of us two, and we always shared a room. Was he still sleepin' in till lunchtime? I wondered.

I tapped on her shoulder. "Come on, Case. Let's get movin'."

As we prepared, our energy grew and grew. The call with my old man had been slept off like some bad dream, and I ain't never seen Casey get dressed so fast. The only thing on our minds was findin' a trace of Bryan's scent. So we strolled into the Phoenix Police Department with our chests high, feelin' pumped.

Place looked bout how you'd expect, real gray, real gloomy, and when we got to the front desk, we were immediately block-aded by a big ol' Black woman. Casey led the way and said, "Hello there, ma'am, we're looking for a police record."

The lady looked pretty useless to me, by the way she was sittin' and by her general disposition. I stepped forward and opened my mouth to explain the situation in greater detail, but then Ms. Karsety snapped to life. Her eyes grew wide, and she said, "Oh, hi there, little darling. You looking for a police record?"

Casey nodded, and they got to work. Casey showed her the '01 *Phoenix Nation* article. "We're looking for the Billy Wilcox from this article."

"Well, we can look through the arrest logs and see what turns up. I can't promise anything that far back, but I'll sure try."

I leaned against the wall with my arms crossed, watchin' her. I never had much experience with nobody that far out west. Had to be careful. She clicked away at the keyboard.

"Casey," I said, "we gotta keep our expectations in check."

But then Ms. Karsety went ahead and said, "I know exactly who can find this!"

"Really?" I asked, my heart lightin' up. "Is it that easy?"

She disappeared into the back, and Casey said to me, "We'll find Uncle Bryan in no time."

I grunted. Didn't wanna believe it, but it looked like it was gonna happen.

Turned out, it was just gonna take a helluva long time. Ms. Karsety told us we could have a seat, that they were lookin' for the record in the back.

Hour by hour by hour, probably took us two and half hours of just waitin' around. After a while, I told Casey, "I'm gonna ask what the hell is takin' so long."

I pushed past some sketchy-lookin' folks and went up to Ms.

Karsety. "How much longer is this gonna take? We don't have all day."

"Let me check." She went to the back, and I heard her voice raise up at some poor clerk to "hurry the hell up." Then she returned. "It'll just be a minute."

"Thanks."

I sat back down and closed my eyes and tried to calm down. I could almost feel Bryan right there, right there with me. I started gettin' a big sweat. Guess my body thought it'd never actually happen, that we'd actually be able to find him. That moment, I could picture him better than I'd been able to years. There he was, just seventeen-year-old Bryan right in fronta me with a great big smile, ready to take on everythin'.

Then Casey tugged on my shirt.

I opened my eyes, and Ms. Karsety held a sheet right in fronta me. "Here's a copy of the arrest log from that incident." She turned around and said, "Have a nice day!"

Casey squeaked out a thanks while I said nothin'. I couldn't focus. My hand was twitchin'. May been sweatin', even. The arrest log had an address, and it had a name. Well, technically it had two of both, but I only needed one to get my head spinnin'.

Record of Arrest
Department of Police, Phoenix, Arizona

Name: Billy Wilcox
Crime: Disturbance of the Peace
Race: White
Sex: Male
Weight: 187 lbs
DOB: March 6th 1983
Height: 6'2"
Home Address: 10411 N 35th Ave, Phoenix, AZ 85051

Name: Adam Isiah
Crime: Disturbance of the Peace
Race: White
Sex: Male
Weight: 154 lbs
DOB: October 22nd 1984
Height: 5'10"
Home Address: 699 W Fillmore St Phoenix, AZ 85003

Hustlin' outta the office, I said half-heartedly to Casey, "Come on, sugar." Then I repeated, "Come on!"

I grabbed her hand and pulled her out the door and handed her the paper and said, "Look up this address. The Billy address!" Runnin' to the truck, I hollered, "Look it up quick! We're gonna ride hard." I hopped into my seat, while Casey tumbled her way in, and I started Mrs. F-150 up.

She handed back the phone and said, "Here, this is the location." I took a quick glance—*only ten minutes away.* "Let's go."

I started drivin', barely able to concentrate on the road. My head was feelin' all hot, but it sure wasn't from the weather. I could barely contain myself. I wanted to smile and shout and holler. So I did, a little. After rollin' down all our windows due to the lack of AC, I turned to the window and hollered, "Woot!" Sounds dumb, I know, too excited for my age, but I didn't care none. Casey was gettin' into it too—smilin', grinnin', lookin' like a silly little kid again.

We broke all kindsa speed limits, but it was worth it. I thought bout all the things I'd say to him. There was so much to catch up on. I wondered if he'd looked different, how'd he take to Casey.

In seven minutes, I pulled into where the phone told me to go. You wouldn't believe how hard my heart beat. I just hoped it wouldn't choke and fail before our reunion.

But then I stopped.

I glanced outside. I checked the address on the street. Then I double-checked it. "Casey, you sure you put in the right place?"

She nodded. "I'm sure."

I took the phone from her and checked it again: *10411 N 35th Ave, Phoenix, AZ 85051.*

Yup, we had arrived. However, we had a tiny issue. We were at a strip mall.

I started scratchin' at my scalp. There was an even bigger issue. We were in fronta a Pizza Hut.

"This can't be right." I slumped into my chair, thinkin' I shoulda known it wouldn't be that easy.

Casey inspected the report twenty different ways, but each time she came up with the same answer: It sure as hell looked like we were at the right spot. "Maybe they put in the wrong address in their system," she said.

"I dunno," I mumbled. I started thinkin' bout what Bryan had put in his letter way back when. Hadn't really crossed my mind he wouldn't be in Arizona no more. Maybe I just didn't wanna think it.

"Come on," Casey said. She opened her door. "Let's go get some pizza. Maybe they have apartments above the shop or something."

I glanced up. Didn't look like there was nothin' but a flat roof and some pipes.

She walked out, so I groaned and clambered out and followed her. My legs felt heavy—I was basically draggin' them against the concrete. Sandra was right. My old man was right. My head started goin'. I kicked an empty Pepsi can down the parkin' lot.

Casey turned around and said, "Come on, Daddy, maybe he'll be right here."

I trudged in. Sure smelled like pizzas, not much of Bryans.

There were just two Mexican-lookin' teenagers drinkin' some Coke in the corner and one tired lookin' one of them workin' the register. Coulda sworn her eyes were pink, druggy. Looked like if she'd been poked, she woulda fallen right over.

"Excuse me," Casey started in, "we're looking for a family member, and we were wondering if anyone lived here."

"Please, baby," I said, "don't confuse the lady. We'll take two pizzas."

Then the cashier went in too, with a smile. "Which is it? Looking for family or pizza?"

I sighed.

Casey said, "Both."

The girl kept smilin', but I didn't trust it one bit. She was just foolin' us. "No one lives here, unfortunately."

Immediately, I turned to Casey and said, "Told you so."

"But," the woman continued, "this is a new Pizza Hut. Actually, I think the whole strip mall is only like four years old. They redistricted the area. Maybe there were apartments here before."

"Lady, does anyone live in this area or not?"

She shook her head. "Not anymore. Anyone here would've moved. It was a pretty rundown area. Lots of temporary living situations."

"That's just great. Just two pizza slices is all we need. Please, *now*."

Judgin' by how fast she found our slices, I reckon she got the message. They were too small, wouldn't fill me up at all. "Can you get us a full pizza, actually? *Please*."

Casey tugged at my shirt and said under her breath, "You don't need to be so *rude*."

Like I cared. These people had lost my brother.

I paid up and waddled my way to the corner of the Hut. I plopped down on a seat, bent a slice in half and swallowed it whole.

Casey followed and my, *her*, phone went off. She answered it, and I groaned. Sandra.

"Fine," Casey said. "We're in Phoenix... yes, ma'am... fine... I'm fine... yes... okay... I love you... Bye." She hung up, and I raised my hands.

"She didn't ask to talk to me?"

Casey shook her head. "No, she didn't. Sorry, do you want me to call her back?"

"No," I muttered. "I didn't wanna talk to her anyhow."

We ate in silence. Well, mostly I ate. I got four slices down while Casey barely finished nibblin' on her first. Somethin' distracted her. She was lookin' at the arrest log all funny-like, like she was some kinda detective, and it annoyed the shit outta me, if I'm gonna be honest.

After a good three minutes of it—her readin' and rereadin' and rerereadin'—I finally demanded, "What is it?"

"There was more than one address on that sheet."

Dejected, I grabbed the sheet back from her and glanced it over. "Whatcha talkin' bout?"

"Look." She pointed. "Adam Isiah. We have his address."

I shrugged. "What good will that do? That ain't Bryan."

"He might know something, he might know something about Bryan, or where he is. They worked together. Remember? The other waiter?"

I grunted, an annoyed grunt. "Course I remember that." Honest, though, I'd plumb forgot. "But that was so long ago, he probably has no idea."

"Well, it was so long ago when Uncle Bryan, or Billy, or whoever, got arrested, but we still tried to find him here. There was a good chance he wasn't here, but we tried anyways. We have to keep trying."

She was starin' at me with her big, googly eyes. Same face when she was askin' to get a dog. I sighed and swallowed down the last pizza slice like a human vacuum. Then I said only a single word. "Okay."

She had an amazin' attitude, gotta give her that. Guess it don't come from me.

WE DROVE, real slow this time. I didn't feel like I was in any real rush. We ended up at 699 W Fillmore Street, and there was this old, ugly-lookin' buildin'. To make a long story short, no Adam Isiah lived there no more, at least accordin' to the landlord, but he happily offered us a *White Pages*, which Casey accepted. A fuckin' White Pages. You woulda thought he was handin' her a Bible the way she so graciously accepted it. She'd probably never seen somethin' of the sort.

So, I sat lackadaisically outside on hot steps tryin' to relax while Casey flipped through this big, thick book. There was no use in goin' back to the car, not while it was boilin' us like a bowl of soup. Instead I glanced up at the sun and listened to Casey flip page after page.

Even as we headed deep into the afternoon, it was still too bright, still too much. Sun didn't quit for no one. The street had a little bit of everythin' under that dry scorcher: beige, red, yellow, and green. Had these nice bright-green palm trees and big bushes. Not to mention these smooth maroon-lookin' bricks under your feet. Though Phoenix didn't look nothin' like the Wild West of my imagination. Too many chain stores and shippin' trucks for that. The cowboys were long gone.

At least a cute mamacita came crossin' the street with barely anything on to cover two bouncin' balloons, if you catch my drift.

Yeah, I thought while I leaned back, *it ain't that bad of a place with her around*. A curious idea came across my head then. Maybe I could just walk up and leave. Yeah, I'd call Sandra and we'd set somethin' up for her to pick up Casey, but maybe *I could just leave*. It wasn't like she wanted me anywho. Neither of them did, really. Seemed Casey was gettin' older every day—becomin' a woman—she didn't even really need me one bit. Everythin' I tried was just a screwup. I could just leave, maybe live in Arizona forever. Get a real nice tan. Maybe even talk to that mamacita. We'd chat, she'd teach me a little Spanish, then we'd make our Wild West—get our salsa on and make love by a pool or maybe in the desert. The heat probably would help me lose some weight. *Yeah, that wouldn't be too bad*. Better than wanderin' aimlessly for a brother who seemed to be nowhere with a kid who didn't even wanna talk to me. So I was like that, goin' bout it in my head, daydreamin' of another me, another life, when Casey tugged my shoulder and woke me up.

She had a big dumb smile on her face. "Look!"

She stuck her hand right in the middle of the white book with a big fat finger so I couldn't see nothin'. I pushed it away and glanced down. *Adam Isiah (602) 555-1683*.

"Huh?"

With that wide grin still plastered to her face, she said, "Let's call him!" She pulled out *her* phone, before I whipped it outta her hand.

"Let me do the talkin'."

I punched in the digits, hopin' she wouldn't be too disappointed when we didn't get nothin', since you can't expect nothin' much from the White Pages, so you can imagine my surprise when I heard a friendly, "Hello?"

Stammerin' a bit, I spat out, "Hello?"

"This is Adam."

"This is Forrest."

The line went quiet for a second. Then he asked, "Who?"

"Forrest." I swallowed. "Bryan's brother."

Again, the line went quiet. "Bryan who?"

Meanwhile, Casey started shakin' her head at me. She mouthed some kinda word, but I didn't understand a lick of it.

I held the phone down by my chest and asked her, "What? What are you tryin' to say?"

"BILLY! Ask him if he knows Billy!"

"Oh." I raised the phone back up. "Billy's brother. I'm Billy's brother."

"Billy?" Adam asked. Then he raised his voice a bit, "Billy *Wilcox?*"

Suddenly, I found myself noddin', shakin' my head right up and down at Casey. "Yessir, Billy Wilcox. I'm his brother."

"Are you serious?"

"As a heart attack."

"Well, I'll be. I had no idea Billy had a brother!" That stung a little more than I'd care to admit. He continued, "Are you just touring Arizona or are you on your way to California to visit him?"

California!

"We're actually lookin' for him."

"We?"

"Yessir, I'm here with my daughter."

"Billy has a niece?"

Damn, Adam sounded more excited than me. "Yessir, he does."

"Wow, this is incredible! Please come over for dinner. I'd love to host any family of Billy's."

"Well, actually, we're kinda in a hurry. You see—"

"Nonsense. It's no trouble. It's almost evening anyways. You guys can stay the night if you need to. It's no problem."

I glanced up. He wasn't wrong—dawn was headin' to dusk. We'd wasted the whole damn day in Arizona.

"Well, if you insist."

"Great! You got a pen? I'll give you my address."

I tried pullin' out the Notes app, but then I got all confused, so I put the call on speaker and handed it back to Casey, who jotted down the address, then gave the phone back.

Adam finished with a peppy "See you soon!" then hung up.

For a second there, I sat in simple shocked awe. Casey probably thought I had a stroke or somethin', with the way my eyes glazed over.

"So?" she finally said. "What's going on?"

"I guess we're back on track."

CHAPTER 27

As we approached Adam's house, the excitement trickled back in me some. My foot took on a little shake, a light tap. I knew meetin' Adam alone was gonna be a good time. Any friend of Bryan was certain to be a friend of mine. And if he could tell us where Bryan was? Good God almighty.

While we cruised to the outer Arizona suburbs and the desert cooled down to comfortable nighttime weather and the wind blew like a whistle callin' us, I realized it'd been so long since I talked to anybody mano a mano, if you wanna stick with the Spanish theme. The last *real* man I'd spoken to in days musta been my old man, considerin' I couldn't count those prep-school bastards from the hotel or smartass Tom as men.

Passin' some big southwest ferns wavin' at us, I asked Casey, "You excited?"

"Not as much as you," she said, smilin'.

"Whatcha mean? I'm cool as a clam."

She let her mouth hang open, actin' like I'd just said dumb nonsense. "Daddy, your leg's been shaking since the second we stepped in the truck."

I glanced down. My left leg looked like it coulda been havin' a seizure. Immediately, I locked it up. Let out a little puff of air from my nose, then a grunt. It'd be good to have a change of pace, I thought. The womanly influences of Sandra and Casey combined were startin' to get to me, gettin' me far too emotional bout this whole ordeal.

WHEN WE REACHED THE HOUSE, I must admit, I was quite impressed. Mr. Adam Isiah had done mighty fine for himself. Looked like somethin' you'd see in the movies, the oldies where the family's perfect and has seven kids and practically a mansion and the only real dilemma was how soon the widowed father would marry the beautiful new nanny or adopt another little girl. Sandra always loved watchin' those movies. She'd watch them over and over and over again.

The house musta had three floors, with nice windows and a big tall gray chimney. I parked out front, and when I hopped out, I whistled into the dry, quiet desert. It rolled away with the wind.

"You really *are* excited," Casey said.

I grinned. "Naw, I just felt like whistlin'."

To be honest, I was sweatin' a little. Goin' into a stranger's house, you never know what to expect, and in the driveway there was a '14 Lexus IS F. Worked on one myself. Nice zippy little pricey sports car with classic Jappy quality. Man had some taste, can't lie bout that.

I dragged myself up to the door, which looked to be pure mahogany. Then I took a deep breath and knocked.

"*Coming!*" His voice was so high pitched, I figured he musta been pretty excited to see us too.

I turned to Casey. "Don't do nothin' weird now."

"*Me?*" She sounded so disbelievin'. "*You're* asking me to not do anything weird? Are you serious?"

"Shush," I stammered. The door was openin'.

As smooth as the sunrise, the first thing I thought was: *Damn, Adam Isiah is one well-dressed man.* He had this fancy dark-red bowtie on, lookin' all suave, and a nice button-down sweater vest, plus fitted khakis. Made me glance down at my own beat-up dirty jeans and the hole on the top of my right tennis shoe for a second there. He was probably a coupla years older than me, by the look of his house and everythin', but I coulda sworn he was younger. His skin looked better: no grime, no lines, no nothin' but cleanliness. Crossed my mind he seemed like the kinda guy that'd run a lot—enter marathons and all those things —but I was too amped up to pass judgment on that.

He had a big ol' smile plastered across his face, big and bright enough that it convinced me to smile back. "Oh my gosh," he said, "you look just like him."

I didn't know what to say to that, so I just stood like an idiot, tryin' to think of somethin', when Casey went ahead and said, "Really?" as she walked into house.

Adam nodded at her. "Yes, don't you see the resemblance? They have the same hair, the same nose. The only real difference is the build."

She snickered. "Uncle Bryan is a little skinnier?"

"Uncle Bryan? Oh, you mean Billy? Yes, he was pretty trim, at least the last time I saw him." He grabbed me by the shoulder and gestured around. "You have so much to tell me!"

Still, I was too dazed and confused to respond as I took in the house. *Adam's woman did right by him.* His whole place was spotless—had these huge elegant windows that dripped the night's desert starlight right into the livin' room, and the walls had long paintins of random colors and scattered shapes (not that I understood it much, but I'm sure it was impressive), and their kitchen was this massive open terrain—coulda fit my entire truck there with some wiggle room left over.

"Wow," I finally said. "You've got a wonderful home."

He tapped me on the back again. "Thanks, buddy!" Then he moved to the kitchen.

Casey'd already found herself relaxin' by the Isiahs' velvet couch, so I went over and kinda fell onto it and rolled next to her, till she pushed me back.

I half shouted, half said, "Adam, do you have an address or number for Bryan?"

"For Billy? I may. It would be buried somewhere," he called out. "I'll check after dinner!"

Hell yeah. My grin was just growin' and growin', couldn't help it. I relaxed a bit. We were gonna find him.

Next, I asked, "Is the missus home?"

He laughed a tiny faraway laugh. "Oh, no, my partner works at the hospital but should be back for dinner."

"Partner? Like business partner?" I asked, but I don't think he heard me cause he didn't respond.

Casey pointed around the house and raised two thumbs up and whispered, "This place is nice."

"Yeah," I said, "this place is nice."

Adam came back with two cups of water and gave them to me and Casey. I started sayin', "Ah thanks, we're good, thou—"

He just shook his head and said, "Nonsense," so I took it and sipped, and honestly it tasted like it came from the Fountain of Youth itself, with a nice little hint of bubbles sprinkled in.

Casey agreed. "This water is *soooooo* good."

"Thanks." Adam smiled. "We get Mexican mineral water. It's got a natural carbonation to it."

Natural carbonation? Fanciest man I mighta ever met, but to be honest, I didn't much care. The bubbles tasted nice. Whole thing felt like I'd entered a dream. Just earlier, I'd thought we were doomed and broke, but now someone had invited us in, just off the good will of Bryan. I released a small burp, and that finally got me talkin' again.

I asked, quick and friendly, "Mr. Isiah, thanks so much for invitin' us. When you told us you knew Bry—uh—Billy, you can't imagine the joy it brought to my heart."

"Joy? Well, I'm glad I brought you joy! I'm ecstatic that I got to meet you! Billy's brother. He was such a good friend over the years, but it's been too long since we talked... has it really been a decade? Wow. Your call brought back great memories."

"When..." My speakin' stumbled. "When did you meet him?"

He smiled, then rolled his eyes. "I was working as a waiter at this shabby restaurant right here in Phoenix, Steve's Diner. God, I was so quiet and shy back then. Then one day this big Southern guy came strolling in and went right up to Steven and said, '*I need a job!*' I remember watching him and thinking, *What bee is in his bonnet?* But that turned out to be the beginning of our friendship."

Casey nodded, real excited. "We read about that! We read that you two got arrested!"

I nudged her, but then Adam broke into hysterical laughter. "Oh my God," he said with the words all stretched out. "Is that how you found me?"

"Yes!" she said.

"We did get into a little trouble. He actually left Arizona pretty quickly after that. But he taught me so much while he was around. He didn't care what others thought. If he thought Steven was being—excuse my French—shitty, he said, 'Hey Steven, you're being real shitty right now.' Or this one time where some father was berating his little girl for not finishing her breakfast, he went up to him and said to the guy, 'Sir, you should reevaluate your parenting abilities.' Then he told him, 'If she's full, and it's got to be finished, I'll finish it for her.' He grabbed the plate and threw a whole pancake into his mouth and got it down in one bite. Steven almost fired him on that one, but Billy managed to talk him out of it."

"Yup, that's Bryan alright." I could barely contain myself. "So, so, where's he livin' now? You see, our family's lost contact with him recently, so we're tryin' to get a location on him."

Adam scratched the bottom of his chin. "I'm not quite sure where he is now. We fell out of touch after the wedding. Probably still in California."

"*Weddin'?*" I burst out. "*There was a weddin'?*"

He looked at me, all curious-like. "Yes, about twelve years ago in Santa Ana." Then a timer dinged. He stood up. "Oh! The chicken's ready."

Once he was in the kitchen, I turned to Casey and whispered, "Can you believe it? There was a weddin'."

She shrugged. "Of course there was a wedding. How else would I have my cousins?"

I laughed and pushed myself off the couch. "Hey, Mr. Isiah, you need help with that?"

"No, no." He came out to the dinin' room table next to his livin' room with a one fat rotisserie chicken and laid it down on a center plate.

I approached it. "You got that at Costco?"

He laughed and came back with some mash potatoes, green beans, some fruit I didn't recognize, and forks and knives. "No, we have our own rotisserie."

Woah. Fancy, fancy.

After he put all the food on the table, he gestured at Casey. "You hungry?"

"Yes!" She jumped up and clambered toward the table.

I started shakin' my head, sayin', "This is too nice for us, Mr. Isiah—"

"Please, call me Adam."

"Okay, Adam, this is too nice for us. You really didn't needa go all out like this." But when I looked at the golden chicken and the lush fixins, and all I could think was: *Thank the Lord.*

"Nonsense! Anything for Billy's brother!"

Casey pulled up her chair, her mouth practically waterin'.

Damn. Sandra never made nothin' this good.

Soon enough, I found myself around the table while Adam took the head. "Looks like we'll be eating alone tonight," he said.

"I guess so." I began to reach for the fork, when he closed his eyes and said grace. I nudged Casey to stop her attack on the green beans and pointed at Adam.

"Bless us, O Lord, and these, Thy gifts, which we are about to receive from Thy bounty. Through Christ, our Lord. Amen."

"Amen," I repeated with Casey. Then we both jumped right into the chicken. She took a leg, and I cut a bit off the thigh.

"So," Adam said, "tell me about Billy. What was he like as a boy?"

Us tell him bout Bryan? More and more, it seemed he had far more to share. "Well," I said in between bites, "he was like you said, *strong*, strong-willed. Him and our old man would clash, would fight somethin' fierce."

I put my fork down. "I never told you this story neither, Casey. There was this one time, we were all just sittin' at the dinner table. I musta been twelve, maybe eleven." I started cacklin'. "And that boy just goes right ahead and stands up. He'd been sulkin' all day, not sayin' nothin' after a big fight. Then durin' dinner he just went ahead and stood right up and didn't say nothin'. We're all waitin' for him to say somethin', but finally Daddy gets sick of the whole thing and asks, 'What the hell you standin' for?'"

I kept on chucklin'.

"What was he standing for?" both Adam and Casey asked.

"Bryan said, 'I'm standin' till you apologize.'"

"Daddy came back and asked, 'Apologize? Apologize for what?'"

"'Apologize for bein' my father.'" I burst out laughin', rubbin' the tears comin' outta my eyes. "He was always a firecracker, helluva firework."

Eventually I got control over myself and realized neither Adam nor Casey were laughin'. I rubbed my eyes again and then let out a long, stretched-out sigh and a final chuckle. "Guess it was just somethin' you needed to be there for."

"Yes," Adam agreed, "I suppose it is."

Then the front door started to swing open. "Ah," Adam said as he jumped up and went over, while I turned to Casey and told her, "Don't get too excited now. We gotta focus on findin' Bryan —gettin' his number."

"You're worried about me getting too excited? Look at yourself."

I waved her off. It was good seein' her happier, but we needed to focus on the mission.

I turned toward the door to thank Adam for the delicious chicken, when I saw the most surprisin' sight of my life. See, this Black guy walked right through the door wearin' scrubs and a white coat. A Black doctor.

"I'm sorry I'm late," he said.

And that was when I got the shock of my life.

"It's fine," Adam said, then he leaned in and he *kissed* the man. Right on the lips.

Suddenly, I glanced around in a panic and realized all I'd been missin'. *The great fashion sense, the decoratin', the high-pitched laugh. How could I not realize it?* Their kiss lasted so long, way longer than I'd ever kiss Sandra in fronta guests. Damn, how could I not see it? Adam Isiah was a queer.

I looked over to Casey, and clearly she could see some level of fright in my eyes, cause she whispered, "You didn't realize? He said 'my partner.'"

All I could do was shake my head. I couldn't believe they'd do that in fronta a child. I found my belly explodin' with all kinda nerves that hadn't been there before, like little worms crawlin' around, eatin' up all the good feelins I had.

When they finally stopped suckin' lips, they turned to me with great big smiles. "So," the newcomer asked, "is this the brother of the famous Billy I've heard all the stories about?"

I mustered a muffled, "Yep."

He came over and extended his hand, and I raised up a dead fish of my own. He squeezed it pretty hard, while I couldn't make a fist even if I wanted one.

"I'm Jamal."

"Hi... Jamal."

Then we were surrounded. Casey's left—Jamal. My right —Adam.

Casey started talkin', but I wasn't listenin' much. "Seventh grade... It'll be okay... The teacher is supposed to be better..."

Is this the closest I've ever been to a queer? Have I ever seen one in the flesh? Yeah, we made fun of Timmy, but I never actually believed he was a gay. Maybe that one kid Rick. He was always pretty weird.

"What about you, Forrest?" Adam asked

They were all lookin' at me. "What about me what?"

He laughed. "What do you think of the food?"

I looked down. My hand was tremblin'. Terror had taken my eyes. After I put down the fork, I gulped, then yelped out in one loud burst, "Is Bryan... gay?"

Everyone looked at me like I was from Mars.

"I mean Billy."

"No," Adam said. The word came out sharp. With a new thin layer of disgust.

I breathed a massive sigh of relief. I mean, while Bryan was still around, he had a girlfriend or two, or three, and he'd been caught sneakin' around quite a bit, and I caught him in some more than precarious circumstances with one girl named Amy, but my thinkin' was you have no idea what can happen out west, especially when the queers were infiltratin' every corner of American life.

They were all still lookin' at me with their jaws dropped, Casey included, so I said, "Oh, the food? It's great. The chicken's real good." Then I buried my face in another bite.

Slowly, the conversation got goin' again, just without me. Apparently Jamal was a surgeon, who woulda thought, and had a nasty day of slicing up a lady's guts. She needed "a small bowel resection" accordin' to him. Sounded like a blocked butt to me.

And as they kept on talkin', Casey kept sayin' how much she wanted a dog, which I ignored while I crunched and sipped and bit and chewed, tryin' to stay low-key, till, at long last, Jamal, of all people, asked me a question.

"So, Forrest, what do you do?"

I swallowed my piece of chicken and didn't look him directly in the eye. I didn't like the sound of the question. Here he was askin' me what I did while he wore his whole surgeon getup, felt like a trick somehow. "I work on cars. Family business."

"Oh." He smiled his brown smile. "Adam loves cars."

I bet he does.

"Tell him. Tell him about your collection."

I raised an eyebrow. "Collection?"

"Yes," Adam said, real slow. "We actually have a garage out back."

"Is that so?" I asked as polite as I could. "I noticed the Lexus out front, mighty fine car."

Jamal clapped his hands. "You should show him, Adam."

I didn't particularly like the idea of Adam showin' me

anything *"out back,"* but I didn't feel like I was in no position to argue, so I just grunted. An *agreement grunt*, just to be clear.

Adam let out this long, exaggerated unpleasant, *"Sure."*

"Great!" Jamal said. "I'll give Casey a tour of the house."

Normally, I'd argue against leavin' any man alone with my daughter, but seein' these two were part of the funny tribe, and Jamal seemed to be playin' the wife role of the two anyhow, by the way he talked, I decided it'd be alright.

Adam led me down another one his fancy hallways, fulla weird-lookin' paintins. They no longer looked so good to me.

"Forrest?"

"Yeah, buddy?"

"I don't appreciate the way you look at Jamal."

I tried to think of somethin' to say but nothin' bubbled up. Eventually, we got to this white door, and Adam pressed on a bunch of secret key codes, and the door swung open.

"Wow." I couldn't help myself.

A 2009 Camaro, a 2011 BMW 7, and a 2015 Aston Martin V12 Vantage.

I went up to the Vantage and gazed into its black surface. It was spotless. "Wow, Adam, this is one beaut."

"Sure is."

I snickered. "Y'all ever considered a rainbow paint job or somethin'?" I glanced back at him. He didn't look so pleased. "I'm just messin' with you," I said.

Turnin' back to the car, I asked, "How much did this run you back?"

"A lot."

"A lot, huh? How much is a lot?"

"Just a lot."

Didn't like the way he said it. Annoyin', pompous. Sounded like he thought he was better than me. Like I couldn't afford it.

Pissed me right off. "Well," I muttered under my breath while I admired the car, "you don't needa be all faggotty bout it."

Then I realized what I said and froze up. Nothin' happened immediately, so I thought I was in the clear. Slowly I reeled my head back then turned around. And that was when I cringed. By the look of his face, you coulda sworn there was smoke comin' outta his ears.

"Uh... sorry."

He began to tap his foot. "You know, Forrest, you know, you know what?"

"Uh... what?"

"It's your type I dislike the most."

I took a step back, leanin' against the $200K car. "I'm sorry?"

"It's you, so callous, so blind, with so little regard for others, that you don't even recognize when you're being an ass. At least people who blatantly hate gay people are clear about it. You're right on that line where you're still a homophobic asshole idiot, but would never admit it."

"Me?" I asked loud as I put my hand on my chest. "You think I'm afraid of the gays? No, no, it's just... I don't really..." Then I ran outta things to say.

Adam sighed. "I want you to leave."

"Wait, wait, I'm sorry bout the rainbow joke," I said while I walked up closer to him. "At least tell me where Bryan is, or gimme his number if you have it. Please, me and my girl have come a long way."

He looked me right in the eyes. No fear, no hesitation, just cold brutality. I couldn't never seen it comin' from a queer, at least back then. He said, "No, Forrest. I'm not going to do that."

I stumbled a step back and hollered, "What?"

"Clearly your brother left Virginia for a reason."

I closed my eyes and balled my fists. All I could think was: *Bryan invited these sissy boys to his weddin' over his own flesh and blood. Over our old man, over Mama, over me?* Can't lie to you, the realization stung. Cut right to the heart. Felt like drinkin' poison.

He kept on talkin'. "I take back what I said about you looking just like him. You two might have the same nose, same hair, but you're *nothing* like him. He's a good man."

"You stop talkin' now—"

"No, I want you to leave. I don't want any of your energy in our home anymore. I feel terrible for your daughter."

That got me to burst open. I jumped like a cheetah and opened my eyes wide. "Well, well," I stammered. "Well, at least I ain't fuckin' another man in the ass!" Then I socked him right on the side of his face and ran off back into the house.

"Casey! Casey!" I yelled. Finally, she came runnin' out from the livin' room.

"What? What?" she asked.

I grabbed her by the hand and pulled her to the front door and said, "Time to go."

Jamal looked confused as all hell, but when he saw Adam enter with a bloody nose, he didn't argue none.

I tripped a little on their fluffy rug, then hopped, skipped, jumped, and hustled outta there and didn't look back. I heard Casey yell, "Bye, thanks for the di—"

Then I slammed the front door behind us.

CHAPTER 28

After we got in the car, I slammed the wheel. "Fuck!"

I turned the key and switched to drive and blasted outta there.

"What was that all about?" Casey asked. She sounded all nervous, skittish.

I rumbled in my seat, slushin' around my weight. "Just a dumb argument. Don't worry bout it."

After one street, I turned left, then right, then left again.

"Where are you going?" she asked.

"He said the weddin' was in Santa Ana, didn't he?"

"Yeah, but—"

"Well, we're going to Santa Ana, then."

"Yeah, but he said he wasn't even sure if he was still there."

"Where did your sense of adventure go? Just put it in the dang phone. S-A-N-T-A A-N-A and add a Billy Wilcox B-I-L-L—"

"I know how to spell Billy."

I waited a bit. "Give it to me."

Santa Ana flashed on the screen. *Bingo.*

"Look, darlin', it's only five and a half hours away!"

I immediately accelerated toward I-10 W.

"Daddy!"

"*What?*" You don't need me to tell you that I didn't need any attitude from her at that moment.

"It's the middle of the night. We can't drive right now."

"Why not?" I raised my hands off the wheel. "Look how easy it is, I'm drivin' with no hands. The road's completely clear."

"Daddy!" she screamed as we veered ever so slightly.

I took control back and then exhaled. "Look, there ain't nothin' you gotta worry bout. I'll get us there in no time. You can go to sleep."

Soundin' all pouty, she said, "I liked them. Why don't we just go back and ask them where Uncle Bryan is? They seemed to know."

I waved her off. "We'll find him ourselves. We got this far, didn't we? Don't worry bout it. Just remember: Billy Wilcox, Santa Ana."

She muttered somethin' under her breath, somethin' that sounded an awful like, "You're crazy."

"What? What did you say?" I shouted.

"I didn't say anything," she squeaked. "Can you just focus on driving?"

"Huh, okay," I grumbled. "I thought you said somethin'." I drove for five more minutes, just gettin' angrier and angrier, not really sure what I was gettin' angry at, but it only got worse and worse. Then I slammed on the wheel again. "FUCK."

"What?" Casey cried.

"I forgot to call Grandmama." I sighed. "Gimme the phone again, please." She started fidgetin', tryin' to pull it outta her pockets. "Now, please," I said. Finally, she handed it over.

With one eye on the road and one eye on the phone, I found the house's contact info. It rang and rang and rang, then went to voicemail. "Damnit."

I called again. It rang and rang and rang, and finally someone picked up. "Forrest," the old man started in with me, "what the he—"

"I wanna talk to Mama. I said I'd call Mama."

"Yeah, ya dumbass. Ya said ya'd call her in the mornin'. It's the middle of the night. I'm goin' to sleep. Don't call again."

He hung up. I called again. He hung up on the second buzz. "Casey, what time is it back home?"

She pulled out her finger calculator and went ten digits plus three more. "One a.m."

"Dammit. Just screw it all." I drove for another two hours till I parked us on the side of the road.

Late into the night, I could hear her soft breath, but I couldn't fall asleep. Nothin' felt right. I put my hands on my face, tryin' to keep the emotions inside, while all these sounds came twistin' and twirlin' in my noggin, like some goddamn circus firework show, throwin' out as much noise and color as possible, just to keep me up.

Adam's anger pierced me, red hot and furious. Daddy's yell —echoin' across three decades—rang in my ears. The frat boys' laughter, Mama's coughin', and Casey's cryin' all buzzed and whined. There in the night, they all layered on top of me, weighin' down every bit of my body, every ounce of my soul.

Then, in the middle of it all, starin' at me strong, were two wide brown eyes. They looked too sad and alone, watchin' me in my rearview mirror as I drove away. That damn boy from Jersey —why was he still stuck in my head? *Where the hell did you end up, Tom?*

But, hard as I tried, I couldn't remember the color of Bryan's eyes.

That night, one thought kept circlin' back around: *Why do I fuck up everythin'?*

CHAPTER 29

The last two days were like yin and yang. You know, those blacks and whites swirlin' around each other? One day we're talkin' and happy, the next day no one wants to say nothin'. We were back in the black, and even though it was bright as heaven outside, in the car it felt only like dark times.

I'd woken up pretty early and gotten us movin', needin' a piss break and all. At around ten, I asked Casey for the phone. She'd already called her mama twice, who still didn't wanna talk to me none. Honest, at that point, I wanted to chat with her, just to hear her voice, but I wasn't gonna say that.

Then I called my parents, and the phone rang and rang. It was the middle of the week, so I knew my old man wouldn't be around. On the third call, it rang for a long time, but finally, I heard her voice.

"He...llo?" Damn near teared up, but I held it back. Didn't wanna let Casey see me like that. She sounded awful, like a creaky bench fulla holes, just waitin' to explode into splinters. It threw me off so much, hearin' her like that, that she repeated herself. "Hello?"

"Mama? It's me, Forrest."

"Forrest," she said, real slow and happy, like a satisfied mama bear after the family's gorged on a ginormous dinner of honey. "Where are you now? Utah?"

"No, Mama, we're in Arizona. We're headin' to California."

"Describe it to me. What does it look like?"

"Mama, I called to check up on you."

"Just do a favor for your dear old mama."

I sighed and glanced out the window. "It's mostly brown, you got dry dirt. Lotta little bushes all over the place, basically litterin' the place. And I see some mountains in the distance. Flat mountains, no peaks, just fat and wide and huggin' the ground."

"What about the sky?" she asked. "What does the sky look like?"

I glanced up. "It's clear. No cloud in sight, just pure blue. The sun is beatin' hard, though." I cut myself off. "Mama, I don't wanna describe you the dang landscape. I wanted to know how you're doin'."

"Don't use that tone with me."

I waited some more. I expected somethin' wittier than that, but she just sounded tired. She sighed, then asked, "What did your father say?"

Holdin' the phone even closer than before, I whispered, "He told me you weren't doin' so hot."

"Well," she started in, "that's what Dr. Sheffield said. But who knows if he's right. I've dealt with worse. I had to deal with raisin' you and your brother and makin' sure your daddy never went off the deep end, and you remember that one time I found you after you broke your arm—"

"Mama." I almost broke out into tears, but I blinked them back. "Daddy told me to come home. He said there ain't no more time to find Bryan."

The line went quiet for a long time, longest three seconds of my life. It seemed every second coulda been ten years, one decade of life at a time, feedin' me back all kindsa memories, even memories I didn't know I had: playin' at the playground, havin' her yell at me for doin' somethin' stupid, havin' her yell at my principal for treatin' me like someone stupid, her cryin' at my weddin', her cryin' after Casey's birth. They came at me in a whirlwind, and in the last second, all I could wonder was why the hell I hadn't called her the entire car ride. Why the hell wasn't I with her right then? I woulda described her every rotten state if she wanted me to.

Then she said, "How close do you think you are?"

I sniffled. Musta had some kinda allergy to all the dust in the air. "We're pretty close, Mama. Bryan's in California. We're bouta be there. We'll bring him home."

"Okay, baby." She sounded so warm, so confident. How could she be so cool? "Put Case on the phone. I wanna talk to her."

"Okay, Mama."

I handed the phone over, and they talked for a long time. Casey mentioned Tom, hotels, dogs, Bryan, and Disneyland. I noticed she skipped over jacuzzis and Adam.

When she handed the phone back, I was all wired up to talk, ready to tell her every single event, give her the detail I'd always refused to offer when I was young. But she only said, "Forrest, I'm tired. I'm goin' back to take a nap. I'll talk to you later."

"Wait, Mama."

"Yes?"

I stopped. I didn't know what to say. I went silent. Somethin' had stopped inside of me.

She filled the gap. "Everythin's gonna be fine, baby."

I gulped. "Okay. Bye, Mama. I'll talk to you soon."

"Bye-bye, baby. I love you."

"I love you too," I whispered.

Then I hung up, waited a second, and shivered.

DURIN' the final leg to California, Sandra wouldn't leave us alone. Well, she wouldn't leave Casey alone. I already told you bout those two calls at the start, but two more came quickly after. And when we were only an hour away from Santa Ana, she called *again*. Each time, Casey would talk less and less and less. That got me worried.

In the final call, Casey said only one word: "Mama." Then she went dead silent. A full minute, silence. What the hell was Sandra tellin' her? After the second minute, I just couldn't take it no more.

"Baby," I said, "gimme the phone. I wanna talk to your mama."

She looked gray-cold and said into the phone, "Daddy wants to talk to you."

Again, ten seconds of quiet from her.

"Baby, let me talk to her."

"Mama, I'm giving the phone to Daddy."

Another five seconds.

"Phone, please."

Finally, she handed it over. I sighed directly into the speaker, then asked, "What's up, honey?"

"Forrest, I've been talking with Casey."

"Yes, I've noticed."

"And I don't like this. I don't like any of this. I don't like that you haven't called me—"

"Well," I cut her off, "I gave my phone to Casey, so she's in charge of it. It ain't mine no more to do cal—"

"Listen, just listen. I don't want to fight with you. I told Casey to take a cab once you get to Santa Ana. She's going to go to John Wayne Airport. I bought her a ticket to come home."

I started rubbin' my forehead. "John Wayne? Like the singer?"

"Can you just be serious for once?"

God, just smite me, I willed. Just send a lightnin' bolt and get it over with.

"I am bein' serious. I just can't tell if you are."

"It's all set up. When she told me you were going to Santa Ana, I bought her a ticket. You'll be there three hours early, and she has what she needs."

"Has what she needs? She ain't even got a passport!"

"Forrest, have you ever even been on a plane?"

I refused to answer that question.

"Kids don't need an ID, just a boarding pass."

I groaned. "All I want is for the girl to meet her uncle. Is that really so bad? I just want her to meet her family."

"This is not about Casey and you know it."

"Oh," I howled into the phone, "yes, you're right again. How stupid am I to not know what I want for my own daughter? How could I have forgotten I am so dumb? Please, oh wise one, please teach me."

"Forrest, just shut up! Just shut up for once! Dammit."

I heard her cry over the phone. Again, always makin' me look like the bad guy, when it seemed I was only tryin' to do right by my family. It got me so frustrated. *How could she not see it?*

Finally, she said, "Just make sure Casey gets on that plane. I know you're upset, and I'm upset too, but I want to work this out, and I can't do that while you're driving off to some fantasy."

Some fantasy, huh? "Sand, I'll call you later. No, scratch that. We'll video chat you. Yeah, me and Casey and Bryan. Bye." I hung up.

I tossed the phone back to Casey and passed a fat truck to get us onto I-215 N. Less than an hour away from Santa Ana.

"Baby," I asked, "do you wanna go to the airport? Do you wanna go home?"

She didn't speak for a long time. Then she whispered, "I don't know."

"Well, listen to me, honey. Okay?"

She didn't say nothin'.

"You search on the phone. Billy Wilcox, Santa A—"

"Daddy, I already did that." She sighed. "I think I already found where he is."

I slapped my wheel and smiled. "That's great, honey! Why didn't you tell me?"

She turned the phone toward me. It read: *Fairhaven Memorial Park & Mortuary.*

CHAPTER 30

"If this is some kinda joke, I don't like it, not at all."

Her voiced cracked a little as she yelled at me. "I'm not joking! This is what Google said for the top search for Billy Wilcox Santa Ana. First result was the obituary."

"Are you sure it don't say arbitrary or orbitary?"

"No, Daddy, I meant an obituary! O-B-I-T-U—"

"Alright, alright, calm down. I was just jokin'."

I didn't know what to say. Guess I was just feelin' all hot, flustered and confused, rash-like inside. I started tappin' my right foot and kept drivin'. After a minute, I said, "Read it again. Read it again, honey."

"I don't want to."

"Just do it."

She tapped around the phone and started, "*Billy Wilcox, age twenty-two, born in Virginia Beach, Virginia died in Santa Ana, California, buried at Fairhaven Memorial Park & Mortuary. Survived by his wife, Jenny Lee.*"

I stayed quiet for a second before I said, "Well, that just don't sound right to me."

"It doesn't sound right to you?" she yelled. "What do you mean?"

I shrugged. "It just don't sound right."

"Who else could it be?"

I shrugged again. "There's probably twenty Billy or Bryan Wilcoxes or Wilsocks or Wilknocks in this city alone. Plenty of them coulda come from Virginia. Could be anyone."

"I don't know," she said awful quiet.

Watchin' California unfold before my eyes, passin' Corona, Chino Hills, seein' the brownish-green valleys and the puffy white clouds, I had no idea what to say. Words just seemed to not wanna leave my mouth. We'd both gone dead quiet.

After thinkin' bout it for a long while and considerin' we didn't really have any leads, I finally gave in. "Okay, okay," I said, "we'll check out this Fairhaven Park, just calm down. Please just calm down."

"What do you mean calm down? I am calm."

"Sure, baby, just calm down." I accelerated to seventy miles an hour. "We'll get there soon, and you'll see there ain't nothin' to worry bout." Then to eighty. "Just stay cool."

As we drove into the cemetery, I must admit the day was quite nice. I didn't see none of those California girls I'd heard so much bout, just one grandmama starin' at a grave, but I did feel that patented California sun and blue skies. Reminded me of bein' back in Disney World all these years ago. Plus there were some palm trees too.

After I parked us on the side of the road, we stared down a maze of gravestones. I said, "Honey, maybe you oughta do some more googlin'. It could take us forever to go through all this."

"Daddy, I told you, I looked up and it said—"

"Alright, alright, relax." I remember thinkin', *Damn, are these the teenage years I've been hearin' bout?*

We walked into the park, cemetery, mortuary, whatever you wanna call it, and as I watched the rows and rows of gray graves, I got real tired all the sudden. I leaned over and held myself against a big stone stickin' outta the ground. It had a little angel carved on it, nice little bible in the middle, and read: Alice Marwood 1932–2005.

"Come here. Look at this, honey," I called out.

Casey came over, all shy and timid-like. From the moment we got there, I could tell the graveyard wasn't her favorite place to be. She walked real slow, tiptoed around practically, like she was gonna wake up the spirits.

I waved her over, and she asked, "What is it?"

"I want you to read this here gravestone."

"*Alice... Marwood...*"

"And what I wantcha to see is that there ain't nothin' to worry bout. Nothin' to be scared of here. Take Mrs. Alice over here, she lived a good life. What's that, eighty, eighty-three years?"

"It's seventy-three."

I counted it back up. "Yeah, you're right, seventy-three. She was alive for World War II. She woulda been right around your age, in fact."

"What's your point?"

"See, I got two points: one—don't be so afraid. The folks around here lived long, full lives, so there ain't nothin' to be sad bout. And two—this woman was old, old as heck. See, people die when they're old. Bryan ain't dead. Bryan's only, like, thirty-three right now."

"But what about Pete's daddy? He died, and he was the same age as you."

How the hell did I forget bout Lil Pete's daddy?

Real quick, I said, "Don't worry bout Lil Pete's daddy. He had some serious problems. Got himself killed. Bryan ain't got no problems."

"What about Papaw and Grandmama, then? They're pretty old."

Why the hell do I talk at all? Frustrated, I hollered, "Don't worry bout them neither. They're fine." I shook my head and leaned on Ms. Alice's gravestone some more. "You understand?"

"I guess."

"Good." I straightened and stretched myself out. "Well, in that case, we'll look around for a bit, and you'll see there ain't nothin' to see, and we'll move on." I nodded. "Okay?"

"Okay," she said quietly.

"Okay, then. Let's have a look around. I'll go right, you go left."

We parted, and I ambled around the gravestones. I wasn't lookin' real hard, just glancin', enough to satisfy Casey.

PAUL WEBB 1929–2010

SUZIE HERNÁNDEZ 1911–1987

MICHAEL MARTÍNEZ 1950–1993

Poor bastards. One day you're strummin' along, just livin' life, the next you're all pooped out.

DAVID FOSTER 1934–2013

ELIZABETH WALKER 1929–1999

NAOMI HERNÁNDEZ 1899–1976

I started gettin' a little bit of the chills. I rubbed my hands together—they were all clammy. Maybe I was gettin' sick or somethin'. We'd been on the road for a long time.

CAROL RODRIGUEZ 1925–2001

ERIC WHITE 2000–2009

SAMUEL BROWN 1933–2010

After walkin' around for a good while, I was gettin' over it, gettin' real tired, real bothered. Maybe my size and the sun were gettin' to me.

PAULA GARCIA 1956–1978

ISABELLE WILLIAMS 1943–1999

BRIANNA MILLER 1912–2000

I sat on the grass and leaned down and started breathin' heavy. I closed my eyes for a second. For some reason, I thoughta Mama's salmon and rice. It never was that good—coulda used a little more spice—but she'd make it pretty often, and it always made me feel ready to go. I'd asked Sandra to pick up the recipe for us, me, specifically, but she preferred cookin' burgers, and I didn't complain. I wished Mama coulda fixed me up some of it then. I peeked my eyes open.

ISAAC FREEMAN 1901–1978

AZEL JOHNSON 1922–1998

EUGENE LEE 1954–2008

Who were all these damn people? Were they happy?

Then there was a scream.

All the hairs on my head spiked, and I jumped like a live fish on a fryin' pan and hollered, "What hell was that?" I turned around and saw Casey standin' over somethin'. She was cryin'.

I ran over, ran like a zombie was chasin' me, as the spirits possessed me.

"It says Billy Wilcox!" she yelled.

"What the hell ya talkin' bout?"

She pointed toward the ground. "It says Billy Wilcox."

I crouched down and stared at the grass. Embedded in the dirt was this most pathetic silver plaque you ever could damn see. You wouldn't even notice it if there was any shade at all. Probably smaller than my shoe, and I ain't even got a big foot.

Engraved in the metal, it read: *BILLY WILCOX.*

I stumbled back, then crept back toward it. It still read: *BILLY WILCOX.*

Casey was just cryin' and cryin' and cryin'. I examined it for a long time, then snapped my fingers.

"Stop cryin', baby, stop cryin'."

She started snifflin'. "What?"

"I said stop cryin'." I jumped up and pointed down on it and yelled, "Look at the date. Look at the damn date!"

"What?" she asked me again.

I took her hand and pulled it toward the metal and little text under *Billy Wilcox*. I said, "Look at the date."

She read, "*March sixth, 1983.*" Then she looked up at me.

"March *sixth, 1983,*" I emphasized. I stomped on the ground. "That ain't right! Bryan's birthday is March *ninth,* and he was born in '82!"

Casey looked at me like I was crazy, then shook her head. "Daddy, he changed his name. He could've easily lied about his birthday."

I hopped. I really hopped! Wavin' my hands over my head, I hollered, "Yeah, but why would he change his birthday by three days if he was gonna change it? Why change it then? His favorite season was always fall anyhow. See? It don't make no sense. No one would change their birthday by only three days. And why wouldn't Adam know? Why didn't he go to the funeral?"

Then in a sudden burst, I saw her like I ain't never seen her before. She *screamed*, "I don't know, Daddy! I don't know! This is what Google said. I don't know!" She sat down and cried into the grass. She was always such a calm kid, never had no terrible twos or tragic threes. But this? Total breakdown.

She just lay down and started bawlin'.

"Baby, don't cry."

But that didn't help none.

"It's alright."

"No..." she said in between her tears, "it's not all right. We... we came all the way here... and he's not even here... and Mama is so angry... and I'm missing my trip home... and school's starting in a week... and... and... and..."

"Baby." I held her by her shoulders. "Don't cry, don't cry. It's alright."

She sat back up and kept snifflin' while I said, "Everythin's gonna be okay."

Lookin' up, she asked, "It is?"

"Yes." I smiled.

"How can you know that?"

"Cause, honey, everythin's gonna work out."

"How?"

I stood back up and went up to that pathetic little plaque in the ground. When I had her attention, I stomped my shoe all over it. "Don't worry bout this, baby. We're gonna find the real Bryan in no time at all."

Her eyes went real wide, and she started cryin' again and fell into the grass.

CHAPTER 31

I drove for five minutes till I realized I had no idea where I was goin', so I completed a stupid circle. Then I parked again and put my hands on my head. "We gotta brainstorm."

I'll tell you, ever since we got back into the car, which was hot as Hades by the way, Casey just sulked. She said, "Daddy, the flight leaves in two hours."

I looked at her with my patented stink eye, tryin' to keep the situation above water. "I guess we'll needa find Bryan in two hours. then."

Think, Forrest. Think. What would Jesus do?

"Well," she said all glum-like, "we could talk to Jenny Lee."

I raised an eyebrow. "Jenny Lee?"

She got all antsy with me. "Jenny Lee, Jenny Lee! The woman from the obituary!"

I still didn't get it.

She pulled the phone out and pointed to the fake obituary, "...*Survived by his wife, Jenny Lee.*"

Ding. Ding. Ding.

I tried to give her a big ol' bear hug, but she pushed me away.

"Genius girl." Leanin' back in my seat, I asked, "So where we goin'?"

She scrolled lazily on the phone, purposefully takin' forever, then finally said, "There's a Jenny Lee who's a doctor in Santa Ana, a hair stylist in Los Angeles, someone living in Anaheim... We could go to Disneyland."

"Who else?"

"I don't know. A Jenny in Irvine." She put the phone down and looked at me. "Daddy, it could literally be any of these people, and we don't know anything about California."

I grabbed the phone and said, "I know aplenty bout California." But when I looked at the Jenny Lees, I had no idea. I picked the one in LA, cause why the hell not?

We headed toward I-5, cause that was what the phone was tellin' me to do, when I noticed Casey was all slumped against the window.

"What's wrong?"

"Nothing," she mumbled.

Whatever. I put a hand out the window. If she was gonna act like that, she was gonna act like that.

So we cruised, and I got a nice look of renowned California as the sun started dippin'. *Damn, we wasted too much time drivin' and at the cemetery.* It did look pretty, though, but still lotsa gray from developments and such. America the free, more like America the freeway.

Then I heard a click. "Shit, do you hear that?"

"Do you have to curse so much?"

"I'm the one who's supposed to be askin' you that. Be quiet now. Do you hear that?"

"Hear what? I don't know what you're talking about."

"Shush."

There was a clickin' sound, a whir, one I'd never mistake. All the sudden, the truck went all fritzy. Suddenly slow, then back to speedin' up.

Immediately I turned toward an exit.

"What are you doing?"

"I'm takin' us off the highway."

"Why? What's wrong?"

Moment I started dippin' down, my check engine light went on, flashin' at me like I was some kinda idiot.

"What's wrong?"

"I said shush! Let me think."

After we got off the exit, the truck started slowin' down heavy. I barely got us to a side street before it gave up entirely.

"What's going on?"

I glanced outside. It was gettin' too dark for my likin'. "Somethin's wrong with the truck. I'mma check her out." I opened the door and hopped out, then turned and said, "Gimme the phone. I need a light."

Casey sighed and handed it over, then followed me out. "Daddy, we need to talk."

I opened the hood to check if the engine mighta overheated. "Talk? Talk bout what?"

While I searched around in the darkness, tryin' to figure out what the hell was wrong with my baby, I couldn't pay attention much to Casey. "I bet the fuel filter's gunked up," I mumbled.

She stomped her foot. "Listen!"

I pushed myself back up and pointed the light at her face. "What? What's it?"

I could see her strugglin' to talk. She was between tears, chokin' on words, while tryin' to get in some air. Wish I could say it made me feel bad, but at the time, cause I was so stressed out, it just made me mad. Madder than a wet hen.

"I was excited to go on this trip with you..." She trailed off. "And it was fun, seeing America and all, like you said. I also really liked meeting Tom and trying to go on our hike and meeting Mr. Isiah and all, but now... Now I want to go home."

I took a step toward her. "You wanna go home?"

"Yes."

"We ain't even found your uncle yet."

"I know, Daddy," she went off. "And if you want to keep looking for him, that's okay. I just want to go home."

I glanced up at the twilight California sky. Oh, the Lord was frownin' on me, I knew it.

"You wanna go home?"

"Yes."

"You just don't believe he's around here. You think Bryan's somewhere else, or maybe that really was him in the ground."

"That's not what I said!" She stomped her foot. "I just want to go home."

Leanin' against the truck, I crossed my arms. "Well, Casey, is you really gonna be a *quitter*?"

She looked shocked. "What?"

I raised my hands. "You really gonna quit now? When we've come so far?"

"Uhh... I don'..."

"I didn't raise you like that, to be a quitter. I'm surprised at you. Is this your mama talkin' for you?"

"That's not what I me—"

I raised my left hand real casual and said, "Enough. That's alright. I get it. The Wild West got to be a little too much for you. Don't needa say nothin' else." I turned back to the truck's engine. "You can just wait in the truck."

She stared at me with her big eyes gettin' watery and wet and salty and all that, then she cried, "We should've just stayed home! You go crazy and get so angry, but you won't even listen to me about anything! Not Tom, not Mr. Isiah, not the dog—"

I damn near lost it. "You're still on that dog crap?" I punched a warm metal door. "Stop talkin' bout that damn dog!"

The floodgates opened, and she started cryin' and cryin' and cryin', and I felt like cryin' too, even though there was no way I could, which just got me even angrier.

Even as the sun set, everythin' was too damn hot. I was sweatin' like her goddamn dog.

"You know why Bryan left?" I said.

"How could I possibly know that?" she whimpered.

"I was sixteen, he was seventeen. And for the last decade, he'd told Daddy he was gonna get a dog, over and over and over again. Of course, our old man said no every time, cause he knew a dog's a damn hot mess. But it didn't matter to Bryan. Bryan always wanted what Bryan wanted, and if he wanted somethin', he sure as hell made sure he got it. Well, this one night, he turns up with a dog. A little white fluffy whatcha call it? Samoya? He came home with his big dumb smile holdin' her and said her name was somethin' stupid 'Chimney,' or maybe 'Biscuit.' Real stupid name for a dog. I coulda done better.

"Well, Daddy took one look and said, 'No. No way.' I was just sittin' on the couch wantin' to pet the damn thing, but you know that woulda only brought disaster.

"So Bryan and Daddy started arguin' like they'd never argued before. Brought back disputes I didn't even remember. The time Bryan broke one of our windows, the time Bryan swapped out a bottle of Coke for liquor. And I'm just sittin' there, shushed.

"Mama yelled at them to calm down, but they didn't listen, not with their war of words escalatin'. Meanwhile, the dog just wandered around, and the two didn't even notice. Then, in the middle of their battle, she came over to me and jumped on my lap.

"Daddy and Bryan looked over at me. Both said, 'Gimme that dog.'

"I'd no clue what to do, so I stayed quiet and turned to the pup. She was cute and all, white and fluffy, but I knew it wasn't gonna end well.

"I scooped her up in my arms and walked over to them. I could feel its little heart beat so fast. But the more I thought bout it, the more I knew that if I gave it back to Bryan, the old man would just light up and we'd back to square one, or worse, even. Wouldn't fix nothin'.

"So I stood up and said, 'Bryan, it's Daddy's house. A dog's a big decision.' And I gave the dog to the old man."

I breathed heavy. The California night had gotten so dark. Too dark. "Well, Daddy took the dog outside, while me and Bryan followed him, and Bryan kept yellin'. Then he threw the pup down, kicked him hard in the leg. The dog started cryin' like all hell. 'Shoo!' he hollered. 'Shoo!' And sure enough, the dog ran away, limpin' a little."

I put a hand over my face, tryin' to not break down in fronta Casey. "I tried to explain it to him, why I sided with the old man, over and over and over again. I kept tellin' him, but he wouldn't listen. All that over a stupid dog."

I slumped over the truck. "In the middle of the night, Bryan took Daddy's car and left without a word. Never came back."

Exhalin', I said, "And, Casey, that's why a dog's a bad idea."

I waited for her response, but she didn't say nothin'. Just looked sadder than ever.

I put my hands on my head and groaned. I hadn't thought bout that night for a long, long time. Just tracin' over it gave me a headache. Got me angry. "I'm just tryin' to get my goddamn family back together!" I screamed. "Does no one else see that? Everythin's gotten so rotten. You look around, Casey. You look around, and it's all trash. Ain't nobody watchin' out for us no more. This whole country ain't the same. It's all people who just don't give a shit, pretendin' to care. It's the same thing with family now—that word's lost all its meanin'. Naw, now it's people just tryin' to squeeze each other for every cent. Well, I ain't willin' to accept it. I can't accept it. And see, everyone's actin' like I'm crazy, while I'm the only one who still cares. I'm the only one tryin' to fix things! Is that too much to fuckin' ask?"

I punched the exposed radiator. Hurt like hell. "Now wait in the truck. Go!"

She walked away, silent.

I waited, perched up over the hood. Took a good ten seconds, but then the truck door finally slammed.

At long last, I was able to focus on the problem again. I put on the phone light and looked at the engine. It all checked out. Indeed seemed like the fuel filter. I'd have to go under and take it out and try to shake it clean till I could get a replacement. Then I sighed. *Ah, fuck.*

"Casey," I called out. "Casey, I'm sorry." I turned the truck's corner and yanked open the door. "Casey, I shouldn't have yelled."

But then I saw there was no one inside.

CHAPTER 32

I yelled down the street, "Casey?"

Oh shit, oh shit, oh shit. I ran up to the nearest corner and looked down. Nothin'.

"Shit, shit." *Where are we?* I glanced up desperate, searchin' for any sign post.

Rocket Drive. Who the hell names a street Rocket Drive?

I didn't know what to do. I musta looked like a chicken with my head cut off, runnin' up and down the street like some kinda deranged drugged-out hobo.

How far could she have gotten? Will she come back? She might just come back. Just stay by the truck.

I jogged back to the truck and worked faster than I'd ever before. I got my tools from the trunk, then removed the switch under the driver's seat and started her up till she gave up to depressurize the fuel lines, then went under the truck, removed the fuel lines, unhooked and removed the fuel filter, shook it as best I could till tons of gunk dripped out, air sprayed it, and put everythin' back, all at the speed of lightnin'. Then I made sure the truck started—she did—and I went outside and waited.

She must come back. I played with my phone, pointin' the light into the night. *She left me with the phone. Why the hell did she leave me with the phone? Why the hell did I throw her old phone out the window?*

After bout a half an hour without a soul in sight, my heart started racin'. I put my hand over my chest. I couldn't take it—my fat fuckin' body couldn't take it. After another fifteen minutes, I decided I had no choice: I had to go and find her.

I hopped in the truck and drove around the block, turned a corner, turned another corner, ended up goin' down W Katella Ave, a damned freeway. *What the hell am I doin'?*

I pulled off and started searchin' side streets: S West, Ricky Ave, Wakefield Ave. Nothin'.

I bent over in my car. I couldn't fuckin' breathe. *Police. I haveta go to the police.*

Big globs of sweat filled up my hands as I searched up the police station. Fifteen minutes. *Fifteen minutes, okay. I'll get there in eight.*

I started drivin' like I was a teenager again, shaky hands all the way, but I went fast, easily twenty-five past. Folks honked at me all the way, but it didn't fuckin' matter, couldn't even hear them. The gong sound of my heartbeat blocked them out.

I got there and rolled up and did a shitty parkin' job. I ran into the office and up to the front desk.

"What's wrong, sir?" this young Mission-Impossible-lookin' guy with a square jaw asked me.

I stumbled out, "My daughter... she's missin'."

"Okay, sir, we'll fill out a report." He grabbed a paper and pen. "Where did you last see her?"

"Well, she was right next to me... On Rocket Drive, I think... we ain't from here... I don't know how she coulda run away. She was just supposed to wait in the truck."

"And what were you doing, sir?"

"Well, I was tryin' to fix the engine. That was after we had our little fight, and I thought everythin' was alright."

"What do you mean by 'little fight'?"

"I dunno, it was just a little fight. We was talkin' 'bout my brother, and she started cryin', and I yelled at her some."

"Was there any physical contact, sir?"

"Was there any physical contact? Whatcha mean... *Wait.*" I stumbled back, barely able to speak. "What are you sayin'?"

The guy said, "I'm just trying to get all the facts, sir."

I put my right hand against my face. Hadn't even realized it, but my lips were twitchin', quiverin' all over the place. "My daughter's missin', and you ask me if I smacked her? Are you fuckin' crazy?"

"Sir, please calm down. Can you give me a name, age, and a physical description?"

I started hyperventilatin'.

"Sir, a name, age, and physical description."

Holy shit, I lost Casey.

"Sir, please calm down. I need a name, age, and physical description."

I leaned over his desk, tryin' to regain my breath. "Her name is Casey. Casey Wilcox... She's twelve... She's got brown hair and the most beautiful blue eyes you've ever seen."

He kept jottin' everythin' down. "Does she have a phone? A number?"

What the hell is goin' on?

"Sir, a number?"

"No... no. She doesn't have a phone on her."

"Okay." He finished writin' his report. "Do you have a picture of her and a number we can reach you at?"

"Yes, yes, I do." I pulled out the phone and started flickin' through photos to show him. "See, this is the time we got ice cream after she hurt her knee when she was five. We got vanilla." I flicked to another. "This is a photo with her and her grand-mama. Grandmama was tryin' to teach her to bake muffins... and this is the ti—"

"Sir, please find a recent photo with just her and email this address." He gave me a slip of paper with an email.

"Okay, okay." I scrolled till I found a good picture—her elementary school graduation photo. "She's in junior high now."

"That's great, sir. Have you emailed the photo?"

I started tappin' at the screen to try to figure it out, but there was no way in hell that was gonna happen with my brain workin' the way it was. "Sorry, Casey usually does this kinda stuff for me."

"That's fine, sir. Can I have a look at the phone? And can you record your name and number right here?" He pushed a sheet in fronta me.

"Yeah... I guess." My writin' was all scraggly cause my hand shook so damn much.

After he handed the phone back and looked over all the information, he said, "Okay, now, what's going to happen is I'm going to file a missing person report, and our officers will start a search. You did the right thing coming here first. Please keep your line of communication open. We will reach out as soon as we have an update, or if we have any further questions. Do you have any questions?"

"No... no questions."

"Okay. Thanks for coming to us, Mr. Wilcox. We will help find your daughter."

"Yeah... got it..." My body felt drained, my head went on a low buzz.

I walked out and slumped into the truck.

Oh my God.

My head hung down and I stared at the brake pedal.

Oh my God.

Then I put my hands over my face and started to scream. It echoed all around me, a wind of panic rattlin' the truck. Then the phone rang.

The police? Already? I grabbed it and read: *Sandra Wilcox.*

I started hyperventilatin' again. I threw the phone up in my hands like it was a hot potato. I couldn't answer it, but I also couldn't *not* answer it. After I couldn't wait any longer, I swiped right to answer and put it up to my ear and tried to calm down my breathin'. *Calm down. Calm the fuck down.*

"Baby, is that you? Are you at the airport?"

Holy fuckin' Jesus Christ, this woman is gonna eat me alive.

Slowly, I leaked out, "Hi, Sand, it's me."

"Forrest? Are you at the airport with Casey?"

Just kill me, kill me, kill me, kill me.

"No... we're at a hotel... she's asleep."

She clicked her tongue. "Why do you do this to us? Do you know how much that ticket cost? What are you thinking? How much longer do you want her to stay out there? School starts in a week."

I started feelin' my hair. I swear to God, it was just fallin' out —the stress had reached my damn follicles. "I know, I'm sorry, Sand."

She musta realized I was talkin' honest, cause she paused for a second before she asked, "Can you wake her? I want to talk to her."

"Naw, I don't think that's a good idea. She's pretty sound asleep right now."

Another pause. *Oh crap.* "Forrest, is there something wrong?"

How the hell does that woman always do it? How does she always know?

"Whatcha mean? Ain't nothin' wrong. Well, except not gettin' her on the plane, but that's totally my bad, and I'm sorry bout that, like I said."

"Please put Casey on the phone."

My body felt like it was gonna burst. "I can't, baby."

"Why not?"

Shoot me. Shoot me. Shoot me. "She ain't here."

Dead pause. Pure pain in silence. Till finally, "What do you mean?"

My heart bounced to the sky and back. "She ain't here."

"Well, where is she, then?"

I whispered into the phone, "I'm unsure."

"What did you say? I couldn't hear you."

"I said, 'I'm unsure.'"

Then, real normal, she said, "Okay, that's what I thought you said." I waited a long time for her to say somethin', anything, and when I finally opened my mouth to check that she was still there, she screamed, "What the hell happened, Forrest? Where the hell did she go? What do you mean you don't know where she is?"

Can sweat go through cellular towers? We sure were puttin' it to the test. Mine just dripped all over the phone.

"What happened?"

"Well... I was fixin' the truck, and she got upset, and when I went back to check on her, she wasn't waitin' for me no more."

"Oh my Lord, you cannot be serious right now. Forrest, you're freaking me out."

"Sand, I know what you're thinkin', but I went to the police, and they're out lookin' for her right now."

"Oh my God, oh my God, oh, Jesus."

"Sand, please relax. Be sensible."

"Relax? *Be sensible*? Forrest... Forrest... I think I'm having a panic attack."

She was havin' a panic attack? "Baby, I'm goin' to find her, just gimme me a day or so."

"I got to go... I got to lay down and think."

"Baby, I know it sounds bad, but I'm gonna fi—"

Line went dead.

I fell back into my seat and lay like a corpse.

What the hell do I do now?

I glanced out the window and witnessed the faraway lights of LA. Each one so colorful. Everythin' got quiet. Finally, I had a chance to breathe. And I realized one thing:

I needed a drink.

CHAPTER 33

My thinkin' was I needed a drink to think straight, or I wouldn't be able to think at all. And I'd needa think to find Casey.

I looked up the nearest ABC Store, but it turned out they didn't have any of those in the frilly state of California, so I swung by the nearest grocery store, some place called Albertsons. Inside, I grabbed a six-pack of Bud Light and a handle of vodka. When I got to the register, my debit card no longer worked. I pulled out all the cash I had left in my wallet. $22.53. Not enough for both. I left behind the six-pack and bought the vodka. $4.27 left in change.

Back in the truck, in the parkin' lot, I rested the drink in the shotgun. It looked at me funny, so I took a sip—nothin' so big to get me drunk. I ain't a maniac. Just needed enough to get me goin'. Tasted like pure acid on my tongue.

I crossed my arms and started gettin' nervous again. Skittish. Still couldn't think straight. Another sip.

Goddammit, goddammit, goddammit, goddammit.

I banged my head against my wheel, then looked up. It'd

gotten so dark. At least it was the summer, thank God for that. She wouldn't be cold, at least.

Soon, my mind started playin' tricks on me, things I don't even wanna describe to you. Anything coulda happened, anything could be *happenin'*.

What if she disappears? What if someone took her? Fuck, fuck, fuck. I ain't fuckin' Liam Neeson. I ain't got no particular set of skills.

This is California. She's either with the gangs or the druggies or the nerds. I didn't know which was worse.

I took another sip and decided I needed to keep lookin', that there was no use in just hangin' around. I turned on the engine. Started up fine. I took another sip in celebration that Mrs. F-150 was back in proper motion.

First stop: Rocket Drive. No one was there. I took a swig.

I drove in a circle around the block. Still no one there. Another swig. No longer tasted that bad.

For some reason, my memory gets a little woozy at this point, but I remember my eyes gettin' watery, and somethin' bout drivin' in circles, up and down the highway two or three times, and maybe I farted. Also, I passed Disneyland one or two times on the highway, but I couldn't see shit. Everythin' was hidden behind a fence. Couldn't even get a castle to cheer me up.

I took another swig. I decided I'd drive forever.

But somewhere in my stupor, I finally reached my goal: bein' drunk enough to trick myself into thinkin' I could think straight. Maybe a quarter down the bottle, everythin' started gettin' a little slower, a little straighter in my head. The edge was gone, the panic was gone, all that was left was rawness. I started accel-eratin' down... Freeway 91, I think? Like I said, I ain't remember much then. Just a couple things stayed in my head.

I thought bout how old Casey had been actin'. How she'd grown. I shoulda just taken her to the damn airport.

Another swig.

I thought bout how Sand would never forgive me.

Another swig.

I thought bout how Mama was dyin'.

Another, another, another.

At some point, I realized I was practically alone on some highway. I glanced down at my speedometer: 95. Whatever.

I was runnin' low on gas. I guess I decided I'd drive till she emptied out. I stared out the windshield. Billboards went flyin' on by, one after another. First, somethin' bout losin' weight. The guy on it looked like me.

Second, some ad with a divorce lawyer who looked too good to be in law. Coulda sworn they were just makin' fun of me at that point.

Then the third came *weird*. Came from a long ways away, but I noticed it instantly. Somethin' bout it sobered me up. I slowed down some to try and make it out, but that didn't help much, cause of the liquor and all.

I can tell you this—there was this guy. A white guy, well-dressed, suit and tie, the whole getup. It said above him, "Get Your Used Cars Today!" And he had this big grin across his face.

Then when I squinted, it looked even more peculiar. I tried to make out the guy's name. It was plastered right above his head... *Will Li?* I turned the truck toward the sign.

No, Bill Lee. Billy Lee? Yes. I stared at the guy's big white forehead, and my whole body started shakin'.

I pumped the gas and yelled, "Bryan?"

I kept racin' ahead toward the sign. "Bryan! Bryan!"

Faster, faster.

"Bryan! Bryan! Bry—"

A horrible crashin' sound. A shakin'. Then everythin' went black.

CHAPTER 34

"Daddy?" I mumbled.

Someone was leanin' over me while I lay on the ground, flat. I looked up and it was Daddy. He opened his mouth like he was screamin' at me for somethin', but I couldn't hear none of him. No words came out.

"What's that? Whatcha sayin'? Am I in heaven?"

He got closer to me and pulled out his left hand. Then he slapped me soft across the cheeks, back and forth.

"Whatcha doin' that for?" I mumbled. It was pretty fuckin' annoyin'. I felt real tired. I whispered, "Knock it off," then closed my eyes again. But right after I did so, I heard:

"Wake up, wake up."

I groaned and kept my eyes closed.

"Wake up, Sleeping Beauty."

Again, I mumbled, "Daddy?" But this time when I opened my eyes, I saw this bald Black guy standin' over me with his hand by my face. I said "Holy shit" and rolled over.

"There you go." He slapped my back like I was some kinda infant, and by God, I felt like one. If you told me I had to stand up to save my life, you might as well have shot me and got it over with. I couldn't do nothin'. I couldn't move a muscle or I might just puke on the spot. Everythin' hurt like a grenade had gone off in my belly, hurt like it'd never hurt before.

"Am I... dead?"

The guy laughed. "No, you aren't dead. You probably should be. You're lucky to be alive. You're lucky your limbs work. The first responders said you are the luckiest man on the planet. You hear that? The luckiest man on the planet."

I didn't feel like the luckiest man on the planet. "What the hell happened?"

The guy stood up and leaned against a wall, this gray chipped wall. "Well, they pulled you out of your truck, expecting to take you to the hospital, but then apparently you got up and started screaming someone's name, and then you almost slapped someone. Your vitals checked out, so our boys in blue picked you up instead."

I tried to screw my head back on right. It was hard to piece together what he was sayin', with every word ringin'. "So... where am I?"

Black baldy laughed at me. He was wearin' some kinda guard uniform. Beige, button-down. "You're being held in Orange County Central Men's Jail."

I slipped back on the ground and lay on my stomach. Then I groaned.

"Now there, now there," he said. "It isn't all bad. You didn't hurt anyone—you're lucky as hell for that too." The guy stretched out and laughed at me again. "Do you remember how you crashed? You ran right into a billboard post."

"I remember some—" But then I stopped myself. *Billboard.* "What billboard?"

"I don't know, some billboard off 91."

I started scratchin' my head as I sat up. "Wait, wait. Whose name was I callin'? Was it Casey?"

"I don't think so." The guy started headin' toward the cell door. "I got to go. Just sober up. You won't be here long."

I crawled toward him. "Wait," I begged. "Wait. Please. My daughter's missin', and there's somethin' I'm tryin' to remember. It's really important."

"Well, you probably should've thought about that before your little drunk joyride. Maybe CPS can help you with your daughter." He shut the door closed and locked it up. "I'll check up on you in a bit."

"Wait!" I yelled. "I remember!" But he just left.

BOUT AN HOUR LATER, after I'd already become acquainted with the steel toilet in the corner, and it became acquainted with my green upchuck, they dumped a new loser into the holdin' cell.

When they pushed him in, I yelled, "I needa talk to someone!" They ignored me completely.

Instead, I got a new roomie by the name of Bob. I knew his name was Bob cause the first thing he did was walk up to me and grab my hand with the strongest grip I'd ever felt and say, "Hello, my brother. I go by Bob."

His head was plumb shaved, and each of his white knuckles except his thumbs were tattooed: BLUT on the left, EHRE on the right. Had some aggressive ink slidin' up on his shoulder and his neck too.

I shook his hand. "Uh. Yeah. I'm Forrest." Then I turned to the door again and yelled, "Can I get my call?"

No answer.

For the next while, I tried to keep to myself, but Bob insisted to keep makin' conversation.

"What you in for?" he asked.

"I guess," I said while rubbin' my head, "I have a DUI."

I didn't ask him what he was in for cause I didn't wanna talk no more, but after bout ten seconds, he smiled. He had two silver teeth. "Aren't you wondering what I'm here for?"

"What?" I whispered.

He grinned. "I split a faggot's spine in half."

For some reason or another, I didn't find myself likin' Bob much. But he kept talkin'. "You know what the issue is, Forrest?" he'd always start, and of course I couldn't just ignore him, so I'd ask, "What?"

"The issue is this country has gotten too soft. Today's men are boys, you know?" Or he'd say, "The deep state controls everything now. Can't trust anyone. How else do you think so many spics get past the wall or how the Jews got in control of Hollywood? You watch out, my brother. We can't let the Great Replacement destroy our people."

Each time, I'd just say, "Yeah, yeah." But somethin' bout what he said really bugged me. Maybe it wasn't *what* he was sayin' but the fact that *he*, Mr. Bob in Orange County Jail, was sayin' them. The topics sounded mighty familiar, but they felt a little weird comin' outta this guy's mouth.

To make matters worse, an hour later, another guard came and dropped a third patron to our lovely little cell, and unlike me or Bob, this guy had dark-brown skin. The moment the gate closed, I glanced back at Bob. His eyes had gone snake-like.

I spent the next hour inchin' toward the exit while Bob and Alejandro, apparently, got this tension brewin'. Finally, things broke open when Alejandro had this nasty sneeze. Mucus flung right across the walls. Little bit got on me, even.

Bob stood up. "You sneezing on me?"

Alejandro shook his head. "Sorry, sorry. English no good." But Bob would have none of it. He started kickin' him, kickin' him hard, right in the legs.

I stood up. "Hey, man, just cool off." Bob looked at me like I'd called his mama a whore. He started yellin' at me too, somethin' bout betrayin' my race and bein' a cuck, and I thought I was finally gonna get killed, but then Mr. Black baldy from my initial wake-up finally showed up. He ran up to the cell and hollered, "Hey, hey!" Then another one of his buddies followed. They broke up the fight, and I went up to him and looked him straight in the eye and said, "Sir, I needa get outta here. I have a daughter who needs help."

He paused, studied me up and down. "You got some puke on your shoe." I glanced down. *Shit.* I scrapped it against the ground. As they dragged Bob to a new holdin' cell, he said, "Come on."

He sat me in a chair next to his desk where my phone, wallet, and keys were. "Thank God," I said.

"Don't thank God. Thank the Orange County Police Department." He slid some paperwork over, a white piece of paper and a pink one. "Fill this out, then you can call someone to pick you up."

I glanced it over: The white one just needed my name, address, and social, but the pink one said *Temporary License and Notice to Contact DMV.* I pointed to it. "What's this? Y'all took my license?"

He laughed. "You thought we were going to let you keep it? You had a .2 BAC."

"Yeah... but... I ain't from here. I'm from Virginia."

"So what? Your case will take place in your home state. You can get a new license there."

I didn't know what to say, so I just started fillin' out the paperwork. I wrote real slow and said, "I remembered what I was tryin' to tell you this mornin', on that billboard."

"The billboard? The billboard you hit?"

I swallowed the lump in my throat. I'd been thinkin' bout it all mornin'. It played over and over in my head. "I need the number from that billboard. It's the number of someone I needa call."

He looked at me all confused. "Is this some kind of joke?"

I shook my head. "No, sir."

"Explain yourself."

"I believe... I believe the number on that billboard is the number of a dear friend of mine. Someone who moved to California. I need that number."

He rubbed his eyes. "I can't believe what I'm hearing."

I finished fillin' out the report. "Please."

He sighed, then stood up and yelled across the room, "Derek, do you have any pictures from last night's crash? Something with the billboard in the shot?"

"Uh," said Derek, "no, but I can search the spot up on my phone. What do you need it for?"

Black baldy just shrugged. "Personal interest," he said and sat back down. "You better thank me."

"Yes." I squirmed in the seat. "Thank you. Didn't catch your name."

"John."

"Thank you, John."

Derek walked over and showed the phone to John. "Here."

I stammered and gestured toward it. "Can I look at it?"

Derek gave me a stink eye and pulled the phone back. John peeked up and wrote down the number. "Thanks," he told Derek.

He slid over the number and gave me my phone. "Okay, Forrest, one call."

My hands started shiverin' and clammed up. I grabbed my phone and turned it on. The first thing I looked for were any missed calls from the police. None. Sand, four; Daddy, seven. Any texts? Sand, eleven; Daddy, three; Lil Pete, two. My belly became all nervous again, just like last night.

"Well," John said, "are you going to call?"

"Yes, sorry bout that." Slowly, I tapped in the digits. Nothin' bout it felt excitin' no more, just scary.

I raised the phone to my ear, and the call got picked up instantly. I heard: "Hello, welcome to Billy Lee Used Automobiles and Motorcycle Dealership. Thanks for calling, this is Trixie, how may I help you?"

Honest to God, despite everythin' that was goin' on, my first thought still found a way to be: *Trixie, really? Is everyone a porn star in California?*

"Hello...?"

I snapped back awake. "Yes, yes, I'm Forrest. I'm lookin' to talk to Billy."

"You want to talk to Billy?"

"Yes, ma'am."

She paused for a second. "Well, Billy's not in the office right now. He runs several dealerships. He's always on the go. Can I take your name and number?"

"Ma'am, you don't understand. Billy will wanna talk to me. He *needs* to talk to me."

"Okay, I understand, sir, but he's not here right now. Can you give me your name and number?"

I sighed. "Tell him... it's Forrest."

"Last name?"

"Just tell him it's Forrest. My number is 757-555-0112. I'm bein' held at the police station. Orange County, I believe."

"The police?"

"Please... Trixie." I leaned into the phone and bent over. "Please tell Billy as soon as possible."

Again with the pause from her. "Okay, then, Mr.... Forrest. I'll be sure to let him know. Bye-bye."

"By—" Call went dead.

John leaned over and took the phone back. "Your friend coming to pick you up?"

I stared at my shoes then put my hands over my eyes. I didn't want him to see me that pathetic. "I don't know." I groaned. "What happens if no one comes?"

"We'll hold you for a couple more hours, then release you, and you'll get a court date and a fine, and you could get up to six months in jail, maybe longer, depending on Virginia law."

I rocked back into the chair and blinked back my tears and tried to open my eyes. *Six months?* "I fucked up, but I don't drink and drive. This is the first time somethin' like this has happened. I needa get outta here. I needa get out now. My daughter's missin' and I needa find her. Ask your buddies in the other station in Santa Ana, they'll kn—"

"Save your sob story for the court hearing." He stood up. "Come on, we'll put you in a different holding cell."

As he led me, I just stared at the floor. When he finally closed the cell, he sighed and said, "For a first-time DUI... no one got hurt... no prior convictions... white guy... they'll probably downgrade it to reckless driving." He nodded at me. "It'll be all right."

I nodded back and whispered, "Thanks." But things bein' "all right" seemed impossible.

AGAIN, I got left alone in a cell.

On one hand, I was lucky—I'd sobered up. On the other hand, I really did feel like I coulda used another drink, as shameful as it is to say. There, alone, my imagination stirred again, got me thinkin' bout how Casey could be all cut up or maybe kidnapped or maybe sold into white slavery or maybe or maybe or maybe or maybe...

That's the one shame bout becomin' a parent: You naturally become a worrier. At least that time seemed more justified than most. I tried to shake it off, but it was hard when everywhere I lay down was plumb exposed. Even takin' a shit involved a peep show. Ain't no way no one can calm down in an environment like that.

At some point, though, maybe after another hour, I curled up and closed my eyes and tried to rest. But I couldn't. I could only think. I thought back, way back, back to right before I smashed into Macy... *Ah, shit, I didn't even ask if the truck survived the crash...*

I thought back to when I was on the beach alone, just gazin' out at the ocean. It felt so good, watchin' the waves, imaginin' Bryan out at the other end of the sea, but this time I tried to see somethin' different. I tried to picture myself back on the same beach, but this time with Casey, with Sand not totally wantin' to eat my brains, and with Mama and the old man. I wished we were all just sittin' together, while Casey played with the little waves as they hit the sand. She would still have a smile on her face. We could forget this whole thing happened. Maybe I'd even go to that damn doc, for Sand's sake. Would let him touch my balls and everythin'. We'd cook up a little brother for Casey. We would put all the pieces back together. Everythin' coulda been fine, if I didn't ju—

"Forrest?"

I opened my eyes. Bryan.

CHAPTER 35

I didn't say much while we were leavin'. He didn't say much neither. I guess we didn't know what to say. At least I found out what happened to the F-150. John told me she was outta commission, banged up, dead, probably. Towed away by some kinda racket operation a mile away or so, if I wanted to pick her up. At least they gave me the rest of my stuff.

Outside, the sun hit real hard. High noon. I could barely stand. I felt real tired.

Bryan pointed to a truck. "Here."

The vehicle woke me up a little. He had a F-150 of his own. It just happened to be eleven years younger than mine and a good deal shinier.

It was weird, walkin' beside him, like it was too weirdly familiar but too completely different, so it made the whole thing awkward. He was still a few inches taller than me. I thought he mighta shrunk by that point. Or I woulda finally grown taller. He was also wearin' some corporate-lookin' clothes. A polo, nice khakis.

I guess all I'm tryin' to say is I didn't know what I expected. Maybe I thought our reunion would be like one of Sand's chick flicks where the guy catches the girl at the airport right before she leaves. Like we'd run at each other in a wide grass field and at the end of it we'd have a big ol' bear hug. Or we'd meet in the woods around a campfire. Or maybe out at sea. Shoulda known that wouldn't happen. If either one of us was gonna give a bear hug, it woulda been Bryan, not me, and he sure seemed too confused by the whole thing to get animated.

That said, when we finally got into the car and I slid, and I mean slid, into the shotgun and Bryan closed the door, he turned to me and smiled. "Forrest. I am so glad to see you." He reached over and grabbed my shoulder and gave it a shake.

I shrugged him off. "Good to see you too."

Seemed like that opened the floodgates. He just started talkin' and laughin' and goin' off, just like when we were kids. He was always the talker of us two.

"What are you doing here?" he exclaimed. "You would've never believed how shocked I was when Trixie texted me that I had a 'Forrest' call. We were playing mini golf, and I was like 'What did you say, dude!'"

"Dude?"

"Ah, sorry." He smiled. "It's something I picked up from the kids, I guess."

I jumped up in my seat. "Kids?"

He smiled again, his big stupid Bryan smile, shit-eatin' grin. Flash of old him for a hot second, high-school him. Only minus some hair. "We got a lot to talk about."

I leaned back down again. "Yeah, I guess we do."

Bryan started tellin' me everythin' bout nothin' that really mattered, like how he now owned a buncha used car dealerships, eleven, in fact, all across Southern California, and a nice ranch-style home out in the 'burbs, and that the wife and kids were still out mini golfin', and he couldn't wait for me to meet them, and, and, and...

In the middle of it, I just said, "Bryan, that's great. I'm happy for you, but we can just... be quiet for a second? My head is hurtin', I need some rest."

"Oh, sure. Oh, sure."

I leaned my head against the window and tried to close my eyes and get some sleep, but it didn't come. I didn't get it. Don't get me wrong—I was happy, happy as a clam, but, well, I wasn't that happy. I just felt weird. It all just felt too strange, seein' Bryan for the first time in forever. And he owned *eleven* car dealerships? I mean, I was glad for him, but it was hard to think of the kid who ran away as this successful business tycoon type a man. I couldn't really believe it.

After thinkin' for a while and bein' unable to fall sleep, I finally mumbled, "I thought you died."

"You thought I died?" He laughed. "Why would you think that?"

"Your grave." I paused, then added, "My daughter found it."

His hands twisted on the wheel. The truck nearly spun. "Daughter? You have a daughter?" he hollered.

"Yeah," I said, real quiet. I woulda thought he'd been keepin' track of us over the internet. I guess not.

"Wowee, Forrest. That's amazing! What's her name? How old is she?"

"Her name is Casey. She just turned twelve. Bryan... Billy... what the hell even *is your* name?"

He laughed again. "I'm Billy Lee these days."

I repeated it slowly, "Bill-EE L-EE." Felt odd on my tongue. "Why? Why Billy Lee?"

"Well, it goes back to that grave you were talking about. I'd almost forgotten it."

"Whatcha talkin' 'bout the grave?"

He scratched the side of his head. His skin looked damn near orange. California sun was even worse than Virginia, I reckon.

"Well, you see, Forrest, I had some... problems with creditors. A couple of my early business ventures didn't go so hot. So let's just say, Bryan and Billy Wilcox got put in the ground, and Billy Lee was born."

"What you sayin'? Did you fake your death?"

He laughed. "You said it, I didn't."

I stared at him. "That's the craziest fuckin' thing I ever heard."

With the way his face was fidgetin', I could tell he didn't wanna smile, but he just couldn't help it. "Well, it all worked out."

"I guess." I closed my eyes again. "It's fine. I knew you didn't die. The birth date was wrong. It said March sixth, '83 on the stone."

He paused for a second. "What do you mean?"

"On the stone, I saw that you put it off a couple days and a year. I thought that was real clever, to give the people who really know you a signal and all."

The truck started slowin' down at a red light. "Forrest, March sixth, 1983 is my birthday."

IT TOOK round ten more minutes to finally get to Bryan's house, and by God, I don't even know how to describe it to you. It was far bigger than Daddy's house and even bigger than Adam's house. Honest, mighta been the biggest house I'd ever seen not on the television screen.

Though it was more than just the size of the house. He had this fancy lawn too, with so much green and cut grass all around. Land on land on land. "Bryan," I asked, "how much did this place cost?"

He laughed, cocky as usual. "Let's just say it didn't come cheap. By the way, I'd prefer you call me Billy around the kids."

It was a damn mansion. I grabbed my bag while he opened his truck door and whistled, loud. Then somethin' started rustlin' from the other side of the house. "What's that?"

"Relax, Forrest," he said with a smile.

Outta the grass came these three dogs barrelin' toward us. One was huge—big and brown—another a golden retriever, and the last a white small fluffy one with black eyes and a wide grin.

Bryan went on his knees, and they jumped all over and around him before they spotted me a coupla feet away. Then they barreled at me, lickin' my legs, smellin' my feet, humpin' my foot. Bryan laughed again. "Rex, Apollo, Chimney, stop," he said.

They didn't listen, runnin' around me as I marched toward the house, till Bryan picked up a ball in the yard and sent them flyin' in the other direction. "Great dogs," he said.

I just looked ahead. "Yup."

"Can I help you with the bag?"

"Nope."

He opened up the house's front door, an unbelievable ten-foot wooden rectangle, lookin' like some kinda fort entrance, and asked, "Can I get you water or something?"

"Naw, Bryan. It's alright."

It looked like he was fixinta say somethin' else, but then he stopped himself. I tried to ignore it. His livin' room looked like the inside of a fort too, and his leather couch the size of a moat. I threw my bag on it and collapsed on top of it. "Aren't you worried bout the dogs runnin' away or somethin'?"

"Nope," he said, shakin' his head. "We got an electrical fence." He sat down too, on a big leather seat.

I stared into his TV. Coulda fit six of mine back home in its screen.

"Can I get you some water?" he repeated.

"No."

"Gotcha, gotcha." He twiddled his thumbs. "So what are you doing here? Like I told you, the message from Trix came as a real surprise." This time he didn't ask with so much vigor.

"What day is it?"

"What?"

"What day is it? Like is it Tuesday? Or Thursday?"

"It's Saturday."

I grunted, then started slippin' down the couch. When my head hit the back rest, I grumbled, "Believe it or not, *we*, me and my daughter, Casey, were out lookin' for you. Big surprise, I'm sure. But I'm too tired to talk bout that right now."

"Ah, gotcha. Where is the little girl? I want to meet her."

I sighed and then fell into the couch some more. "That's the pressin' issue." I paused, then said, "She disappeared last night. She ran away."

Bryan leaned forward and tipped his chin toward me before he said, "She ran away?"

"Yes." I crossed my arms.

He paused, then asked, "Why?"

"Does it matter?"

A loud stinky quiet came over us. Fortunately, one of the dogs started barkin' outside.

"Listen, Forrest, that's terrible. How can I help?"

Again, I sighed. Seemed to be comin' naturally to me at that point. "I don't know. I told the police to call me if they found a trace of her."

"And they arrested you for that?"

"No." I put my hands in my face. "They arrested me cause after I couldn't find her, I started drinkin' and drivin'. Then I crashed into one of your damn billboards."

"Oh."

I peeked an eye out between two of my fingers. "How many you got, anyhow?"

"What, dogs?"

"No," I said with some passion. "Billboards."

"Oh. Two."

"I guess yesterday truly was my lucky day," I muttered.

He looked at me again like I was some kinda fat alien, then stood up. "I'mma get some water for you, buddy."

I was gonna tell him I didn't need none, but then I realized how dry my lips were, so I didn't say nothin'. As he came back and handed it over, he said, "Where did your girl go missing? I can help look. I have friends everywhere."

I gulped the water down in four seconds flat. "Yeah, you do have friends everywhere, it seems. We met one on the way. Adam."

Bryan banged his foot against the floor and slapped his knee. "You saw Adam? Adam Isiah?"

I nodded. "Yup."

"How the heck is he doing? And what was his name, his husband, Jamal? How's he? I haven't seen them since my wedding, I think." He laughed. "Man, what a nice guy."

I glanced at him, hard and long. "He's doin' good, it seems. Casey went missin' somewhere in Santa Ana. I don't know. Rocket somethin'?"

"Rocket Drive?"

"Yeah..." I trailed off. "Somethin' like that."

"Okay, Forrest." He pushed himself up. "I'm gonna make some calls. I'll tell everyone to be on the lookout. Don't worry, brother, we'll find her."

Brother. It felt so off to hear him say that. Like there was somethin' between us I couldn't even see, like some kinda glass. The moment the word came outta his mouth, I felt like my whole life was a goddamn joke. I wanted to glance around and check if there were cameras. Maybe this was one big way of my old man gettin' back at me for not turnin' back around and goin' home. Put me on a show where I was the biggest damn fool on the planet. Instead, I just said, "Thanks."

"Now you rest up."

I didn't say nothin' to that one. He pulled out his phone and went outside, and the dogs barked around him again.

I curled up and pulled out my phone. I found Sandra's contact and tried to call her. It immediately went to voicemail. Then I turned the phone off, closed my eyes, and instantly fell the fuck to sleep.

CHAPTER 36

I woke up to someone hangin' above my face. Why'd everyone see that as appropriate to do to sleepin' men all the sudden? I blinked twice, then my heart got a little quicker. The face had slanted eyes. I pushed myself up and said real fast, "Tom?"

After blinkin' again, I realized it was not Tom—the kid in fronta me was half of Tom's height. Close enough face, though. Wide eyes, yellowish-but-white skin, not exactly a Chinese but similar. Probably bout ten years old.

"Whatcha doin' here?" I babbled.

Suddenly there were two more of them behind him— another boy and a girl, all black hair—climbin' over everythin', with the dogs dancin' around them too. Then behind them, a tall one appeared.

Wait, I realized, *that ain't no child. She's holdin' a baby.* She looked pretty young, though, and more Chinese than the rest of them. She came over and put the baby in one arm and stretched out the other. She smiled and said, "Hi, I'm Jenny! I've heard so much about you."

I was dazed, so I reached out slow and shook it soft. "Pleased to meet you." Her voice didn't sound like a Chinese.

Lastly, Bryan came barrelin' in with his big grin plastered across his face. "Meet the family!"

I shook my head. "You didn't tell me you had four kids."

The two with the dogs ran to the other room, while the tallest boy, my original greeter, kept his eyes peeled right on me.

"No? I could've sworn I did."

"You said you had a 'little family goin'.'"

"I guess you could say I have a medium family going. Four kids isn't too much," he said with a cheeky smile.

Jenny walked over and gave the baby to Bryan. "You have to stay for dinner, Forrest."

I glanced at Bryan to try to gauge his reaction. He was too busy rockin' the baby. Jenny looked so damn happy, and not in a tricky way like I woulda expected from Sandra sometimes, so I said the only thing I knew how to say, cause my brain was goin' too damn fast. "Okay."

The two younger kids got bored of the dogs, I guess, cause they returned and all bunched up around me.

The middle one, a girl, asked, "Are you our dad's brother? He told us you are our uncle."

"Uh, yeah."

The youngest, the other boy, said, "Why have we never met you before?"

"Uh—"

Jenny butted in. "Hey, Isaac, Forrest is a guest. Don't bug him so much."

The oldest still lurked around me, right outta the corner of my eye, like some kinda shark decidin' whether or not to bite me. "Are you a criminal?" he asked.

I blinked. "What?"

The youngest, Isaac, added, "Our daddy said he was going to pick you up at the jail."

"Hey," Jenny jumped in again. "Enough."

Isaac just shrugged, then him and the girl disappeared into another room, while the oldest kept starin' at me. His arms were crossed.

I looked at him and asked, "What's your name, little man?"

"Freddie," he said, then he ran off too.

Jenny went over and took the baby back from Bryan. "Sorry about that," she said. "They're all just hyped up on mini golf."

I grunted. Bryan asked her, "Who won?"

She smiled at him. "Who do you think?" Then he smiled at her, and they didn't say nothin' else. That pissed me off. How the hell was I supposed to know who won?

"So, Forrest, did you come to California alone or...?"

I glanced at Bryan. "My daughter is here too. Just not right here, specifically, right now."

"Oh," she said. "Will she be joining us for dinner? Should we prepare for one more?"

I scratched my head and kept lookin' at Bryan. "Uh, I don't think so."

"Okay." She turned and smiled at Bryan for just a tad too long. I was freakin' her out, I could tell. "Well, I'll just start preparing something and leave you boys to catch up." And then she waddled outta the room.

I stood up and peeked into the dinin' room. Coast seemed clear. Then I turned back to Bryan. "Didn't realize you were into the Chinese."

He laughed, but not his usual laugh. More a soft, uncomfortable laugh. Awkward-as-all-hell kinda laugh. "Actually, Jenny was born in California. Her parents are Korean, though."

"Ah." For the first time, I started walkin' around and really examinin' the room. A dang bear skin dangled above the TV.

Beautiful pictures of the family—*his family*, the kids and Jenny —hung everywhere. And on the back wall was a small trophy, with a golden soccer ball at the top. I approached it: *Orange County Junior Soccer Club Champion 4th–5th Grade.*

"Your kids play soccer?"

Bryan walked up behind me. "Yeah. Freddie does." He touched the trophy. "His coach says if he keeps it up, he could play college ball."

I grunted. "Kid got any interest in football?"

He laughed. "I'm sure he'd love to play if we let him. It's too dangerous."

Took me a moment to process. "I see."

I stepped back and turned my attention to the big windows next to his door, showin' off all the wide greenery under his control. Heard one of the dogs rustlin' around somewhere in the house.

"Forrest?"

"Huh?"

"Why were you looking for me?"

I reached into my pocket and pulled out my phone. "Sorry, Bryan," I said as I walked to the front door. "I gotta call the old man. Gimme a second." I exited the house and let the door clatter behind me.

Had to call two damn times before anyone picked up. "Daddy? It ain't even that late yet."

Heard nothin' but heavy breathin' for a clean five seconds. "Forrest." Pause. Another pause. "Do ya know how many times I called ya?"

I glanced down at the phone. "Yeah. Seven."

"Forrest, I swear to all that is ho—"

"I found Bryan."

He didn't say nothin' for a long time, so I repeated myself. "I found Bryan."

"So what?"

I leaned down and sat on the grass and peeked over my shoulder. One of the kids was lookin' straight out the window at me. The girl. She turned around instantly.

"So, what's the plan? When does Mama wanna see him?"

"Where do ya reckon yer mama is right now?"

"I don't know. In bed? In the kitchen?"

"She's at the hospital, Forrest."

I exhaled into the phone.

"Are ya on yer way back? Sandra called me, in some kinda panic. Somethin' bout Casey. Now she won't pick up the phone."

I leaned down and let my head sink into the grass. "I just can't. I just can't deal with this right now."

"*YOU* can't deal with this right now?" His voice suddenly got all harsh, a typhoon of sound. "What the hell ya talkin' bout, boy?"

I didn't say nothin'.

"My wife is out there fightin' for her life, yer mama, and *ya just can't deal with this right now*? Have ya lost your goddamn mind?"

"Daddy—"

"No, no. I'm sorry the pressure's gotten to ya. I'm soooo sorry. I shoulda minded yer feelins. Didn't realize I raised such a sissy."

Again, the phone went quiet, till he muttered, "Forrest, can Casey and ya get on a flight home in the next few hours? I'll pay for it." He paused, then added, "Bryan can come too."

"I can't do that."

"Why? Why not?"

"I have pressin' matters here."

"Pressin' matters? *Pressin' matters*?" He went and rattled on and raised hell for another good thirty seconds. I'll let your imagination fill in the blanks. It got awful ugly. Finally, he finished with, "What the hell could be so pressin'?"

I mumbled, "I don't know where Casey is."

"Ya serious?"

"Yes."

"By all that is good and holy, are ya tellin' me my grand-daughter, my only granddaughter, is out missin' in God-knows-what country? Is that what yer tellin' me right now?"

"She ain't your only granddaughter."

Silence.

"Listen," I said, "I gotta go. Tell Mama to call me from the hospital."

"Forrest, I swear to the good Lo—" I hung up on him.

I called the police after. No leads.

CHAPTER 37

Later in the day, the police officers called me again—told me they hadn't found her and were still lookin'. They asked me where I was too. Told them I wasn't quite sure. They seemed to not like that answer.

No word from Sandra neither. I called her twice and got nothin'. Went straight to voicemail both times.

As for my truck? Well, the towin' company said she was good as gone. The pole ran right through the shotgun seat, destroyed the entire engine, transmission, ripped apart everythin'. Even that damn fuel filter I'd worked so hard to unclog. They were willin' to buy it for a hundred bucks and turn it into scrap. I told them I'd think bout it. Bryan offered me a new ride, a loaner. I didn't accept or deny.

Somehow, a whole day had gone by since I'd last seen Casey.

I spent a coupla hours just tryin' to hide away from Bryan's whole... posse. The little ones pestered me with questions every chance they got: "What is your favorite color?" "Are you going to live with us now?" "Are you married?" "What's your job?" "Do you have any kids?" Didn't answer most of them. I'll tell you what—I was never so bold at that age. Guess those two got it from Bryan. Figures, they both had his damn movie-star eyes. He had hazel eyes, I relearned. I was more like the oldest one, Freddie. He spent the whole day just quietly watchin' me, not sayin' a word, probably tryin' to figure me out. Casey woulda liked him.

By dinner, I was strung out, piss tired, generally just not doin' so hot. So when I smelled somethin' like noodles, my belly woke up real good. I realized I hadn't eaten all day.

I'd been hangin' outside, takin' a walk back and forth while my phone charged on the porch, waitin' for a call, when the scent hit me. It came peekin' out through the window, flowed down with the breeze. "Forrest?"

I turned around. Jenny was hollerin' at me. "Dinner's ready!" She was a natural smiler, just like Bryan, I reckoned. Real peppy, though I got the sense she had a better head on her shoulders than him. You nearly wouldn't be able to tell, but I could—my ears had been becomin' pretty sensitive. Her voice had a drop of anxiety.

When I got inside, all the kids were already at the table, even the baby, who I must admit was damn cute, sittin' higher up than all of us in his booster. Couldn't tell if it was a he or a she, but I couldn't stop starin' at it. Big eyes, short hair, pink chubby cheeks. I'd missed that.

"Forrest?" Bryan called out to me. I realized everyone was waitin' on me. I sat down, and we dug in after sayin' grace.

To my left was the little girl, the second oldest, to her left the baby, and then to my right was the second youngest, then Freddie. Kid. Kid. Me. Kid. Kid. Somehow, I'd ended up in the children's section. Freddie kept starin' at me.

I felt all awkward all the sudden—no one was talkin'—so I tried to break the ice. "So," I said, lookin' to my neighbors, "what are y'all's names again?"

The young boy said, "Isaac."

"Oh yeah, I did know that one."

Then the girl said, "Emille."

"That's a pretty name."

Jenny smiled and put the bib on the baby. "And this little guy is Jackson."

"Ah," I said, "goin' with the white names, I see. Probably a wise choice."

You woulda thought I killed someone. They looked at me like I was the antichrist. Bryan in particular had his mouth basically hangin' open, while Jenny shot him a glance.

I leaned over and grabbed a ladle outta the big pot and dipped it in and said, "Well, anyhow, anyone hungry?"

Slowly but surely, everyone sprang back to life, shovin' plates around, while the kids talked with their mouths half full and the baby spat and drooled everywhere. I tried to stay quiet and focus on the food. I'd had Chinese before, but never quite somethin' like that meal. She'd made these crazy noodles with thick slices of pork. They said it was called "gee gai," I think? It was red all over and kinda spicy. Not gonna lie, it was awesome. I started forkin' it down, slurpin' every bit I could. I was just too damn hungry.

"So, Forrest," Jenny said.

I flicked my head toward her and sucked down my noodles.

"What do you think of California?"

"Oh, California?" *Goddamn hot wasteland of kid kidnappers and hippies.* "It's alright."

"Did you visit anywhere? The beach? Disneyland? You could drive up and see the Golden Gate Bridge too."

"No, nothin' like that." *Maybe I could go and visit the beach then jump off the Golden Gate Bridge. That'd work.*

Freddie, still starin' at me, eyes ever lasered on, finally spoke. "What do you do for work?"

Jenny seemed pretty surprised that he asked me that, but I answered real smooth, "I'm a mechanic. I work on cars."

Bryan jumped out. "You ended up working with the old man? That's awesome!"

Workin' *with* Daddy? I got all gritty. "Somethin' like that."

The kids seemed interested. Little Emille asked, "Your dad worked with cars too?"

Then Isaac added, "Why have we never met him?"

Bryan looked uncomfortable, so he just shrugged, while Jenny took over and laughed. "The car gene must run in the family."

Well, it did for him. My head hurt again. Casey woulda done so much better with those kids.

I glanced at Bryan. He seemed more squirmy than I'd ever seen. Pansy-like. It bugged me. I decided to see how much I could push the issue.

I turned to the little ones. "So, kids, did your daddy ever tell you bout our time in Disney World? Or maybe the time he infected one of our old man's cars?"

They jumped up. "What? No!"

"So, this one time, he'd convinced our mama to fix us up some apple pies. See, she's a master baker, and it was spring-time, and in his words, 'It just felt right for apple pies.'"

Bryan half laughed. "I don't remember that."

"Well, I do." I leaned in. "See, kids, back then, we were boys, and me and Mama were bakin' up the pies. She liked to teach me, but your daddy was too stubborn for that. He preferred to spend time in the garage, watchin' our old man examine every inch of his new convertible. At some point, Mama called for food, and your daddy came burstin' in, grabbed some pies, said him and our old man were busy, and went away. Of course, I went in runnin' after him into the garage. There I saw our old man under his shiny car.

"He hollered, 'Hand me a slice,' so your daddy handed him a slice. Then, while we waited for our old man to reemerge, your daddy leaned over the open hood, tryin' to figure it out for himself while chowin' down. He grabbed slice after slice. I pointed out to him that he was gettin' crumbs everywhere, whole chunks, even, but he just waved me off. I swear by the end of it, he'd gotten a whole pie's worth of food in the internals.

"Then our old man finished his work, closed up, and everythin' was fine after that, and we all enjoyed our pie. But a coupla days later, we were sittin' down for dinner, waitin' for our old man. He was busy in the garage, doin' his thing, lookin' at the convertible one more time. He never really drove it much. Always said it was too pretty for that.

"Then, while we were waitin', we heard this *shriek*!" I said it in a real high-pitched and loud and nasally voice, like I'd do when Casey was younger. The kids loved it.

"What happened?" Isaac asked.

"What was it?" Emille followed.

"We all got right up from the dinner table and ran to the garage, and backed into a corner was Daddy. Our mama hollered, 'What's wrong?'

"Daddy pointed into the car and muttered, 'Bugs.'

"We all peeked inside, and sure enough, there were more than a few cockroaches dancin' around. Even a rat too—waltzin'. Y'all can guess what they were snackin' on. Me and your daddy glanced at each other and immediately started dyin'.'"

Gigglin' outta control, I wiped my eyes. "Bryan Wilcox was a wild child."

When I said that, the kids looked at me funny. Real confused. "Who?" Isaac asked me.

"Bryan, your daddy."

All the sudden, Bryan looked at me all angry, with hard eyes, while the kids looked confused as hell.

"What, your parents never told you?" I asked in between bites. "Your daddy's real name is Bryan, Bryan Wilcox."

Freddie was enchanted. He turned to his father. "Really?"

Then the baby, Jackson, started wailin'. "*Gaga wah wah! Gaga wah wah!*" Jenny scooped him up and tried to calm him down and disappeared deeper into the house.

After that, it seemed all the kids' eyes were laser-focused on Bryan. As for me, well, I just focused on the food and tried to not panic, cause Casey was still missin'. "Forrest," he said, real cool. "Can I talk to you for a second, outside?"

I shot the kids a glance, then shrugged my shoulders and raised my hands in innocence and followed Bryan out the dinin' room and out the front door.

"Why the hell you actin' so weird?" was the first thing he said to me when we were outta earshot.

"Ah, finally, I get a glimpse of the Bryan I know."

"Stop that."

"Stop what?"

"Stop callin' me Bryan. The kids know me as Billy. Billy Lee. That's my legal name."

I blew into the air. "Listen, Bryan, I ain't never gonna stop callin' you Bryan. Bryan, Bryan, Bryan."

"Forrest, grow up."

I scoffed, tried to think of somethin' clever to say, but couldn't find nothin', so instead I said, "At least I didn't sell out."

"I sold out?"

"Yeah, ain't it obvious, Mr. Soccer Dad? You sold out."

He shook his head. "What did you expect, Forrest? Did you expect me to be on the road for the last fifteen years? Maybe you thought I woulda joined a band and been tourin' and whorin' and drinkin' every night?" He shrugged. "I settled down. Seems like you did the same. Maybe you're just not doin' as good a job of it."

I spat onto the ground.

"Come on now," he said. "Are you really bouta pout?"

Still said nothin'.

"Goddammit, Forrest, you always do that. Can't you ever talk somethin' out? Why you always gotta clam up?"

"What do you know bout me? Like you said, I ain't seen you for fourteen years." Some crickets filled our silence. Then I sighed. "You wanna know why I came here? I came cause Mama asked me to come and find you."

"Why'd she ask you to do that? Why now?"

I opened my mouth to speak, but the words were too afraid to come out. Slowly, I muttered, "She's sick."

"Sick? How sick?"

I turned away from him. "Real sick. Now, listen—I don't have time for this. I needa find Casey, and you needa come home. You can bring the whole family on the trip, make it a summer getaway."

"I can't do that."

"Why not?"

"Look, Forrest," he said slowly, "I'll help you find your little girl. I want to meet her, I really do, but I left for a reason. There's nothin' there for me. And I feel bad about Mama—"

"Feel *bad* bout Mama? You feel bad? She's your mama." I laughed a rough, chokin' howl. Realized how much I sounded like our old man.

Then he snapped too. "Do you really think I can just pack up and head outta here? I run a business, I got a family to manage." He started walkin' up, gettin' in my face. "Maybe you got time to just lollygag around. What's the old man got you doin'? Oil changes? Well, I ain't got any time for that, and I certainly ain't goin' to Virginia." He pressed a finger on my chest. "And I don't appreciate you comin' in here and screwin' with my family. The first thing you do after meetin' them is be disrespectful to my wife and kids, and I don't appre—"

I shoved him back, then he dashed forward. I raised my right hand, but then we both heard a door swing open. We instantly turned toward the house. On the porch was Freddie, just starin'.

Bryan let out a little groan, then scratched his head. "Hey there, buddy."

Freddie just kept lookin' on, all confused, so Bryan dashed up to him and hugged him, while I watched them. Bryan crouched down and whispered into his son's ear and then gave him a light, playful noogie. And for the first time I'd seen it, little Freddie smiled.

I started walkin' away, back to the road.

"Forrest," I heard Bryan call out behind me. "Where are you goin'?"

I kept walkin'. "I'm goin' to find Casey."

"Wait. Stay. Don't you need your stuff, at least?"

I waved a hand. "Naw, keep it. All it is is dirty clothes, anyway."

"Stop, stop." I could hear him joggin' right up to me. "Where are you gonna go? How will you get there?"

"She'll be somewhere in Santa Ana, I'm sure. And she showed me how to use those dumb apps. I'll get a taxi, and I'mma find her."

"Forrest—"

"Stop." I turned around with a flat face. "It's alright. I can tell when I ain't wanted." Then I walked down the road till I was sure they weren't able to see me no more, and I played with the app to get a cab and made sure it was set on our old credit card. I put in Rocket Drive, Santa Ana as my end destination, but that didn't work. Turned out it was Rocket Drive, Anaheim. Guess I didn't even realize what city I'd lost her in. I sat down in the dirt and put my head in my lap and waited for the car.

CHAPTER 38

Durin' the cab ride, my phone kept goin' off. Not from Bryan, mind you—I'd never given him my number. No, it was the old man. He called me twice, but each time, I let it go to voicemail. Instead, I watched the outside scenery. As crappy as California had been, I had to admit it was mighty pretty at times. The sun kinda glowed on the horizon, shiny on the palm trees. Made me wanna hit the beach again. But then I noticed how many ugly buildins dotted the landscape. They sucked away the green, sucked it right outta the earth. California's dirty secret, I realized, were the dead forests buried under her highways. All of America, really.

Eventually, the cab reached Rocket Drive, and I made my quick escape. I don't really know what I was doin'. I kept walkin' in circles for a bit there, back and forth on the street, thinkin' I'd find her or somethin', but of course, I didn't.

Daddy kept callin'.

It was gettin' late, with the sun settin' on America, and I'd seen a hotel while walkin' by a coupla times, so I said what the hell, and I went in. This pimply ginger teenager at the desk gave me some trouble in the lobby cause my debit card didn't work, but then I started yellin' that I could pay him tomorrow. He glanced around a couple times for his boss, then said if I gave him fifty bucks under the table, he could gimme a room if I left by mornin', cause they had so many empty. Well, I told him I didn't have any cash neither, but like I'd told him before, I could pay him tomorrow. He got all red and angry and told me to get out, so I told him I'd give him two hundred dollars tomorrow if he let me stay the night. Finally, he gave up and gave me a keycard. I wasn't so certain on where I'd get the two hundred dollars, but if I got lucky, I woulda paid up, I swear.

In the room, I tried to get some sleep, but I couldn't. Not with the phone goin' off from the old man and not with my head buggin' out. No calls from the police neither. After the fifth call from Daddy, I finally picked up.

"What's up?" I said, real quiet.

"Forrest... I've tried to call ya four times."

I sat up. The old man sounded sadder than I'd ever heard him before. Sadder than a sinner in church on Sunday. Sadder than a starvin' squirrel. Sadder than sad. "What? What's it?"

He just sniffed over the phone. "Here's your Mama."

"Mama? What's goin' on?" I didn't hear nothin' so I yelled, "Mama!"

"Forrest, is that you?"

Holy shit. She sounds awful. Her voice was like an engine bouta blow, on its last puffs. She could barely get any words out. Hell, it sounded like she was strugglin' to sound out even a vowel.

"Wait, Mama," I whispered. "I think there's somethin' wrong with the phone. Can you video call? Click the video button, Mama."

"Forrest, Forrest, it's great to hear your voice," she croaked. "Tell me, have you had a good trip?"

I glanced around my tiny barren hotel room. "Yeah, Mama, it

was great." For some reason, I found myself snifflin' too. "Where are you? Are you feelin' okay?"

"Forrest, I'm in the hospital. I'm feelin' okay. The doctor gave me somethin'. Can you put your brother on the phone? Your father said you found Bryan, thank the Lord."

I put the phone down and pulled hard at my hair, then smacked at my head twice. Tears flowed like rollin' boulders. I considered lyin' to her, makin' up a voice, pretendin' he was right there, but I decided I couldn't, not to my mama, not then. "Sorry, Mama. I found him, but we got separated." I swallowed the lump in my throat. "He ain't here."

"Oh."

She stopped talkin', so I started. "Mama, he's so happy. He has four kids. You hear me? You have four more grandkids. They're the sweetest bunch. There's Freddie, he's eleven, then there's Emma—I think that was her name—Isaac, and baby Joshua. Three boys, one girl. Really sweet kids."

"Oh my Lord, are you serious?" She sounded real happy for a second, but then she coughed for a long while. I heard the phone rustle.

"Forrest? Forrest?"

"Daddy? Is that you?"

"Listen, yer mama is in the ICU. We gotta go now."

"Wait!" I heard her yell in the background. She shouted, "Is Casey there? Can I talk to Casey?"

I couldn't tell her I lost her, I couldn't, I just couldn't, I couldn't, I couldn't do it. I hate thinkin' 'bout this part of the story.

I don't wanna tell you no more of this story.

Just lemme get a breather.

I know you don't fuckin' care none how this affects me. You just want your inners tickled. Treatin' me like your show pony. Your fuckin' hick, just cause I made some mistakes and talk different. I'm only a man. My mama asked, "Is Casey there? Can I talk to Casey?" It rang in my ears:

"Is Casey there? Can I talk to Casey?"

"Is Casey there? Can I talk to Casey?"

"Is Casey there? Can I talk to Casey?"

"Is Casey there? Can I talk to Casey?"

"Is Casey there? Can I talk to Casey?"

Damnit all. Goddammit.

I hate this part.

I told my mama, "She's in the bathroom."

"Can you get her?" she asked, nearly beggin' me.

I put the phone down and waited a second, takin' a deep breath to try and stop my shakin'. Then I picked it halfway up and yelled, "Honey? Honey? Grandmama wants to talk to you." Then I waited another second and picked the phone up and said, "She's really stuck."

"Oh." More coughs. "What about Bry—"

Suddenly the phone went fuzzy, all static. "Hello? Hello?" I screamed.

Daddy said quick-like, "Forrest, yer mama dropped the phone. We needa go now."

"Wait! Wait!" I screamed. But the phone was already dead.

I pushed myself to the back of the bed and scrunched up. I toyed with the idea that none of it was real, everythin' had just been a big nightmare ever since that day I hit Macy, one big nightmare. Casey wasn't really missin'. I hadn't never really looked for Bryan. Mama wasn't dyin'. It couldn't be real, it couldn't be real. I started hyperventilatin', if I'mma be honest. I couldn't breathe. None of it, none it could be real. I tried to focus. Turned on the TV, but I didn't catch nothin' they were sayin'. It was like it wasn't even English, just went through one ear and out the other. I turned it off.

It can't be real.

It can't be real.

It can't be real.

Then I got a ping from the phone in the quiet. A text from the old man. It read: *Hope your trip was fun. Don't bother coming back. It don't matter now.*

I wrote back quick: *What do you mean?*

Nothin'.

I wrote again: *What do you mean?*

Nothin'.

I put the phone down.

Oh my God. Oh my God. Oh my God.

I cradled myself on the bed.

Oh my God. Oh my God. Oh my God.

I blinked back more tears.

This can't be happenin'. This can't be happenin'. This can't be happenin'.

Why me? Why'd it all haveta happen to me?

I thought I was goin' crazy, everythin' seemed to be meltin'. I tried to stand up straight, but each time, I fell back to the bed. My head hurt. My eyes couldn't look straight. My heart started burnin'.

Then there was a knock at the door.

"Casey!" I screamed. "Casey? Casey?" I ran to the door. "Casey!"

I opened the door. "Casey?"

In fronta me was Sandra.

CHAPTER 39

I blinked twice and stumbled back onto the bed. "Am I dreamin'?"

She came forward holdin' a small bag, then she leaned against the television stand. All annoyed, she asked, "What are you talking about?"

"Like, am I dreamin'?" I started curlin' myself under the covers. "Is this all one big nightmare? Am I gonna wake up back in Virginia?"

She put a hand on her face while I pinched my skin. She didn't disappear. "Forrest, I don't have time for this. I'm here to find my daughter."

"How... How'd you find me?"

"I tracked your phone. Our whole family has trackers on our phones. I've told you this before."

"Oh." I pulled out my phone and threw it on the bed. Felt poisonous in my hand, after the call with my old man. "But how'd you get here? To California?"

"I flew, obviously."

"But how'd you know what room I was in?"

"I asked the kid at the front desk, and he told me some fat

idiot yelled at him earlier. Figured it was you." She tapped her foot against the floor. "Forrest, during the flight, I tried to think up what I was going to say to you, but every time, I couldn't. I... I just can't believe you."

"Sand—"

"Stop. Just stop talking."

She trembled. Honest to God, I wanted to hug her then and tell her everythin' was gonna be alright—that we'd find Casey in no time, that I'd go to the damn doctor and have him check on my balls, that'd we get to work on that second kid, and we'd all be the happiest family ever till the end of time. But I didn't. Not with the way her voice wavered, not with the way I couldn't look her straight in the eye. I only tell stories true.

Instead all I could do was whisper. "It's over, ain't it?"

She waited, then said real soft, "It's been over for a long time."

I pulled the bed sheet over my legs. "I found Bryan."

She looked down upon me and took a long second. Then she said, "I don't care."

Everythin' fuckin' hurt. Felt like my body was drownin', drownin' into the bed. I sniffled. "You know I love you? You do know that, right?"

"Forrest, stop crying. I'm not here to help you feel better."

I raised my voice. "Then why the hell are you here?"

"I wanted to ask you where you saw Casey last, and what exactly happened."

"You couldn't just call?"

"No, I needed... to check that Casey wasn't with you."

I cocked my head. "What's that mean?"

"It doesn't matter."

I raised my voice some more. "No, it does matter. Why the fuck did you come here to check on me?"

She inhaled sharp, opened her eyes wild as two hounds bent

on destruction, and began her assault. "Forrest, you kidnap my daughter and then tell me she's missing!" she screamed. "I can't trust you. I can't trust anything you say! You throw her phone out the window, you have no idea how to handle her problems. Who packs her lunch? Who takes her to tap class? Who knows what supplies she needs for school? Who gets her those damn chicken nuggets? *Me*. It's all me. *You're* completely unreliable. *You* drink too much. *You're* a fucking judgmental loser who thinks he's the greatest thing to walk the earth, when you're not. All the fuck you can think about is high school and football and Bryan and who you wish you were while you sit on the couch. You know what they call that? Selfish. You're selfish, Forrest Wilcox. All you guys are like that. Like father, like son. Why do you think you're supposed to run the world? Why can't you just be happy being a father? Why can't you just be happy being *her* father? Why couldn't you just listen to me when I asked you to do one thing? All I wanted was for you to go to the doctor. Was that really too much to ask?"

She wiped away a few straggler tears. "I can't deal with it anymore. So, I came to make sure you weren't lying to me some more, and now I'm going to go to the police to find our daughter, whose fucking birthday you couldn't even make it to on time!"

Her words echoed through the small hotel room and cut into my skin like fallin' splinters, with each one goin' deeper and deeper than the previous, till they pushed all the way into my heart and ripped it through and through. Cause—hard as I may have not wanted to believe it, hard as I wanted to deny it—we both knew every single word of hers was true.

"My mama died," I whispered.

She exhaled. "What?"

I looked up at her, my eyes full. "Mama died."

She waited, then said, "I'm sorry, Forrest. Maybe if you'd listened to me and your father, you would've been home with her, and Casey wouldn't be scared and alone and in danger right now."

She walked to the door real slow. "I am assuming you've told the police and they're out looking for her."

"Yes," I said quietly.

"Good. At least you did that right."

Thinkin' she'd left, I leaned into the bed and covered my eyes in the blanket. Then I sobbed.

All I could see was Casey, scared somewhere in the summer's dark, and all I could hear was Mama's coughs over the phone.

Bryan fuckin' hated me, Daddy fuckin' hated me, Sand fuckin' hated me, and Casey fuckin' hated me. I'd fucked up everythin'.

Then I heard the door creak open. "Forrest," Sandra said.

"Yeah?"

"I am sorry your mama got sick. She was a sweet woman." Then the door closed.

I left the hotel a coupla minutes later to find some food. There didn't seem to be much reason to hang around there any longer. Wouldn't been able to sleep anyhow—place felt kinda haunted.

When I returned my keycard, I thought the kid at the front would gimme more trouble, but he told me it was fine. A nice lady had paid for my stay, he said.

Outside was dark, a pitch-black night. Made me stress on how Casey was doin'. I started walkin'. It was work. This country ain't fair to pedestrians, and through my own foolishness, I'd become one of them. As I wandered, I spotted closed restaurants and churches. Ain't no food there.

Every step hurt, weighed so heavy, my feet slow and stupid. Somethin', maybe someone, was pullin' me down, pullin' me into the earth.

I spotted a park, a playground, Ponderosa Park, and it got me ponderin'. When I looked inside, the night's dark shifted. Couldn't tell if it was an animal, a light movin', or just my eyes playin' a trick on me. I yelled, "Casey?"

Then I saw two bodies rise and shudder like twitchin' shadows. One had a straggly beard, the other had somethin' stickin' outta his head—maybe a hat or maybe a tumor—I couldn't tell, and I didn't stay long enough to find out. I ran, occasionally checkin' over my shoulder along the way. Didn't wait for the crosswalks to change, just glanced down the road and dashed between the cars rollin' by. I heard more than a few honks, but I ignored them and just kept goin'. Kept runnin'.

At some point, though, my body broke down. My weight got too heavy. The devil wanted me so bad. Wanted to drag me all the way down, down the farthest down that anyone can possibly go down.

I bent over, heavin' and gaspin', then I tipped and fell into someone's yard. I stayed there, crawlin' on their warm grass, and there I cried. Right into the green.

Snifflin' and makin' a mess, I turned over and stared at the night sky. There was only the moon. The city blocked out the stars.

After all the fightin', after all the ridin', after all the workin', after all the strugglin', after all the searchin', and after findin' Bryan, I'd found what I'd been dreamin' 'bout for years: I was alone.

I could go anywhere. I could restart.

And it felt terrible.

CHAPTER 40

Lyin' there, weighed down under a dead sky on some stranger's grass in a place too far away from home, the night felt weird. Like my heart wished I was in a dream, but my brain knew it was real, and the two couldn't get along. The summer heat, plus the dark, plus California, plus my complete state of discombobulation made me wanna scream and cry and hush up. Like livin' in a nightmare. I was heavy, heavy with the world, plumb lost, and the devil had me.

I considered what would happen if I let the California freeway traffic decide my fate. How many cars could I dodge? Three? Maybe two, considerin' all my fat. Or maybe instead, I could let the guys back at the park take care of business. That might be quicker.

The hurt grew inside, inflated like a tire, till it damn near burst a hole in my chest. Like I said from the top, I ain't a poet, but I do know my cars. My engine was goin' out.

In the night, as the grass got cooler and I got lonelier than ever, I wanted a voice, any voice, to listen to. Coulda damn well been a traffic report, just anything to take me away from that California cricket-quiet. Maybe they'd listen to me too.

I pulled out my phone and scrolled through my contacts.

Daddy... Casey... Sand... It all just made it worse, so much worse.

Chris... Jackson... Mark... Old friends I hadn't spoken to in years, damned assholes who couldn't be bothered to spend even ten minutes visitin' me.

Luis, idiotic Andy... The kids Casey was textin'... No, no, no, no.

No one wants to fuckin' talk to me.

I grabbed at my hair and pulled at it, and was bouta quit, when I stumbled on a new, unexpected contact. Said it was recently added.

Tom.

I hesitated. Casey musta added him.

I knew there was no way in hell he wanted to hear from me, but the glow from his name on the screen stared at me like a star cuttin' right through that night. I still don't know if it was the explodin' hole in my chest, or if the good Lord commanded it of me, but I clicked on that bright button.

It rang three times. Then I heard: "Hello, Casey?"

I exhaled heavy. "Hey, Tom."

"Mr. Forrest?"

"It's just Forrest, Tom."

Then we both went quiet for a while. The crickets sang, the cars vroomed, but above them, I could hear that boy's soft and steady breath.

"How you doin'?"

"It's been all right. How did you and Casey make out?"

Rollin' onto my side, I held back the brewin' tears. "Not so good to be honest, Tom. Not so good."

"Oh."

More quiet.

"Did you make out okay after I left you?" I asked. "Did you make it out west?"

"I did. I hitchhiked with this great dude in Oklahoma—Miko. Took me all the way. We're actually still driving right now."

"That's great, son. Where'd you end up?"

"Near San Bernardino."

"So you made it to California?"

"Yeah."

"That's funny, we did too. Santa Ana."

He didn't say nothin' after that for a long while. Guess he was waitin' for me to speak, but eventually he said, a little unsure, "Is there a particular reason you called? Do you want me to talk to Casey? Is there a problem?"

"No, Tom, I just wanted to call you." I rolled around again and exhaled. "Listen, if you're in California, you wanna meet up tonight? You could roll by with your new friend. We might could grab a bite or somethin'. I'm just sittin' out here. I'd be glad to talk to you."

He waited a long time to answer. "I don't know, Forrest... I'd have to ask Miko. It's probably an hour away."

I held it in a bit longer.

"Well, I'll be here. I can't move. Your pick. I'll send you the address. Okay?"

"Okay, Forrest."

He hung up, and I sent him the address. Then I groaned loud and hard.

I knew he was never gonna come. I could feel it in my bones. Why would he come? Why would anyone come for me? Tiny critters from the grass started crawlin' on me, but still I didn't wanna move. Everythin' was too tired, too worn down to move.

From the freeway, each vroomin' car's lights flickered in my eyes. They were all goin', rollin' somewhere, on some journey, while I stayed stuck.

Some pesterin' annoyances popped up again, breakin' me

down even further:

Truck's gone.

Bryan and Daddy think I'm a loser.

Sandra hates me.

How disappointed is Mama right now, watchin' me from heaven?

And what if I never find Casey?

I tried to piece it all together, to figure out where it all went so wrong, but my brain was blocked—no energy to think, only worry. All that anger that'd fueled me for so long was gone, all of it snuffed out. Nothin' left but misery.

Just vroom, vroom, vroom.

They're never gonna come.

Vroom, vroom, vroom.

Everythin's played out.

Vroom, vroom, vroom.

It's over.

Vroom, vroom, vroom. Vroom, vroom, vr—

"Forrest?"

I pushed myself up.

There in fronta me, by the side of the road, was a banged-up blue van, and leanin' against it, a tall brown-skinned fifty-somethin'-lookin' fella, with long cheeks and a strong face and black hair. He watched me with some curiosity and a smile. And beside him, two brown eyes shone through the night.

Tom.

"What are you doing lying out here?" he asked. "Where's Casey?"

"Tom," I whispered as I stood up. "You actually came."

"Yeah, I came. You sounded awful on the phone. I wanted to make sure Casey was all right. Where is she?"

I ran over and gave him a bear hug. Didn't know why I was so damn glad to see him, just was. He smelled pretty bad, though, sweaty and stinky. Like donkey dick. Guess we both did.

I pulled back. "Tom, it's good to see you."

You woulda never believed that boy's expression. You woulda thought he'd shat himself right there and then.

"Yeah... sure... It's good to see you too... Forrest. Where's Casey?"

"I ain't sure." I passed Tom and went up to the stranger by the van and reached out my hand. "Hello, sir, I'm Forrest."

He gave it a nice, strong shake, then a wide smile. With a deep, warm voice, he said, "Miko."

Tom ran up behind me and grabbed me by the shoulder. "Forrest, what happened?"

Turnin' to him, I could see the concern in his eyes. The boy really cared, he really did. With my voice shakin', I said, "Can we first go somewhere? Just somewhere where I can think."

"Where?"

I blinked back a tear that had been hidin' somewhere in the corner of my left eye and asked the big brown guy, "Can we go to the beach?"

CHAPTER 41

I crammed my fat body in the back of the van while Miko and Tom took the front. Miko said, "Sorry about the mess." I told him it was fine, but the Big Man had stuff overflowin' out the back: a cot, clothes, toiletries, backpacks, cans of food, water, books, and a plush stuffed dog.

"You tryin' to survive an apocalypse?" I asked.

"No." He laughed. "But the road can stretch pretty far."

As we rode, the van croaked and creaked at every stop, and I could tell Tom wanted to ask me some questions cause he kept glancin' my way in the rearview mirror, but he didn't say nothin'. Not like he had any reason to complain—he had nowhere else to go neither. We, the three wanderers, didn't needa speak. The shiny moonlight and the cool summer wind and the engine's hum said more than we ever could.

And before we knew it, the sea stared at us from the window.

"We're here," said Tom.

As we hopped outta the car and our movement cut up the quiet, I asked Miko, "You native or somethin'? An Indian?"

He grinned. "You could say so. Some people say Indian,

American Indian, Native American, Chickasaw. You can just call me Miko."

"Okay, Miko."

We jogged toward the beach, then ripped off our shoes and socks. The dark sand was cold as hell, but when I smelled the ocean's salty tide rollin' in, I ran harder. I ran and ran, ran right to the edge of the water and started coughin' from the effort, so I bent over to let the ocean run over my hands and cool me down. With my eyes closed, I tried to picture her face. Tried to picture her wide smile from that dumb clown's balloon dog. She was so happy.

"Forrest," Tom called out to me.

While Miko sat down, relaxed and lookin' out at the sea, Tom stood anxious. "We're at the beach," he said. "Now are you going to tell me what happened?"

I sighed, then waded outta the water and sat next to Miko, so I wouldn't needa look at Tom's face. "What bout y'all?" I asked. "How'd y'all end up together?"

Tom mumbled some annoyances, but Miko spoke up. "I was resting in my van in the parking lot outside the Walmart in Ada —you should visit. It's a nice small town, with a nice park, Wintersmith Park. It has its own lake and an entire amphitheater, believe it or not! And the people are kind. This one woman, Denise, she works at the Walmart there, and anytime I come in, she tells me I look handsome, so I tell her she looks beautiful."

"Does she?"

"In her own way," he said with a real soft smile. "Anyways, deep into this particular evening, I woke up from a nap and wanted a snack, so I left my van to go visit Denise. Nutter Butters was my choice. And as Denise checked me out, I said, 'You look so beautiful today, Denise.' But she seemed distracted, so I asked her, 'What's wrong?'

"She pointed out the window and told me, 'You ought to be

careful tonight, Miko.' She said there was a kid resting outside the Walmart that she hadn't seen before, that I should watch out and stay safe. I thanked her, then went on my way, and as I walked out and pulled out a delicious Nutter Butter, I saw this little face sticking out of a sleeping bag behind a tree. It's all flat land out there, so it wasn't hard to make out. I thought he didn't look that scary. I went over, stood above him, and asked him if he wanted a cookie. That's the easiest way I've found to help men bond—Nutter Butters."

The moon was like a damn half face eyein' me all the way from heaven. Hung right there. "So how'd y'all end up all the way over here?"

"Tom told me about his journey. How he was going west for some fresh air. That he'd biked for a while, then hitchhiked around. Why is it that men always need to run away to heal? I've never figured that one out." Miko laughed. "He also told me about this wild man who nearly ran him over and kicked him out of his truck. I guess that was you. But he also told me about the man's daughter, that she was kind. I guess that was your daughter. As for me, I was happy to go. I've been to a lot of places, and California is as good as any."

Tired of listenin', Tom said real fast, "Forrest, tell me—where is Casey?"

The waves waved. The air aired. The crickets cricketed. "I lost her."

"How?"

"I yelled at her and she ran away." The sand between my fingers felt so nice.

"I cannot believe you."

"I know."

The tide came in and out.

"What about the truck?" the boy asked.

"Destroyed it."

"Maybe she's with your wife?"

"Naw. Sandra's out lookin' for her now. And she hates me too. Cursed me out and everythin'."

Tom groaned, then grunted—a furious grunt. "Why do you get so angry at everything?"

"I don't know."

"That's not a good enough reason."

I grabbed at the sand and pressed it into a hard ball and squeezed it tight. The emotion engine seated deep in my belly reignited, rumbled and roared like a V-8, with every piston pushin' down on my pain and pressin' it into passion. "You just can't get it," I yapped as my body shivered. "You're too young. You ain't got no life experience. You're just stuck on that damn chick. All the good stuff is gone. In high school, I coulda done anything, been anyone. Back then, I was still free, and I wasn't so damn fat. Now everythin's closin' in. Don'tcha get it? There's walls everywhere, and they're trappin' me, trappin' me till the only time I can still enjoy is my drive between the time I wake up and the time I reach work. The only time I'm alone. The only time I can fuckin' breathe.

"Goddammit!" I yelled. "And this country—look at this damn country! This country used to save people. Used to mean somethin', stand for somethin'. There were heroes. My grand-daddy fought the damn Germans. Men were men and girls were girls. But now it's just gotten worse and worse, and no one seems to give a shit. No one. Maybe I thought if I found Bryan, it'd get at least a little better. Is that too much to ask? To have at least one person on my side again, like when we were kids? But no, I was wrong bout that too. Guess I'm the goddamn idiot. Every-thin's done gone and changed and broke and ain't nothin' gonna get better, and no one else gets it. So tell me, boy, why shouldn't I be angry?"

I covered my face. The waves kept on comin'. Thank God. I needed their sound to cover up my bawlin'.

But then, outta nowhere, Miko chuckled. "You're funny, Forrest. You really are. You sound like so many of my friends. Sammy, always talking about how his Peruvian restaurant would've taken off, if only his waiter hadn't screwed up the local reviewer's order... Or Selina, what could've been if she didn't get pregnant."

He sighed, then smiled. "They only talk through memories, stories about how good yesterday was. And usually they imagine yesterday to be better than it actually was. None of them can face the present. Then they get gone, scattered, or drunk. Too many. Too many. My grandfather always complained too. Spent whole weekends complaining with me. Said life would've been so much better if it was the way it was as his grandfather's grandfather said it was: greener, cleaner, with good earth and bright skies, back when we were whole.

"I thought about it for a long, *long* time. It made me angry, really angry. I remember screaming at storms when I was young and fighting anyone I could. I'd wonder over and over again: Where was my good hand? Where was my ace of spades? Took too long to realize those cards were already dealt. I'd missed them, missed them by a long shot—they'd already been passed out in the distant past, long before I'd had my chance to even catch a glimpse of them. That got me bitter. And that got me in some trouble. But then, as the years have ticked on by, I realized a lot of people are hurting, and those days Imafosi chewed on won't return. This country isn't going back to the way it was. Time never goes backwards. No amount of wishing or dreaming will make that true. You can love your past, but you can't become lost in it because an old life is a dead life. It dies every morning as the sun rises, and all that's left in its place is a newly born day, which we best not waste."

I sighed and pushed my toes into the dry sand. "I don't know what the hell any of that means."

"Forrest," Tom cut in, "shouldn't we be looking for Casey?"

"There ain't nothin' we can do. The police are already lookin' for her."

He slapped at the sand. "Then why did you ask me to come? To hang out with you on the beach? Because you needed someone to whine to now that you have no one?"

"I guess... I guess..."

"You *guess* what?"

I swallowed. "I guess I wanted to say... *I'm sorry.* I shouldn't have said all those mean things to you. I shouldn't have kicked you outta the truck. That was stupid of me. I don't know why I did that. I don't know why I did a lotta things. I'm sorry. I'm sorry."

Tom waited a while to speak. Think he was surprised to hear those two magic words from me. Then he exhaled, deflated like a balloon, and fell deeper into the beach. "Forrest, you can't just yell or get angry at people, just because you're frustrated. I shouldn't have to tell you that. You're not that kid anymore."

The ocean under the moonlight looked real pretty that night, shinin' and reshinin' with every twirly and twisty wave, and as I watched it, gettin' sucked deeper and deeper into its folds, I realized I'd done somethin' I'd never even dreamed would be possible for me, Lil Forrest Wilcox, the mechanic from the 757. Through all my runnin' and hidin' and drivin' and fightin', somehow I'd stumbled upon *America the Beautiful.*

From Virginia to California, from sea to damned shinin' sea, from her wilderness and mountains and rivers and cities, I'd done it, seen it. America! And she was beautiful, plenty beautiful... sometimes. Cause for every good-lookin' green tree, there were aplenty of warts: gas station bathrooms with shit stains on the toilet seat, backed-up roads, annoyin' frat boys, sketchy guys in jail. But that was what she was! A big mixed bowl of a little bit of everythin': good and bad, pretty and ugly. And she was always changin', her landscape morphin' with new sights replacin' old ones, and new faces arrivin' and old ones leavin' all the time.

And as my toes dug deeper into the sand, I realized us three bozos were a livin' testament of her constant transformation—past, present, future. The Indian, the whitey, the mixed boy, all sittin' as one. *That* was what made her different. Made her special. Where else in the whole entire world, outta all the dumb other countries out there, could I have found myself on a team like that? *Nowhere*, that's where. Only in America. Only in the US of A. And somehow, despite my damn best attempts to screw it all up over and over again, America had still seen me through. Through the days and through the nights, through the dry and through the wet, through the backroads and through the highways, she'd delivered me right there—there to her beautiful shinin' sea.

And who'd been there to see it all with me, the whole way through? And who shoulda been there with me then, on that beach, to see her sea and make some sand angels? Who'd been the one to point out all her beauty? The greatest little girl in all the land.

"You're right, Tom. I ain't that kid no more," I said, my voice risin'. "That kid was happy to do anything, could be friends with anyone. Happy to play in the sand or snow or hike, happy to explore. Happy to laugh with his brother. That little curious kid made his own freedom. And if that kid saw me now, he'd call me a fat-ass asshole."

I spat out a big gob of spit that'd been accumulatin' and buried it in the sand. "Guess Bryan never lost that. Maybe he took it when he left. I don't know, but I do know I can't do this no more. Can't afford to be that angry."

Then I took a deep breath of the salty, crisp air. Tasted good.

"It's funny, even after all the shit I fucked up, I needed you of all people to help make that click." I chuckled. "Shoulda figured. You always were the smart one in the truck. Well, you and Case."

I pushed myself up and wiped the sand off my pants and touched the tide one last time. "I know I ain't who you came to see, but thank y'all for comin'. I've done enough wrong to you, Tom, and for that I apologize again, but I needa bother y'all for one more trip. It'll be the last, I promise. I gotta work somethin' out with my brother."

CHAPTER 42

As the house appeared in the distance, I offered the last $4.27 in my wallet for gas. Miko refused, so I just dropped it in the back of the van as I hopped out.

Tom told me they'd look out for her. Said he'd check online too. I thanked the boy and the Indian, then they drove off, wanderin' into the night.

In the dark, the house looked haunted—too big, too perfect, too wide, too long. Menacin', even. I tiptoed my way over. It was the middle of the night, and I didn't wanna wake up the whole damn family, just Bryan. Needed to talk to him.

I leaned over and grunted, then scanned the property. There looked to be a nice triangle window on the second floor. Bigger than the rest. Figured it was the master bedroom. I picked up a pebble, and it took me back. Back to when we were kids, or more like when I was a kid and Bryan was beginnin' to sneak around. He'd always throw a pebble at my window, and I'd drop a rope, and when the folks asked where he'd been, he'd always say he'd been stuck in the bathroom.

I threw it at the window and missed. Just hit the right side of the panel. I stopped, crouched. Thought I heard a rustle, but it turned out to only be the wind. I bent over and found another pebble and missed again, this time underthrown.

I grunted a second time. Could feel my eyes droopin' down. The only thing keepin' me awake was the fact I *needed* to talk to him. Found a slightly larger pebble, arguably a rock, but I thought it'd do the job. Unfortunately, like most things in the past week, I couldn'ta been more wrong.

I lifted the large pebble and *gently* threw it at the window again. This time I was dead center. Spot on.

And the glass shattered.

You wouldn't believe the sound it made. You woulda thought someone was shootin' up their house, the way it *crashed!* Turned out there was a bigger issue. Immediately, an alarm started blarin':

EE-OOO, EE-OOO, EE-OOO!

And sure enough, the dogs got into the action, soundin' like a pack of hyenas.

WOOF-WOOF-WOOF-WOOF!

Then somewhere, little baby Jackson wanted in too.

WAH-WAH-WAH-WAH!

"Shit." *Why the hell did they need so much security when they got three dogs and a baby?* It was a fuckin' firework show.

I was bouta scream "Bryan!" when I heard his voice from the window. He hollered, "Whoever's out there, I'm givin' you three seconds to back off the premises before I deliver a warnin' shot."

"What?" I asked, but he couldn't hear me over the damn symphony.

"One!"

I peeked up. Right outside the top window, there was a tiny shotgun barrel pointed straight at me.

"Two!"

"Wait, Bryan," I yelled. Lights all over the house flicked on. "I just wanna talk," I tried to yell over the commotion.

"Three!" *BANG.* The shotgun blasted into the night, and immediately somethin' stung.

"Goddammit!" I screamed. "You actually shot me, you bastard!"

Am I dyin'? Is this really how it ends, after all that? Thank God I didn't shit myself.

I peeked down. No bullet holes in my chest. Groin seemed fine. Legs were still in place. But still, somethin' pinched like the sting of a bee that was born and raised in the seventh level of hell. I fell onto my ass and ripped off my left shoe and looked at my sock. Right in its corner was the tiniest bit of blood. Gently, I pulled off the sock and inspected toe by toe.

Big toe: *fine.*

Middle toes: *greenish, but fine.*

But pinky toe? *Gone!* Well... not exactly gone. And didn't exactly have a bullet in it neither. Looked a little bloody, but then I rubbed the blood a little, and it went away. Upon closer inspection, seemed I'd survived a shotgun blast and was left with a scratch.

Made me think: *Guess this is what Tom was whinin' bout before. Still a little too much whinin' if you ask me.*

"Fuckin' Bryan," I hollered while pushin' myself up. "You shot off my pinky toe!" I shouted, while pressin' my sock against it. In truth, didn't feel real bad no more. I just wanted to get his attention, maybe make him feel a little remorse.

I heard more rustlin' in the house, next some clatterin', and then the door opened and all three of the dogs busted out, started barkin' and runnin' after me. Then a coupla seconds later came Bryan, holdin' his shotgun pointed straight ahead.

"I told you to leave!" he hollered. Then he lowered it. "Forrest?"

"Yeah, it's fuckin' me! Who the hell did you think it was?"

"I... I don't know. Whatcha doin' out here in the middle of the night?"

He was wearin' some dumbass pajamas, kind you'd see the fathers in the sixties sitcoms wear when the couples were sleepin' in separate beds. He looked like a geezer.

I pushed myself up, found my balance, and kinda hopped on my left foot. "I just came to talk to you, and you shot me!"

"I didn't shoot at you. I wasn't aimin' at you. It was a warnin' shot," Bryan yelled. Then he glanced down at my foot. "Ah, shit, Forrest, that looks bad."

"Yeah, yeah, it's fuckin' bad!"

He threw the gun down and ambled toward me, while behind him, Jenny popped outta the front door as she tried to shove Freddie and the two other kids back into the house.

"Well, maybe you shouldn'ta been sneakin' around my house in the middle of the night, and I wouldn't have shot you!" he hollered.

I pressed my foot down and sorta limped toward him. "Maybe you shouldn't be shootin' such shitty warnin' shots!" Soon enough, we got right up face-to-face, and I don't know if it was the adrenaline from the wound or my sleepiness flippin' over to anger, or just cause I needed it outta my system, but somethin' compelled me to raise two fists.

Bryan stopped. "What the hell you doin'?"

I wasn't so sure myself, but despite that, I found myself sayin', "What does it look like? I'm sparrin' your ass!"

Bryan started shakin' his bobbly-tired-big head. "Forrest, I ain't gonna fight you!" he hollered. "You're bleedin'! And it's the middle of the night!"

"I don't give a shit. Fight me." I stepped forward and air-jabbed right in fronta his face, laughin'. He didn't flinch.

"This is ridiculous, Forrest." He crossed his arms. "I ain't gonna fight you."

"Pussy!" I cackled into the night, stretchin' out every syllable. "Puss-ay!" I glanced up behind Bryan. Now the whole family except the baby were out to watch. Little Isaac was huggin' his mama's leg.

I looked right up to Freddie on the porch and grinned and hollered, "You hear that, nephew Freddie? Your daddy's too pussy to fight me!"

Bryan glanced over his shoulder and groaned. "Everyone back to bed!" he yelled, but they didn't move an inch. Then he faced me again. "I swear to God, Forrest, just shut up. When did you get to be so fuckin' stupid?"

"I just take after the greatest," I said, now tryin' to hop like a boxer even with my busted toe. "It's in the Wilcox blood."

He grunted. "I guess that means it ain't in my blood no more."

I hopped toward him and punched him playfully in the shoulder, then Isaac yelled, "Hit him, Dad!"

"Stop that," he said.

I did it again.

"I swear to God, Forrest."

The third punch, he grabbed my arm and threw me back. I stumbled over but got up quick and ran toward him, while hollerin' and laughin' like a wildebeest.

He thought I wasn't serious. He said, "Forrest, st—"

Then I tackled him. We started rollin' over, while the dogs barked all around us. He pushed his hand into my face, and I punched his stomach.

From the porch, I could hear the kids yell, "Go, Dad, go!" while Jenny screamed, "Stop it! Stop it!"

But we kept rollin'. Chimney, or maybe Rex, kicked me in the face at some point, but I didn't care. We were goin' blow for blow

—he'd hit the side of my face, and then I'd knee him in the groin. I wish I coulda told you it was rainin' and everythin', to make it more dramatic, but no, instead it was hot and humid as hell, and we became sweaty and sticky as one ball of slick rollin' around under the moonlight. We were probably punchin' at each other for a good ten seconds before Jenny tried to pull Bryan off of me, but he just yelled, "Back off!"

Punch there, knee there, roll some more, you get the idea. But at that point, I was gettin' winded, so I crawled back like a lobster, and that's when Bryan got me in a lock. I tried to nudge my way out, squirm as much as I could, but eventually I realized I couldn't move a damn inch.

He'd pinned me, got his knees on my arms. He'd won. So I stopped movin', stopped tryin' to escape, and finally realized I'd been cryin'. And the tears would not stop.

"What?" he asked. "Did I hurt you?"

I tried to close my eyes, hide from him, but he had me all splayed out. "Why'd you haveta leave like some kinda bastard? You couldn't even say goodbye?"

"What?" he said with a trembly voice. "I wrote to you. Did you not get my letter?"

I wanted to make the faucet stop, or at least wipe the tears off my face so bad, but I couldn't do nothin' but let them roll down my shirt. Looked like a damned fool. "Course I got your letter, you dumbass."

"Then why didn't you write back?"

"Why the hell would I write back? You left without sayin' a word. You just left us."

"Forrest, I told you. I had to go—"

"How could you?" I swallowed my words between my sobs. "How could you?" Finally, I got it. "How could you leave *me*?" All the tears came out then. "Your own fuckin' brother. You coulda easily found me, called me, told me you were alive, anything." I started blinkin' heavy, and through the salt in my eyes, I saw he was cryin' too.

"I waited three months in that spot for you to respond to that damn letter!" he cried. "Three months and nothin'! I waited for you to write back, but you didn't, so I made my peace with it and moved on."

Soon he rolled off of me, and we just lay out on the grass, lookin' up at the sky, both of us cryin' like little girls.

"I'm the one who stayed," I said. "You're the one who left."

"Oh my God, Forrest."

"You changed your goddamn name, moved across the whole country, and pretended to die just to get away. Were we really that fuckin' awful?"

"No, it's not that. The dyin' part had nothin' to do with that. And the other stuff wasn't cause of you or Mama neither, you know that."

"Then what was it?"

"I don't know... I just wanted to go. I needed somethin' else. I wanted to call you, but it was hard, and the longer things went on, the harder and harder it was to call and the easier it became to just... disappear. To move on. I needed to be where I could breathe."

I pushed myself up and spat on the earth. "Breathe, huh? Well, I hope you got in aplenty of breathin'." Then I fell back down on the grass, face-first.

We went quiet for a while, and I listened to me cryin', Bryan cryin', the dogs barkin', and the kids mumblin' in the background.

"Mama died," I whispered. So we kept cryin', and he began to cry louder, while the whole family watched us. "I miss Casey," I added.

All the pain came out then—Mama dead, Casey gone, Sandra ended—it floated up and outta my body with each and every single tear. Considered for a bit lettin' myself die right there, to ask Bryan to shoot his Winchester right into my stomach, but listen to this: after the bulk of Bryan's tears were shed, somewhere between his sniffles, he started *gigglin'*.

I kicked him in the leg. "What the hell you laughin' bout?"

In between his sniffles and laughs, he said, "I ain't seen you cry this much since we went to Disney World. You remember that? You were such a crybaby, cryin' that whole damn ride."

"How could I forget?" I mumbled.

"And Daddy slapped you, and it just made you cry even harder, and then Mama asked us what the hell happened."

I rolled over, and the tears slowed down a little. "Why the hell are you talkin' bout Disney?"

On his face was a big old grin. A classic Bryan grin, only this time a little salty and wet. "This just made me think of it. What on earth would Mama say if she saw us right now? Bet she'd chew us out." He pushed himself up. "I'm sorry, Forrest. I'm sorry Mama died. I'm sorry I didn't listen to you. I shoulda been there. You were always the better son to her."

"It don't matter anyways," I whined. "We woulda never made it to Virginia in time."

He inhaled sharply. "And I'm sorry your daughter is missin'. I shoulda never let you leave this afternoon. I shoulda called you over all these years. It was never about you, you gotta know that. It's just... it's just... I wanted somethin' else. A different life... and I found it here." He laughed. "I guess we've always been a stubborn-headed bunch."

He began to wipe the dirt off his pants. "We should go to the Splash Mountain here sometime. Maybe after you find your little girl."

Wait.

In a split second, a lightnin' bolt struck me from the top of my head all the way down to my bleedin' toe. A damn brain blast of epic proportions sendin' shockwaves through every fiber of my bein'. *What'd that girl been talkin' bout that whole damn trip? Who'd that girl dress up as for Halloween two years in a row? Which were the only damn movies she'd watch over and over and over again?*

"That's where she is! That's where she is!"

"What? Where?"

I grabbed the side of his confused face. "Disneyland!" I tugged on his arm. "Come on. We needa leave!"

But then someone snapped, "How can you two just make up, just like that?" We both turned our heads. Jenny was there, holdin' the family shotgun, all menacin'. She looked so peeved that I thought she might just go ahead and take us both out with one big blast.

"I'm sorry, Jenny," I said with a stupid grin.

Bryan, or Billy, I guess, grabbed me by the shoulder and pulled me in tight. "That's just what brothers do," he said, also with a smile. "Fight and make up, rinse and repeat."

She raised her hands, annoyed outta her mind. "I'm going to bed. You two idiots figure out your nonsense." She walked back to the porch and yelled, "Kids—inside and back to bed, *now*." One by one, they trickled back in, first the dogs sprintin', then the kids toddlin'. Freddie was the last to leave, eyeballin' us the entire way. I gave him a thumbs-up. Finally, Jenny slammed the door behind her.

Once they were gone, Bryan asked me, "Forrest, are you serious?"

"Yes!" I nodded. "Think bout it. Where else would a little girl hide for two days? And we were so close when she got lost!"

"What about your toe?"

I glanced down. It had a good amount of blood tricklin' from it after our little spar. "Who cares bout the damn toe? I'm bouta find Casey!"

"Well," he said, unsure, "maybe we could go. But why don't

you just tell the police? If she's there, I'm sure they can find her in the mornin'."

"No, no," I begged. "I wanna go now. I needa see her now."

He looked at me for a long time, till he finally exhaled, then smiled. "Okay. Just please stop cussin' in fronta the kids."

"Deal."

CHAPTER 43

Bryan drove fast through the night. I appreciated it, despite the fact I kept tellin' him to go faster and faster. I knew we had to get there quick, before the sun came up, and that yellow eye was already startin' to peek out on the pink summer horizon.

"So, Forrest, when we get there," Bryan said, "we'll talk to the staff. They got plenty of folks cleanin' up durin' the night, so if she's there, I'm sure they'll have found her. We'll ask them if they've seen a little girl in the park. Okay?"

"Sure, sure." Bryan didn't say nothin', so I added, "I know she's there."

"You're probably right. I just wanna make sure if they've already found her, we don't confuse them."

"Fine, fine." I could tell Bryan didn't think she was there, but that didn't bother me none cause I knew she must be there. It was in my bones.

We drove on a bit longer before he asked, "Do you wanna call your wife and tell her we're lookin' for your daughter?"

I laughed. "That's a touchy subject right now. I'll call her after we find Casey. I'm sure you'll meet her soon enough. Maybe you remember her. It's Sand, Sandra."

He grunted. "Faintly. She was real pretty, right?"

"Yeah," I whispered. "She is."

As we rode on, I watched the California highways and palm trees and buildins fly by. Some green, mostly gray, a little bit of orange with the sun, but basically bleak, if I'mma be honest. I'd seen all of Ms. America, at least her southern portion, so I felt obliged to evaluate her from cheek to cheek. Got my brain all twisted up, threw back my mind.

In that predawn nighttime summer day, I found memories I'd forgotten—like when I was a kid and first saw the long blue strip off the Chesapeake Bay Bridge, the ocean seemin' to stretch out forever, or when we all went campin' out in some God-forsaken no-man's land state park and the wind and grass twirled around us, givin' me more air than I deserved, and even the pretty Blue Ridge Mountains me and Casey passed along the way. Made me realize Virginia had aplenty of green, plenty of good looks. Couldn't really answer anymore what I thought I'd been missin'.

A little bit later, when we got close, I pulled out my phone to send one last message. I wrote to my old man: *I'm sorry.*

SOON WE FOUND ourselves face-to-face with Disneyland's front gates, and we waved down a guard.

"Sir! Sir!" I hollered.

He was sittin', lookin' bored as hell on a plastic foldin' chair while he played with his phone. He squinted and whipped a flashlight toward us. "What do you guys want?"

I ran up to him, pantin' a bit. "My daughter's here in this here park."

He gave me a you-don't-know-jack-shit kinda look, then

pulled out his radio and buzzed, "Hey, we got a guy here who
says his daughter's in the park. Did we pick up a little girl
tonight?"

He waited a second, the radio buzzed back, and he said,
"Gotcha." Then he put the radio down and went back to the
games on his phone. "There's no way your daughter's here."

"What? Why?"

"We sweep the park every night. We didn't find any little
girls. If she was trying to hide, she would've been found."

"She's a smart girl. The smartest girl. If anyone coulda found
a hidin' spot, it's her. She disappeared in Anaheim a coupla days
ago. She's here, I'm tellin' you."

"Sir," the guard said, not even lookin' at me, "she's not here. I
can tell the staff to look out for a little girl, but I'm telling you
right now, she's not here."

Me and Bryan went back to the parkin' lot, and he said, "Forrest, we'll wait for the park to open, and then we'll look for her."

I tapped my foot. "I ain't gonna wait." Then I gave a *look*.

Took him a second, but then he returned my mischievous
face. "Are you serious?"

"Yeah, I'm serious. I ain't waitin'. Once it opens, there's gonna
be a whole crowd swampin' the place, and we'll never find her.
Or she could leave before then."

He put a hand on his face. "You ain't jokin'?"

"No, I ain't."

"Well, Forrest," he said with a grin trapped across his mouth,
"I guess you'll get to be first in line on *all* the rides."

It was good to see he still had a little mayhem left in his
bones.

We started sneakin' around the edge of the park, which had
fences tall as baby redwoods. Guess they wanted to make sure
none of the magic could leak out. Bryan led me, sayin', "Forrest,
you get in, look around, and get out. I'm doin' this for you, but I

can't get arrested, and I don't want you to neither. If you get caught by someone, just tell them you passed out in the park drunk, and I'm sure they'll let you go. I just don't wan—"

"Bryan." I put a hand on his shoulder. "It's gonna be fine. She's here. I know she is."

He gave me a long look, then nodded. "Okay."

We stopped at a fence on some boulevard. Bryan checked the street to see if anyone was watchin'. Once he saw the coast was clear, he said, "Forrest, over this here fence is Tomor-rowland."

I raised a foot on the edge of the fence. "Got it."

He lifted me higher. "And Forrest?"

"Yeah?"

"I'm glad you found me." Then he pushed me over.

With the wind spinnin' around me, I crashed into some bushes. I got up real quick, and while walkin' away, I secretly wished he'd come with me, but I came to terms with it. Findin' Casey was somethin' I needed to do. I was the one who needed to set things right. But right when I was bouta take another step forward, I heard a whisper from behind the fence. "Wait. Stop."

"What?"

"I changed my mind. I'm comin' with you. Push my foot under the fence. I'll hop up."

Hell yeah.

"Okay," I whispered. I leaned over, tryin' to get my hand under the fence, but there was no gap. "I can't get my fingers under."

"Whatever, I'll get over myself."

I heard a heave on the other side and saw the tips of his fingers graze the top of the fence, then disappear.

"It's fine, it's too high," I whispered. "I'll find her myself."

"No, Forrest. I'm comin'."

Again, he jumped, and this time he got his full hand on the

steel. "Hurts like hell," he complained. Then slowly but surely, he pushed more and more of his body over bit by bit, but then I heard him creakin'.

"Bryan, what are you doi—" I jumped back just as big Bryan's whole damn body came crashin' down with a huge thump, laid out. I stood over him and said, "Damnit, are you tryin' to wake up the whole park?"

"Sorry," he whispered.

We waited, but luckily, no one came. I breathed a sigh of relief, gave a signal, and we began our trek. Above our heads was a rail system, which we followed for a bit, and it led us to the edge of Tomorrowland. There I saw the park in its entirety. Of course, it's a little different than Disney World, but it matched up pretty well with what my kid eyes remembered. I could see roads and signs and futuristic rides soarin' above my head— loopy-loops, domes and all. In the quiet night, the fixtures were a little eerie and shadowy, but they got me excited anyhow. Reminded me of two goofy boys runnin' around with far too much energy.

I also thought: *How the hell am I gonna find her?* The park was damn massive. Lookin' for her on foot could take forever.

Then we flinched. Above our heads, a sound blared.

"Testing PA... 1... 2... 3..."

We both pointed to the speaker simultaneously. Wilcox genes ain't that dumb after all. I whispered, "We'll get to the PA system and get someone to send a message. Or if they don't, I'll do it myself." Bryan nodded.

After crawlin' through some grass and shrubbery real stealth-like, we found ourselves beside the outer fence of a go-cart area, but then we stopped. There were two bozos cleanin' up the space.

"Did you hear what happened yesterday?" one of them asked.

"No, what?"

"Carol caught a couple spending the night in It's a Small World. Apparently they were getting busy."

"Doing what?"

"You know."

He shook his head. "That's just nasty."

I got tired of their blabbin' real quick, but it wasn't like we could make any moves or they might notice the two whiteys crouchin' in the bushes. In fact, the more I looked into the park, the more I realized how much was goin' on. Everywhere there were these bright floodlights and employees runnin' around doin' stuff. Worst part was that the sun was really gettin' high by then. Those summer mornins came early, and I knew we needed to act quick or we'd get spotted.

I shifted closer and closer, while Bryan followed, till we eventually reached the shrubs outside this big space dome ride and were stuck again. The only way forward would be the main path, which I knew would spell doom. Fortunately, that was when our miracle came.

As we kept waitin', tryin' to figure out what to do, Bryan tapped my shoulder and pointed out a third employee, who appeared seemingly outta nowhere. She was exitin' this shiftin' panel on the side of the ride's buildin'—like a hidden painted door, nothin' you'd expect. The door started to close, so Bryan said, "Let's go." He tugged on me. We dashed forward and snuck in, right before it shuttered behind us.

Inside was like a whole new world. There were these gray walls and a staircase goin' down. Reminded me of jail. We peeked over the staircase's ledge, saw the coast was clear, and ran down the stairs.

"I think these are the park's secret tunnels. I've heard of them," Bryan whispered.

"Why the hell do they need secret tunnels?"

He winked at me. "It's to maintain the magic."

Once we got to the base of the stairs, the facility opened up a lot more and became a wide passageway. I also noticed Bryan was startin' to rub the top of his head. "This is pretty crazy," he said.

"Don't worry. We'll be in and out." That said, I had no idea where the hell we were goin'. Fortunately, there was a wall with all kindsa signposts: *Adventureland... Main Street... New Orleans Square... Critter Country... Fantasyland...*

"Let's go to Fantasyland," I said. "I'm sure if there's a sound system, it'll be there." I didn't know jack shit, but it seemed as good a guess as any.

So we set off, turned the corner, but immediately there was a woman. We froze in our tracks. It wasn't just that we were caught. Naw, she was *stunnin'*. She had this short black hair, red rosy cheeks, and this yellow dress. The only reason I didn't think she was an actual princess was the phone in her hand. She put it in her pocket and caught us starin' at her. "Hello," she said, all airy.

"Uh... we're new sound... engineers," I found myself sayin'. "We're supposed to be workin' on the music systems and all that."

She beamed at us. "Oh, your first day on the job? That's so exciting! Are you talking about the computer room? The DACS thingamajig?"

"Yeah," I said, real slow, "that's exactly it."

"Ah, okay." She tapped the side of her plump cheek. "I think there's a bunch of different control rooms. Are you looking for one in particular?"

"Yes, uh, the one with the PA system."

"I think maybe the one on Main Street, near the castle, is the one you want. I can lead you!"

"Okay..." I trailed off. I could see why they picked her as a princess besides her looks. You woulda thought she was takin' us on a damn quest based on her bubbly tone.

As we followed her, Bryan whispered to me, "You've become a much better liar since we were kids. I'm impressed."

I shrugged him off and gave a small laugh. "You taught me well."

Through the gray halls were a hodgepodge of people, some dressed normal, some dressed odd. I glanced at the time on my phone. Already half past seven. We needed to hurry—the park opened at eight.

"Just the staff getting ready for the day," she said.

I really got a sweat goin' at that point as we passed a damn human chipmunk. Guy had bottom-half human legs, top-half rodent head with googly eyes. We'd infiltrated deep.

After another minute or so, she stopped in fronta a room with the door slightly open. "Here we are!"

Me and Bryan peeked inside: massive panels everywhere fulla buttons, screens, more than you could ever imagine, and a coupla microphones. On the televisions, we could see every inch of the park. And best of all? There was no one there but us.

Ms. Princess said, "The guys must be getting breakfast." She started to head out, but then she asked, "Do you want me to show you guys the cafeteria? It isn't too bad."

"No, no," Bryan said, "we'll just wait for the other boys to return."

"Thanks, Princess," I added.

She smiled. "No problem. And I'm only 'friends' with the princess," she said with air quotes.

"Uh," I said, "alright."

Once she was outta sight, me and Bryan looked at each other and then did a major high-five. We were *in*. We got to work.

Bryan lingered by the door and said, "I'll keep watch. You find the speakers."

I leaned over the all the machinery and buttons, but to be honest, I had no idea what the hell I was lookin' at. Over the years, I'd learned aplenty bout engines and transmissions and HVACs, but the computer boxes were a whole other story. There were these two microphones screwed into the desk with a couple buttons around each of them: a blue one, two gray ones, and a red one.

I was sweatin' over which one I oughta press, then I decided: *Fuck it.* I pressed one of the gray ones, waited a second, and said "Hello" into the mic. Nothin'.

I pressed the other gray one, then repeated, "Hello."

Suddenly, a major sound bellowed back to me through the lower halls, boomin' toward us: *Hello.* I glanced up at a screen with some guys cleanin' up Main Street outside and held the button down, and said, "Hello, hello, hello, hello, hel—"

"Forrest, what the hell are you doin'?" Bryan called over my "hellos" echoin' around us.

I lifted my hand up from the button. "I was checkin' if my voice was goin' outside." But it hadn't. The guys on the screen didn't react one bit to the noise.

"Well, hurry up," Bryan said. "They're for sure gonna come back now." And just as he finished his sentence, some clamberin' came from down the hall.

Bryan took a step out in fronta the door. *Oh shit.*

"Hi there," I could hear him say.

It was damn near impossible to focus, with my hands all sweaty.

"Yeah, I'm new. We were lookin' for help on somethin'." I heard him say.

"Sure, buddy," a new voice emerged. "I don't remember interviewing you." A split second later, Bryan burst into the room and pushed the door closed, holdin' it tight.

"What the hell you doin'?" I exclaimed.

"Just hurry up, they're gonna bust us."

Soon they banged on the door. "OPEN THIS DOOR!"

Shit. Shit. Shit. I really needed to focus then. I clicked the green button, yelled "Hello," and stared at the screen. Nothin', no reaction.

The door was really budgin' now. "Forrest..."

It has to be the red button. Red button. Nothin'.

"Forrest, this is fuckin' crazy!" Bryan screamed. He used his foot to pull over a chair and tried to angle it against the knob.

"I'm sorry, I'm sorry," I yelped. *It wasn't any of the damn buttons.* Then I realized: it was the other microphone.

I slid my chair over and smashed the green button there and said: "*Hello.*"

YES! Everyone on the screen stopped for a second, in all corners of the park, and I could even hear it echo down into our dungeon.

Then I hesitated. I hadn't thought bout what I was gonna say. I started scratchin' my hair, tryin' to come up with somethin' elegant, but then Bryan screamed, "FORREST, HURRY THE HELL UP."

I pressed the button and said:

"*Casey, it's Forrest, your daddy. I know you're out there, and I just want you to listen... First of all... Well, before I say that, I guess I oughta say I've missed you, and I hope you're safe and sound. Now, with that said, I wish you hadn't run. It got me really worried sick. And it got your mama worried sick too.*"

I sighed.

"*I'm sorry the trip wasn't what you thought it was gonna be. Ain't what I'd thought it be neither. But I'm glad you came. Honest, we both know if you hadn't come, everythin' woulda turned out a lot worse. I probably would still be out drivin' in the middle of nowhere... and maybe somethin' else worse woulda happened. A lot worse.*

"*But more importantly, since the moment you left, I've done a lotta thinkin'. I got thinkin' bout Grandmama, Granddaddy, your* *mama, Bryan, and just family in general, but most of all, I thought* *bout you. And I realized some things. So I guess, I just wanna say—"*

"Forrest!" Bryan yelled. I turned to him. Then the door busted open, and four guys tumbled over each other, rollin' onto the room's floor.

Quick as a Mustang, I yelled into the mic: "*Meet on Main* *Street! In fronta the castle!*"

Now, I gotta get careful with you on how I tell this parta the story, cause I don't want the mouse comin' after me, but this is where things got *wild*.

It was like everythin' went in slow motion. I got up from my chair and began to run, when I realized the mountain of overweight sweaty sound engineers were gonna swallow me whole, right by the front door, but then, in that moment of uncertainty, there was this split-second look between me and Bryan. An acknowledgment that only brothers would know. He told me: *I* *got you.*

And that was when he jumped head first into the pack and tackled them. He screamed, "Go, Forrest!"

So I ran and ran. I leapt over them as they all tumbled to the ground. I felt some fingers touch the back of my shin, but it was only a graze.

I cleared them. I cleared them all.

I ran faster than I'd run in years. I ran through the halls, laughin' so much that tears rolled outta my eyes. We were just those boys of yesteryear again, runnin' around, gettin' into nonsense. I felt freer than I had in forever as I ran to my little girl.

CHAPTER 44

My first obstacle was a kid with broad shoulders and big black hair. Dude wore a bright-red jacket with yellow gloves. Looked dumb as hell. Problem was, he was in my way. Shoved him to the side.

"Hey, watch where you're going," he hollered.

I didn't care.

Next came a pair of ducks, well, more like a quartet. One with a fancy hat and glasses, then a trio of little ones in different colors. Looked pretty cute with their quackers all open and big eyes and such. I didn't care—I had somewhere to be. I rammed through their middle and broke their line.

Next came another sequence of folks rushin' down the hall, all fine lady princesses. Brown one, black one, white ones, Asian one, all gorgeous lookin', but I had no time for a chat. Lucky enough, they were smarter than the guys and got outta my way.

"Stop!" someone screamed behind me. I kept goin'.

Down the hallway, I saw a staircase with a wide sign that read MAIN STREET. But in fronta me was a whole horde of both regular-dressed and silly-dressed folk who blocked the staircase. No matter.

I pushed past a busty fairy with a blonde bob and a green dress and fake white wings.

"What the hell?" she asked.

I shoved a big yellow bear and a dude wearin' a ridiculous top hat.

"HEY!" they screamed at me.

Threw some space ranger with a big plastic chest toward the wall. "Fuck you, man!"

Up the staircase.

Damn superheroes. Had to clear a big ugly tree thing and a dude dressed in tights with a spider on his chest. Those two tried to get ahold of me, but I kicked them back, and they tumbled down a little.

I can see the light.

Next came the ice queen herself, recognized her aplenty from Casey's shows. Well, she got outta my way, that was for sure.

Then the tall one with the long ears that sounded like a doofus. Elbowed.

Some goobers with light sticks. Busted up.

And finally, best for last, I swept Mr. and Mrs. Mouse off their feet. They fell down the stairs, onto the other characters, but got caught by a man in a damn toy cowboy outfit. I said, "Pardon," to show my respects, but to be honest, I didn't care much. I'd arrived.

I pushed the thick door open, and the light rained down on me.

The sun shone high and bright on Main Street and spilled down onto my noggin. It didn't care one bit bout any of the bullshit I'd done. It hugged me anyways, and it felt so good.

Around me was a ghost town—just a few employees finishin' up as they cleaned their fancy buildins of polished red brick and gray stone and blue-painted wood.

We'd explore it together, once I was done, I decided. But I needed to hurry. I needed to see her.

I spotted the castle in the distance and started runnin', slappin' my slow feet against the clean road as fast as I could go, but the sun burned hotter and hotter onto my neck, and then I realized how gassed I was, how much my run ran me out. I slowed down, tryin' to catch my breath, when I heard, "Grab that guy!"

You know I didn't turn around then. No, I hightailed it, cause I found a renewed strength fuelin' my body. No one on the planet was gonna stop me.

I ran by some big trees and empty benches. "Casey!"

That baby in my arms.

I reached these gardens, fulla pink and purple and white flowers, with each and every petal smellin' like her. "Casey!"

My little jitterbug.

I passed a big shinin' statue of Walt and the mouse. They held hands while Walt pointed out to the horizon, showin' the mouse the beauty of the world, its endless possibilities. Their plaque had one big word inscribed on it: *Partners*. I gave them a little wave. I was sure they'd approve, knowin' my intent. "Casey!"

The angel of my life.

On the drawbridge in fronta the castle, adrenaline coursed through my veins like nothin' else. I coulda beat a bear, assaulted an alligator, defeated a dragon. Anything to reach her. With all the air in my lungs, with all the might in my thick belly, with all the power I possessed, I roared, "CASEY!" It echoed throughout the land and spread into the universe like a call to heaven itself, cause God knew I wasn't messin' around. I was there for my baby girl.

There was just one problem. She wasn't there.

Outta room to run and fully exhausted, I collapsed onto my

knees, heavin' and wheezin', while the footsteps of the squadron behind me grew louder and louder.

"Casey!" I yelled again, lookin' up at the castle. No answer.

Then I felt blood poolin' in my shoe. I'd forgotten bout the cut, musta reopened.

"Casey!"

Suddenly a buncha arms grabbed at me, squirmin' all over my belly fat and chubby legs. "Stop... it..." I said in between my coughs.

"What were you thinking?"

"We're calling the cops."

"Who are you? What's your name?"

I shook my head, not willin' to believe it. *No.*

My grand illusion, my dream, shattered all at once. The pain returned.

She ain't here. She never was. Of course she wasn't. She's still missin'. I didn't find her. I made Bryan go through all this for nothin'. Oh God, what if I never find her?

The guys tried pickin' me up, but soon I found myself stumblin' to my knees. Guess I was too heavy to move, too heavy for this world. There, in fronta the palace itself, I began to weep.

God, everythin's all my fault. I fucked up everythin'. Why the fuck did I think she was here?

They found a way to hoist me, I reckon, cause I started movin' backwards real slow.

"We have to get him out of here before they open," they said to each other.

The castle grew farther and farther away while my tears made everythin' more and more blurry.

I shoulda just taken her to Disney World.

I don't know if I'll ever be able to express how low I was then. Like I said when we began this tale, I ain't the best with words. I guess... I guess my soul had finally left my body. All that excitement from seein' Tom and patchin' up with Bryan had been erased, cause the only thing that mattered, that *truly* mattered, was gone.

I was ready. Ready to be washed away and disappear forever.

But then, like a thunder from the heavens themselves respondin' to my grief, I heard a cry. It was loud and clear and strong and bellowin' and everythin' I coulda ever have hoped for, and till the day I die, I'll never forget it. It revived my life.

"Daddy!"

With my arms pulled behind my back, I looked up. Standin' tall, glowin' under the sun, on the center of the castle's awnin', was her. Miss America. My princess. My little girl. Casey.

She came dashin' down the stairs. "Daddy! Daddy!"

I couldn't believe my eyes. I woulda sworn she was a mirage, but when I heard her shout "Daddy" again, I knew it was real.

She ran to the left, down some hidden staircase, while I turned toward my captors. Just four bums probably not gettin' paid near enough, but they shouldn't have tried to stop me. Some super strength came over me. I fastened my feet strong on the ground, then with all my might, I burst up and twisted my arms, knockin' them outta balance and settin' myself free. Just a daddy reflex, I suppose.

Then I ran up to the castle. All my lost energy returned to me, all my power recouped. "Casey," I screamed.

She appeared at the bottom, tears streamin' down her face, while they flooded my own.

We met in the middle, and in fronta all the land, we embraced. Behind us, a crowd's stomp rumbled in the far distance while the bums screamed at me, but it didn't matter. None of it mattered. I had my little girl.

I cried into her shoulder. "I'm sorry, I'm sorry. I'm so sorry." I pulled back and looked into her big awkward twelve-year-old blue eyes. "You're better than me. You're smarter and sweeter and the best person I ever met." I hugged her again.

"Did you find Uncle Bryan?"

"Yeah," I said, pullin' her in closer. "But that don't matter right now. I'm just glad I found you. I'm sorry I was late to your birthday. I'm sorry I was such an ass. I'm sorry I left Tom on the highway. I'm sorry I punched Adam. I'm sorry I yelled at you. I'm sorry I didn't listen to you. You were right. You been right bout everythin'."

"It's okay, Daddy," she whispered. "I'm fine, I'm fine."

"No, it ain't. It's not okay. You are the most important person in my life."

"Daddy..."

"I'm sorry, I'm sorry, I'm so sorry." I sobbed. "I will never leave you again. Never." And as I held her, I planned on never lettin' go.

Damn, it really is the happiest place on Earth.

At that moment, as I sweated and cried and hugged in fronta all the land, I even regretted hittin' Macy's car and all that nonsense. See, here's the thing I figured out after all the madness that summer: The times are always gonna move on. They're always gonna change. And people are gonna change too. Just the way it goes. Ain't nothin' we can do bout it, so either you gotta learn to treasure it all and everyone, or else you're gonna dry up like some old piece of turd, stuck hatin' everythin'.

I needed to be better—I need to be better—for her.

Guess the last thing I'll leave you with is this: As the guards started to push us away and hollered all around us to get the hell out, me and Casey went real quiet, alone with each other and our cryin' and all that fluffy-duffy stuff.

But toward the end, I yelled out the one thing screamin' in my head—you woulda never believed how it ran through me, how it took me over—it was like I saw her as that beautiful baby again and as the genius girl in fronta me and as the wonderful woman she'd become, all at once, all wrapped together, and she was my past, my present, my future, and would be my everythin' till the day I died, and you coulda sworn the Holy Spirit took over my body and willed me to see the light, but I knew it was no spirit, no, it wasn't even the California sun, not even findin' Bryan, not Sand's wrath, or Mama's death, or Daddy's coldness, or Tom's words, or Miko's hippy advice, or my crazy head. No, instead it was just seein' and holdin' and embracin' my little girl that compelled me, collapsed one message down inside of me and pumped my heart and willed itself to break out, needin' to be heard, forcin' me to shout one thing and one thing alone.

I screamed, "I LOVE YOU!"

Casey Wilcox (Class B)
Ms. McAdams
August 28th, 2016
7th Grade
3 Pages

What I did Over the Summer Essay

Where do I even start?

The beginning of the summer was normal enough, nothing special. I mostly watched TV and hung out with my friends. My friend Peter got a new Xbox which was really cool, but toward the end of the summer is when things got interesting...

See, about a week before school my daddy was like: "You have an uncle." And I was like: "What!!?" It turned out my daddy had a brother and he was out west and my daddy asked, "I'm going to find him, do you want to come?" Of course I said, "Yeah!"

Well we started going and things got a little rocky. My daddy's chubby and when he tried to do a hike, he got all mad when he couldn't finish. Then I made a new friend named Tom, who's in college, but my daddy got all angry at him for asking him about my uncle so he kicked him out and I got a little sad about that, but Tom texted me later and said everything was all right and he wasn't angry at him anymore.

Next he showed me a jacuzzi at a fancy hotel, which was cool, but then some stuff happened which made it less fun and some stupid older idiots bugged us.

I was a little upset then but the country was still pretty. I liked looking out at Texas and New Mexico. Most of it was brown, but sometimes it was very green and it smelled really good. It was super hot though. In New Mexico, we found out that my uncle Bryan was in California from one of his old friends Adam, but then my daddy got super weird and really annoying.

But once we reached California, I found out that Bryan actually died—or so I thought! We went to his "grave," and I started crying and my daddy got really upset. I should add, my mama wasn't happy at all about me going with him on the trip. She was actually very mad and she kept asking me to come back.

At that point I just wanted to go home, but Daddy wanted to keep looking for his brother, and then the car broke down and he yelled at me, so I got upset, so I just ran away. To be honest it was really scary. It was nighttime and I didn't know where I was going and I started crying. I tried to find my daddy again, but I couldn't find my way back, so I kept running around until I saw a sign: Disneyland!

How could I not go? I went toward the sign but it was all gated. Luckily I snuck in trailing another family and hid out in Critter Country overnight. The next morning, it was so cool. There were a ton of people and rides and I went on The Haunted Mansion, It's a Small World, and even Splash Mountain! My daddy once told me about Splash Mountain at Disney World but it was even better than I thought it was going to be!

By nighttime they were starting to shut down and close, and I thought about talking to someone to try to call my daddy, but I got a little scared again and kind of wanted to stay a little longer, so I hid inside the big castle. I almost got caught twice but I managed to sneak away.

And that's when the craziest thing happened. Early in the morning, I woke up and I could hear my daddy! He was on the speakers and he started calling for me! He told me to meet him on Main Street. I didn't quite believe it, but then he kept talking and talking. He was getting pretty emotional.

Of course I went to go and find him, and he was there! He started crying and hugging and kissing me and I started crying too. It was nice, but a little cringe if I'm going to be honest about it.

Well, that day was crazy for a lot of reasons. First they kicked us out of Disneyland and said we were banned for life, but my daddy said he'd sneak me in again at some point. Then it turned out my uncle Bryan was actually alive, and I even have four cousins! Freddie (who's almost my age), Emille, Isaac, and baby Jackson (who's so cute!) and an aunt Jenny!

It wasn't all great though. While we were away, it turned out my grandmama passed away. She had cancer for a long time, but I was still sad and my daddy pretended not to be that sad, but I think he was.

We all—Daddy, Mama, Uncle Bryan, Aunt Jenny, and my cousins—flew back home for my grandmama's funeral, and then Uncle Bryan and my grandfather got into a really stupid argument about some old car but they agreed to fight about it later and seemed all right. My daddy and my mama also got into a big fight and I think they might be breaking up, which I was pretty upset about, but honestly it was a long time coming, anyone could see it.

In general though, my daddy's a lot happier and a lot nicer around me which I like. He keeps calling me silly names in front of all my friends now. It's pretty embarrassing. He also said he's going to quit his mechanic job with my granddaddy and open up a bakery! I thought my granddaddy would be really mad, but he said he might give him some money to start up if my daddy bakes some of Grandmama's best recipes for him. Apparently our family friend Luis will take over the shop when Papaw retires instead.

I hope I get to see my cousins soon. Uncle Bryan told me I have to visit them during fall break. Daddy told them they had to come back and we'd all go hiking (I think Daddy's got to lose some weight first though).

So, yeah, a lot of stuff happened... but do you want to know the best part of the summer? Well, after the first day of school, my daddy picked me up and told me he had a surprise. I was like: "What?" (I didn't want any more surprises), but he said I'd like this one.

So we're walking to the porch and then he ran ahead and said, "Give me a second." I waited and waited, then yelled, "I'm coming in!"

I stepped into the house, and to my surprise, in his hands was a little brown barking baby. I had never before been so happy. He said, "You better walk him," and I said, "Of course!"

I couldn't believe it. My birthday wish came true. My daddy got me a dog!

ACKNOWLEDGMENTS

This novel would have never reached its full potential without the support, feedback, and wisdom of my family, friends, and mentors.

Specifically I'd like to thank:

My editors: Sara Gardiner, Crystal Watanabe, Michele Ford, Janet L. Wagner, and Alex Gray

My book cover artist, Bailey McGinn

Ma (Elayne Kesselman)

Kate Kesselman

Oliver Yan

Brad Houska

Austin Cheng

William Wallace

Alexander Brinkley

Kaitlyn Early

Cindy Dale

Claire Nieusma

Shane McCarthy

And most of all thank you, my reader.

DEAR READER,

Thanks again for reading *Finding Bryan*. I hope it was an enjoyable experience. If you want to help me further, please don't hesitate to leave a review on Amazon or Goodreads. It's the best way for authors to gain exposure.

Also, if you haven't already, I encourage you to check out my first novel, *Buried Vapors*. It's quite a different type of story, but one I believe you may find interesting.

Additionally, please visit my YouTube channel "Matthew Kesselman." There you will find some auxiliary content for *Finding Bryan* which you may enjoy. And if you are interested in any of my future work, please visit matthewkesselman.com. There's exciting things to come.

Lastly, I hope your family is doing well, whomever you consider family. Tell them you love them.

All the best,
    Matthew

AIN'T NO DAY LIKE TODAY

BY TYLER PRESTON

Risin' like the sun in the east,
She'll come back one day, I know,
Even though she's left with the wind.
But I can't stay here, can't keep wonderin' where she's
   gone.

It's time to put the ol' engine to the test,
Time to leave my ol' life behind,
But ain't no reason to be stressed.
We just gonna head out west, yeah, out west.

'Cause ain't no day like today!
The journey will be long,
And all my friends have gone,
But ain't a problem, no, sir,
'Cause there ain't no day like today.
Ain't no day like today!

I hope she's thinkin' 'bout me.
Thinkin' of her keeps my heart free.

I can't look back, no, not today
'Cause goin' forward is the only way

And it's all gonna work out okay.

'Cause ain't no day like today!
There ain't no day like today.
'Cause ain't no day like today!
There ain't no day like today.

No more tears, no more cryin'
Hit the road hard and don't ever stop
I'll keep goin', keep goin', and goin'
No, I'll never stop, I'll never stop.

'Cause remember, baby girl:
There ain't ever gonna be another day like today.
There ain't no day like today.
Ain't no day like today.
Ain't no day like today.

CPSIA information can be obtained
at www.ICGtesting.com
Printed in the USA
FSHW011603080221
78300FS

9 781952 974038